Pinocchio Island

by

Alexandra Wallner

Uncial InPrint   Aloha, Oregon
2019

Pinocchio Island Copyright © 2019 by Alexandra Wallner
Cover art and design Copyright © 2019 by John Wallner

ISBN 13: 978-1-60174-910-9

Ebook published by Uncial Press, Aloha, Oregon
www.uncialpress.com
ISBN 13 978-1-60174-239-1

Pinocchio Island
Published by Uncial InPrint,
an imprint of GCT, Inc.

To Johnnie, Barbara and Jim, the Gang at Casadrala
and to Snooty Ooty who kept us sane.
Special thanks to Judith who has faith in the story.

CHAPTER 1

I could have sworn the yellowish, sea-worn shard on the kitchen windowsill of the abandoned island cottage had not been there a moment ago. I picked it up, wet and ice cold. On one side, "Welcom ... 1901" was printed in faded blue letters. Tingles slid down my spine. How could it have appeared out of nowhere? I loved everything about the cottage but this gave me shivers.

A chill breeze swept from the front door and Max, my husband, walked in. Before he could notice it, I slipped the shard into my coat pocket. I wanted, more than anything, to live on this stunning island but Max had his doubts. No point confusing the issue with the shard.

"How did Ernest react to our offer?" I said.

Max twiddled his moustache. "You know how real estate agents are. He hinted the owners might accept a lower offer, but I don't know..." Max walked to the wall and pushed on it. "No spongy dampness. Good. But unpainted walls, floors thirsty for varnish, no appliances." He shook his head. "Could be a money pit, renovations on top of the hefty asking price. It would take all the proceeds from the sale of the townhouse and business."

"I feel good about this cottage. When you give in and admit that you want to retire, it could be ours. I know it." I gripped his arm. "Let's try."

Max chewed his lower lip. "True, it's charming but something bothers me. Someone started to renovate it then stopped. Why?"

I tried to sound nonchalant. "Maybe someone in the family took ill or they ran out of money." I ran my fingers through my hair. "Not important."

"Or..." he said, with a wicked grin, while wriggling his fingers in front of his face, "There was a grisly murder and the bodies are buried in the basement."

"Come on, Max." I was miffed but determined to keep my cool.

Max knew how I'd pushed for retirement. He said, "You've given a lifetime's work to *Presentation Is Everything*. You want to live in a community. You want to take up painting again. I know you're ready to quit. That's fair. But what would I do? Nothing thrills me except garnishing food and catering. It's my life."

I crossed my arms and looked him in the eye. "You're the icon in the catering business, the legend, the winner of five Golden Radish Awards. You've been moaning about not having time to write your memoirs. Max, it's time to hang up your carrot curler. Do it! Retire."

He rubbed his chin. "I ask myself over and over: have I done all I can for the garnishing industry?"

I groaned. "Same old chestnut. For heaven's sake, Max! Yes, you did it all. You're the elder statesman of garnishing."

He cringed. "You make me sound ancient." He turned and looked out the window. "If we retired, you'd finally have that community you're always talking about."

"Make the offer."

As Max walked outside to talk to Ernest, I got one of my premonitions. This cottage would soon be ours. I just knew it.

Max returned, looking resigned. "Ernest thinks our offer will be accepted." He threw his hands in the air. "I guess we're moving."

"Hooray," I shouted.

"And about the unfinished renovations..."

I held my breath.

"No details. The people who owned it left suddenly and it fell into the developers' hands. They just want to get rid of it."

"You won't regret this." I squeezed his arm. "Guaranteed."

* * * *

Earlier that crisp autumn day, Max and I had ridden on the ferry from the mainland to Martini Cove Island. We sat up top, the wind ruffling our hair. The short trip, invigorating as an ocean voyage, gave us a clear view of the bay. Sun reflected on water, like the bubbles in champagne. In the distance, rocky islands with pines and deciduous trees poked out of the sea. Power boats, barges, sailboats, glided by. Crying gulls soared overhead in clear skies. The air smelled of water and when I licked my lips, I tasted salt.

I had always wanted to live and paint by the sea. Often, during the years I'd worked as manager for *Presentation Is Everything*, I had pictured myself sitting on a rocky ledge surrounded by tubes of watercolor paints, brushes and pads of paper, with gentle breezes sweeping my face. I would buy a portable folding artist's easel and stool, a paint box, and, yes, a hat--a broad brimmed straw hat with a ribbon flying behind me in the wind. I would become an *en plein air* artist, painting stunning scenes.

"Look!" I pointed as we approached Martini Cove Island. Rocky cliffs topped by pine trees rose from sand beaches. The dock and marina harbored pleasure boats glowing in the sun.

I put my head on Max's shoulder and sighed. "It's perfect."

The ferry bumped into the dock, and when the gangplank was lowered, we were the only disembarking passengers. Several golf carts were parked on one side of the dock but the only person in sight was a bent, wizened man with weather-wrinkled skin. He had on the same type of clothes we saw on many of the ferry passengers: a nylon windbreaker with hood, khakis and leather boat shoes. When he shuffled up to greet us, he pulled his hands out of the pockets of the jacket and pushed his sunglasses up on his forehead. He introduced himself as Ernest.

Max pointed "Golf carts. No cars?"

"None allowed, Mr. Saltwater," Ernest said. "Carts are electric. Don't add noxious fumes or noise to the environment."

"How enlightened the residents of Martini Cove Island are," I said, while clasping my hands. "Aren't they?"

Ernest pointed to his cart without commenting.

We climbed in, me in front, Max in back. Ernest turned the key, started the engine and the cart jerked ahead onto a sand road. We bounced along, the wind whistling through the cart. I had to keep myself from jumping up and down on the seat, it was so like an amusement park ride.

"What brings you to Martini Cove Island?" Ernest said, without taking his eyes off the road.

I said, "We're retiring. After reading the Martini Cove Island brochure, we thought the peace here would be perfect."

"Ayuh."

The sand road cut through pines and wound up a hill. Ferns sprouted from boulders on one side. On the other, the land dropped steeply and below, a pond reflected autumn colored trees like a mirror. Pine, earth and leaves scented the air.

When we came to a plateau, Ernest veered right to a road circling a vast, manicured lawn bordered by stately maples. Ringing the lawn and trees, several large two-story brick buildings stood like wardens. Short sets of stairs led to wide porches and front doors painted gleaming white. Ernest explained that these were the condos, but I already knew that from the brochure.

"Ocean views from every condo," Ernest said. "Interested?"

"Just in the cottage we talked about."

As we drove along, the only sound was the shushing of the golf cart's wheels.

I craned my neck around. "Where is everyone?"

Ernest scratched his head. "Dunno. Off-island?"

Max leaned forward between Ernest and me. "The brochure said Martini Cove Island was a renovation. From what? A government facility? Army?"

Ernest shifted in his seat, and tugged at his coat collar. "Ayuh," he said. "It was an institution all right, in the early nineteen hundreds. Right different now." He jammed his foot to the pedal and the cart whizzed ahead. We flew out of the circular road, onto a tree-shaded lane and stopped in front of a cottage. Ernest slammed his foot on the brake. I slid forward, almost bumping my head on the windshield as Max bounced against the front seat.

"Here's the cottage you wanted to see," Ernest said. "A gem." He got out and shuffled to the front porch, where he opened the door with a key.

Max and I climbed out of the cart to size up the cottage. The covered porch ran along the front of the brick building sheltering a Dutch door in the middle, windows on either side. Three windows in a line were evenly spaced along the second floor with a small diamond shaped one at the peak. A chimney stood on the right of the deep slanted roof. Maples, pines, birches and ferns hugged the cottage on three sides. It needed more work than the small photo in the brochure showed. But it looked compact, cozy, and welcoming. I loved it.

Ernest stood in the open front door, slapping the frame with his hand. "A real beauty but people pass it up. Humble compared to the ocean view condos. Guess people get a notion about the kind of home they want in a place called Martini Cove Island. Shouldn't be saying this, but I like this small cottage better than the condos."

The private, quiet woodland setting would be perfect for us.

"Let's take a look," Max said.

I whispered to him, "I won't need a hard sell."

He squeezed my elbow as if to say, "Don't let him know what you're thinking," and guided me up the rickety porch stairs.

Inside, the cottage was flooded with warm sunlight from its many-paned windows. The first room on the left could be Max's study. On the right side, the room with a small brick fireplace would be the living room. In my mind, I was already arranging our antique furniture.

In the kitchen, two bright windows on either side of the corner showed only makeshift plywood counters.

The last room we came to would serve as the dining room. As I looked out the window into the woods behind the house, I saw the sun shining through red and orange maple leaves, looking like stained glass windows.

I pointed. "We can put the antique pine table here to entertain friends for a change." It was the same table at which Max and I had sat, mostly alone, for the past thirty-five years. I jammed my hands into my coat pockets. "Imagine, Max, a real community. People you see every day--neighbors who cook you chicken soup when you're sick. New Year's Eve with friends. Fourth of July barbecues."

Max looked at me over the top of his glasses. "You have an idealized idea of community."

I flipped my scarf over my shoulder. "Maybe, but I'd like to find out by having one."

"I know, my dear," he said. "I know."

When we stepped out to the back porch, Ernest stayed inside to give us privacy. A large boulder sat at the end of the yard, surrounded by ferns. Beyond that, a drop-off into the woods defined the end of the garden.

I tilted my head. "We could sit on the porch in two old-fashioned rocking chairs on summer nights and listen to crickets."

"And plan our wills?"

"Retirement doesn't mean death."

"Rocking back and forth would be good exercise for my heart." He frowned and scratched his chin. "You don't suppose there are bugs and snakes out there, do you?"

"There might be," I said. Was island living going to be too much nature for Max? He was a city man, through and through. His idea of roughing it in nature was taking a walk in a park.

He twiddled his moustache. "What about lions?"

"Don't be ridiculous."

"That's a relief."

"If you're going to make fun, then why did we come here in the first place?"

Max squeezed me. "Just kidding," he said. "Let's go upstairs."

The large room in the front would be my studio. I envisioned shelves holding art books and supplies. In the corner would be my drafting table. I would fill the Italian tie string portfolio Max had given me with watercolors. Through the front window, I saw the sand road and beyond a field of wildflowers circled by birches.

"We're going to have an extraordinary time on this island," I said.

As it turned out, we did.

* * * *

Arm in arm, Max and I walked outside. I knew we had done the right thing. But I had to know about the shard I found on the sill. Back in the golf cart, I pulled it from my pocket and showed it to Ernest. Trying to sound as if it didn't matter, I said, "Did you put this on the windowsill in the kitchen?"

Ernest took it, turned it over and shook his head. "But I can tell you about it. It's from crockery used when this was an institution. The company that made the dishware was called 'Welcomer'."

Max looked at it over my shoulder. "What kind of institution?"

Ernest played with the zipper of his jacket and cleared his throat. "Didn't want to mention that before you saw the cottage." Nervous laugh. "This was once a facility called 'The Welcomer Rest Home for the Treatment of Ennui and Melancholia.' It was built at the turn of the twentieth century, when rich people sent troubled relatives away to rest in fresh air before psychotherapy became popular." He patted my hand. "But don't you worry, Mrs. Saltwater. It closed in the 1950's."

Max clapped me on the shoulder. "Great! Now we can sit on the porch in rocking chairs wearing straitjackets. Considering we've made our living by carving vegetables, we must be a little cracked. We'll fit right in."

I gave him a withering look but held back a retort. I wasn't going to let my beloved Max and his Kasumi knife cutting tongue get to me.

I said to Ernest, "Do you know who lived in our cottage when the institution was active?"

He guffawed. "Don't worry, Mrs. Saltwater. No peculiar people ever lived in that cute place--just staff. Say, does this institution stuff bother you?"

I laughed, and tossed my head back. "Of course not."

Did it? Rest home? People with mental problems? Could their unstable energies be haunting the place? I wasn't going to tell Max my doubts. Once we lived here, everything would be all right. Of course it would.

We had time before the ferry back to the city arrived. "Ernest, do you think we could meet some of our new neighbors?"

He rubbed the side of his nose. "Let's see if anyone is around." He drove the cart only a few yards, stopped, and pointed to deep woods next to our house. "An old woman lives here. She'd be your closest neighbor. Let's stop by to say howdy."

"By all means, let's say howdy," Max said.

I ignored Max's snobby sarcasm. Looking through dense pines, I saw another brick cottage I hadn't noticed before.

We walked toward it, ducking under untrimmed branches. Like ours, this cottage suffered from neglect.

Ernest knocked on the door. Nothing. I cupped my hand to the window glass but saw only faded curtains. Suddenly, a fat tabby cat with large yellow eyes hopped onto the windowsill.

I shrieked.

Max chuckled. "Maybe that's the old lady in altered state. Is there a full moon tonight?"

"If there were," I said through narrowed lips, "the old lady wouldn't be a cat, she'd be a wolf ready to rip your throat out!"

Ernest scratched his head. "Reckon the lady's not at home. Let's see if anyone else is around."

We drove back to the condos and Ernest, looking puzzled, rang a few doorbells but no answers.

Then he looked like he had an idea and snapped his fingers. "Plum forgot. Today is Tuesday, island shopping day. Folks are in town and won't be back until after your ferry leaves."

A loud toot sounded from the dock and Ernest looked at his watch. "There's the ferry now. Better hurry. Darn shame about not meeting your neighbors."

Something wasn't right. When I called to make the appointment to see the cottage, Ernest was specific about only being available to show property at Martini Cove Island on Tuesdays. Why would he be surprised that today was Tuesday and everyone had gone shopping?

I said, "Do you live on Martini Cove Island?"

"Naw. Too rich for my blood."

That explained it. Not being an islander, of course he forgot about shopping day. I made a dismissive gesture with my hand. "I'll meet everyone when we move here. I know a place as special as Martini Cove Island must have extraordinary residents."

"Ayuh," said Ernest. He avoided my eyes. "Extraordinary."

CHAPTER 2

The developers accepted our offer on the cottage and the next few months were a whirlwind. We honored previous business commitments, worked with a local architect to renovate the cottage, sold our house in Philadelphia, sold *Presentation Is Everything,* and packed. It all went well and because it did, I was sure the decision of moving to Martini Cove Island had been the right one.

We did not go to the island again before the move. The architect we hired was well respected and we trusted him. He sent us plans and pictures every few days that we modified and sent back. Everything was timely and within budget.

Our clients, hearing of the end of Max's career, clamored for just one more party from the legend who had won five Golden Radishes. Max turned all offers down, but when a request came from Spec and Bunny Delacorte to cater their fiftieth wedding anniversary, he couldn't refuse. The Delacortes had been our first important clients and paved the way for meeting rich and celebrated people who became the core of our business.

The Delacortes weren't the richest clients nor did they throw the biggest parties, but they had impeccable taste and always wanted the best. They loved good food, good wine and living well. They were the only clients Max actually adored.

When Max signed the contract for the party, Bunny was wearing a green silk suit accessorized with an emerald brooch. Max knew her weakness for precious jewels, so when he unfurled his sketches for the party, she nodded her approval.

He took Bunny's hands. "I'll leave the way I came in, catering to the best," he said, and kissed her on the cheek.

On the night of the party, the Delacortes' penthouse overlooking Rittenhouse Square sparkled like a diamond. Crystal and marble gleamed, silver trays shone, champagne corks popped, flowers perfumed the air, a string quartet played light classical music. Bunny wore a periwinkle blue satin gown accented with sapphire earrings.

I looked elegant too, in a black taffeta dress with a gold brooch in the shape of an oyster shell holding a blister pearl, my parting present from Max as a thank you for managing *Presentation Is Everything*. It was one of many food-themed pins he designed for me over the years.

But the showstopper was Max's buffet table. He had carved and assembled chunks of hard cheese to look like treasure chests holding pirate loot. Cherry tomatoes, pickled beets, baby carrots, scallions, jicama, pitaya and dozens of other exotic fruits and vegetables glazed with a shiny Asian sauce resembled bracelets, necklaces and rings strewn around the table. He had fashioned whole hard-boiled eggs crisscrossed with caviar, sea salt and tiny pieces of vegetables to replicate Faberge eggs. Everything glittered.

When Bunny saw the buffet table, she threw her arms around Max and exclaimed, "Darling, I don't want to eat it, I want to wear it!"

* * * *

After six hectic months, we were ready to move, the van having left ahead of us. At the city dock, a few miles from the island, a barge took the van to Martini Cove Island and the movers unloaded boxes and furniture into our newly renovated cottage.

Max, Truffle our terrier, and I traveled by plane. Our only luggage was an overnight case and a duffle bag filled with my jewelry collection, the pieces Max had designed for me through the years.

It was a rainy, windy night and the plane dipped and swayed all the way on the one-hour flight. Truffle, subdued after a dog tranquilizer and several licks of Triple Sec, was in a carrier case under the seat ahead of us.

I wish I could have put Max into a carrier case, too. He absolutely hates flying, so it took more than a couple of sips of Triple Sec to get him on the plane. Sweaty and gray faced, strapped securely in his seat, he gripped the two miniature bottles of wine he'd bought in his fists all the way, taking intermittent sips. I was tempted to slip some dog tranquilizers into the little bottles.

After landing and getting a cab to the dock, we learned that the last ferry to Martini Cove Island had just left. We wove our way down a plank to a water taxi, heavy rain pelting us, black seawater swirling below. The small boat dipped like a roller coaster car as we churned across the choppy bay, wind howling. As we huddled together in the small cabin, I gripped Truffle under my coat, while watching spray slap against the window. Max closed his eyes and leaned his head against the back of the seat. His skin was slightly green, either from the motion of the boat or the combination of Triple Sec and airplane wine--probably both.

Finally, we arrived at the Martini Cove Island dock. A single bulb on a pole illuminated the slanting, bashing rain. The boat's bobbing light shone on the floating dock where water taxis parked. With the help of the driver, Truffle and I disembarked from the rocking boat to the unsteady dock. Max stumbled off carrying the overnight case, with my jewelry bag slung across his chest.

"Sorry to leave you like this, folks," the taxi driver shouted above the wind, "but I have more fares to pick up." He gunned the motor into reverse and churned away.

We swayed on the small unstable dock unable to see in the dim light. Then Max took a few bold steps forward. "Damn!" he yelled.

"What?" I shouted at his dim silhouette ahead of me.

"No guardrails," he called over his shoulder. "I was almost lost at sea. Keep to the middle."

"Is my jewelry okay?"

"Your jewelry's fine." A pause. "Don't you care about me?"

"I would miss you terribly, dear, but the jewelry is irreplaceable."

Max trudged ahead up the metal gangway. "Wonderful to be

well loved."

"Just kidding."

"Ha ha."

We had not told anyone on the island when we were arriving, so no one met us. Wind whipped the pines above us as we climbed the hill up the sand road, lit by an occasional lamp, toward our cottage and our new life.

I looked at Max, puffing along next to me. "You're very brave, dear," I said. "It gets better from now on, you'll see."

"Harumph..."

When we arrived at the cottage and turned on the lights, we saw it was in pristine condition. I had had the foresight to send emergency provisions ahead in a box with the movers: bottles of wine, cans of pâté, caviar, English Stilton cheese, crackers, coffee and panettone, all emergency rations to get by on until we could shop. After getting out of our wet clothes, we had a merry picnic in front of the fireplace. We were home.

* * * *

Although it was still raining the next morning, light filtered into the house through the new six-over-six windows. The kitchen was small but efficient, with shiny new appliances, cabinets and polished stone counters. I couldn't wait to arrange my antique crockery collection. The floors were varnished and fresh paint gleamed. We explored outside and admired the new roof, pointed up bricks, repaired porches.

I had since learned that on all days of the week, a supermarket in the city packed groceries that islanders ordered into banana boxes and shipped them out on the afternoon ferry. I called the market, and later that day my order was brought to my door from the ferry by resident assistants. Having carried many heavy grocery boxes and bags for our business, this was yet another perk in paradise. Max was in the study arranging his antique garnishing tool collection in the lighted display cases he had designed.

My studio had new built-in shelves. I unpacked a new drafting table, several boxes of new books on watercolor techniques, fresh tubes of Winsor & Newton paints, and brushes, pads of Arches French watercolor paper and other supplies I would need to start my new career.

The rain stopped a few days later and I decided to take a break from unpacking by assessing the garden. As I walked through the wet ferns, I planned a stone walkway to encircle the house. That big boulder near the drop-off into the woods would be a focal point for the antique birdbath. The garden would stay natural, so I could devote time to painting. But I would need a gardener for heavy work and I was sure that manicured Martini Cove Island would have a competent one.

As I dreamed and planned, I became aware of faint humming and the smell of chocolate coming from the direction of the neighbor we had tried to meet. I couldn't see her house because of the thick stand of juniper bushes between our cottages. If she was working in the garden, maybe I could sneak a peek at her. With some difficulty, I pushed the strong branches apart and came to the edge of a garden. Light filtered through trees showing lush beds of plants larger and healthier than any I had seen on the island. Neat stone walkways organized the back yard into a square with crisscrossing paths, intersecting in the center where a large antique iron urn overflowed with ferns and ivy. Daffodils, tulips and hyacinths abounded. Butterflies flitted, bees buzzed. It was like being in a fairy tale. To the left stood the cottage, the back porch looking shabby and neglected like the front, a pitiful contrast to the garden.

The humming came from a far corner where I could see the back of a wraith-like woman, wearing a white, lace-trimmed, old-fashioned summer dress and a ragged straw hat with a wide brim. She did not seem aware of my presence as her right hand clasped and unclasped the handle of a pitchfork. I recognized the tune she was humming as "The Marseillaise," the French national anthem. With quick force, she thrust the pitchfork into the ground at the heart of a clump of flowers--pulling, hacking, tearing and digging up a core of roots. She finished her work and speared the pitchfork into the ground, standing back, hands on hips.

"Hello," I said.

She whipped around to face me, her fingers flying to her mouth, her eyes round with surprise.

"Sorry to startle you." I walked slowly toward her. "I smelled the chocolate, and then I heard you singing and then... Well, I just wanted to introduce myself. I'm your next-door neighbor Sylvia Saltwater." I extended my hand.

She shrank away and stepped back. Stray wisps of white hair escaped from her tattered hat. Her narrow face and thin arms had translucent skin, with a network of wrinkles and veins showing through. Her eyes were faded blue, red rimmed and watery. She was old, perhaps in her eighties or nineties.

I dropped my hand and did not try to move closer. "My husband Max and my dog Truffle and I just moved into the cottage next door." I pointed over my shoulder. "Forgive me for barging in. I wanted to make a formal call. I'm not a nosey person, neither is Max, but I'm anxious to meet my neighbors and since we are so close." I shrugged. "I do hope we'll be friends."

For a long moment, she searched my face. Finally, she said, "Are you her?"

"I don't know who you mean. We've never met."

She stepped closer and stared at me, and then shook her head and looked down. "You're not her. She used to bring me things." A tear fell on her gardening clog, making a clean spot on the dusty shoe. "Sometimes the others come, but they haven't been here in weeks." She put a finger to her lips. "Or was it yesterday?"

She fluttered her hands. "I don't know. I'm never sure about time." She took another step. "I don't have to be afraid of you, do I?"

"I won't hurt you." I smiled. "Please give me your hand."

She hesitated, but then, like a trusting child, she put her hand in mine. I could feel the bones beneath her skin, fragile as a baby bird's but I knew she was strong, too, from the way she dug up the plant.

I said, "Tell me, dear, what's your name?"

Pulling her hand back, she curtsied, holding her skirt out, just as a child from long ago would have done. Then she put her hands behind her back, swaying from side to side and tilted her head. "I'm Fern." Her voice was high and lilting, like a girl's.

"Does anyone live with you?" I said, while glancing toward the cottage.

She put her finger in her mouth. "Just Tansy."

"Who's Tansy?"

"Tansy is my friend." Fern pointed to a large cat sitting on the shabby porch sofa, the same tabby that had jumped on the window ledge the first time we tried to meet her.

Fern was old, yet acted like a little girl. Whatever was she doing here living alone?

"Your dog won't hurt Tansy, will he?" she said.

"Truffle would never hurt anything."

"That's good," Fern said. Her brow wrinkled and she threw up her hands. "Where are my manners? Mother will not approve."

"Mother?" I said, not believing that her mother could still be alive. "Does she live here, too?"

"Oh, no. But she watches me, you know." She pointed to heaven. "You seem all right, though. If I have to have a neighbor, it might as well be you." Her fingers flew to her mouth. "Oh, that sounds awful, doesn't it? I didn't mean it that way." Flutter of fingers. "Would you like a cup of tea and a brownie?"

I never turn down a brownie. "I would love tea and a brownie."

She led the way up rickety porch stairs. The overstuffed sofa where Tansy sat had been elegant at one time but was now sagging in the middle, with stuffing pushing through holes in the worn tapestry fabric.

"Do come in. I'll just go make the tea," she said, and disappeared through a patched screen door.

I followed her inside and saw a combination living room-dining room ringed with bright windows. A few good quality, though worn, pieces of furniture, threadbare carpets and faded curtains filled the small space. In contrast to the timeworn appearance, everything was neat and clean and furniture was polished. Although run-down, the interior was cheerful with bouquets of flowers in chipped vases and teapots. A bookcase held large, well-worn art books. I took one out and flipped through it, noticing several bookmarks stuck between pages. A few good paintings in tarnished gold-toned frames hung on the walls: landscapes, flowers, children and adults in Victorian clothes taking a stroll in a city park...in Paris?

Fern came back carrying a silver tray with a porcelain teapot, two mismatched cups and saucers, spoons, sugar in a bowl without a lid, and a plate piled with brownies.

"Do you like my pictures?" she said.

"Oh, yes. They're very good."

"Mother and Daddy gave me the pictures a long time ago." She sighed. "I wish I could paint."

"I'm an artist myself and want to paint lots of watercolors of the island."

She clapped her hands. "I want to see them."

"Maybe we could paint together."

She shrank back. "I couldn't do that." Primly she arranged cups, saucers, and clean but frayed napkins. She pointed to the chair next to her and said, "Do sit." As she poured the tea she said, "Mint, from the garden."

When she offered the brownies, I put one on my napkin. It was heavy, dense with chocolate, still warm from the oven. I nibbled a corner and closed my eyes. "This is the most delicious, full bodied brownie I have ever tasted." I know desserts and this one was great.

"Thank you." Fern was blushing. "A special recipe given to Mother in Paris by one of her friends."

"Really?" I took another bite. "Have you ever been in Paris?"

She chortled. "I lived there long ago with Mother and Daddy. We had such a good time strolling in parks and visiting museums. There were puppet shows and restaurants with music. Everybody was so friendly." She looked at me and tapped the side of her head with a finger. "I can go there, you know, anytime, in my imagination." Then she stared through the window as if she could see her memories playing before her eyes like a movie.

"Do you still have family?"

She sighed and shook her head. "Just me and Tansy."

"Do you ever leave the island?"

She looked at me, clasping her hands, shrinking away, her eyes wild. "I could never do that. You won't make me, will you?"

"No, of course not, dear." I wanted to pat her hand, but didn't. "How do you get food and things you need?"

"I have a telephone, you know," she said pointing to a black phone on a small table. It looked like a relic from the nineteen forties. "I call a nice young man in a store and then that same day I get a box. It's always on my doorstep. I think Mother and Daddy pay for it."

Fern was still a child, I realized. She had never grown up. Things she needed were always just there.

"The pretty bluebird... I can never remember her name. She used to bring me things, nice things. Boxes of candy, plants for the garden, art books. But she went away."

"A neighbor?" I asked.

She glanced at me sideways. "I get confused." It seemed like she thought she had said enough and had almost divulged a secret.

I had eaten the first brownie and was nibbling another. These were marvelous! Soon I would have to leave and cook dinner but not just yet. I was relaxed, mellow, felt...floating on air.

"The butterfly and the swan bring me things now," Fern said.

"An insect and a bird bring you things?" I giggled. Sure. Why not? I rested my head on the back of the chair and closed my eyes.

"No." She laughed. "Two ladies, but I can't remember their names. They *remind* me of a butterfly and a swan." Then she looked at me wide-eyed again. "You won't tell them to stop bringing me things will you?"

"Of course, not." Fern's face was getting blurry. "Could I ever bring you things you need?. Food or medicine?"

"That's kind of you."

"Sure thing." It was hard keeping my eyes open. "Just let me know."

My glance drifted to the black-and-white and sepia photographs on the sideboard. Curiosity overtook my sleepiness. I rocked myself out of the chair and stood. I swayed, and then wove my way to the photos and squinted at them. One of them, that looked like it was taken in the nineteen twenties, judging by their clothes, was of a young couple with a toddler. The Eiffel Tower loomed in the background.

"That's me with Mother and Daddy," Fern said.

Another photo showed a stout woman with close-cropped hair standing next to a short woman with a slight moustache and dark bob. Next to them, were young Fern and her parents.

"Those are our friends, Trudy and Alice."

Gertrude Stein and Alice B. Toklas?

The rest of the photos showed views of a large, gingerbread style home. In each, Fern at different ages, and her parents stood in front of it.

I staggered back to my chair and fell into it. Out the window, I saw the garden with cartoon flowers that had little faces and leaves like hands waving at me.

"Your flowers..." I slurred, "look...so...friendly."

Fern giggled. "I give them lots and lots of food. Keeps them growing, growing, growing!" She shot her arms into the air like a kindergartner in a school play. Then she leaned toward me, dropping her voice to a whisper. "They hide my house and keep me safe from *them.*"

I whispered, "Them?"

"*Them*," she said, as if I really should have known. She glanced over her shoulder.

I didn't press her. I was more worried about myself than her right now. I realized I couldn't make a fist and could no longer feel my feet.

"I really must be going now." I pulled myself up. "My husband will wonder where I am." I held onto furniture until I was on the porch. "Thanks so much for the tea and brownies." I looked at her, but could not focus. "Oh, dear," I said as I held on to the door frame, "you must think the worst of me." What the heck was wrong?

She held my arm and led me down the porch stairs into the garden.

"Don't worry, dear. My brownies have that effect."

"Must be all that sugar."

"Yes, the sugar."

As I walked out the porch door, I thought I saw Tansy grinning at me. Fern guided me along the path to the thick growth of bushes between our cottages. At the edge, she gave me a slight push.

"Good-bye, dear," I heard her mumble. "Come back soon."

The bushes snapped back together behind me, making a dense screen. It was as if Fern, her house, her garden and Tansy had existed only in my mind.

I don't remember what happened after but somehow I must have found the way back to the house and into bed.

CHAPTER 3

During the night, I awoke to the most pitiful wailing sound I had ever heard, heart-wrenching and utterly lost. Max and Truffle were snoring softly, undisturbed. Maybe it was just my imagination.

As I laid my head back down, the doleful sobbing started again.

I shook Max's shoulder.

"Whazzzzzt?" he said without opening his eyes.

I shook harder. "Listen!"

The crying stopped.

"Don't hear a thing," he mumbled, and turned over. Truffle kept snoring.

I stumbled out of bed. "You two are a big help." Then I remembered Fern, the secret garden and the brownies, but I didn't remember coming home. Looking out the window in the direction of Fern's house, all I saw was the thick growth of trees--no garden, no cottage, no lights. Feeling fuzzy and sick, I lay back down.

Buoy bells ding and the low, sad trumpet of a foghorn sounds, but instead of being charmed by the music of the sea at night, I see the ocean's vastness, the black depths, the murky ocean floor, dark and sinister, strewn with barnacled debris of ship wrecks and decaying remembrances of times past.

I am walking in slow motion on the ocean floor, shafts of light shine through thick bunches of seaweed waving like shadowy traps. Fish with small sharp teeth swim in and out. Slopes drop to obscure depths.

Presently I see two smoky, wisp-like columns ahead, and the wailing starts again. As I move forward, the smoke turns into human forms: a man with grey hair and a woman with long black hair swirling around her head. Their clothes are shredded. Upright, they float in place, arms and legs down, skin pale blue. Their heads hang, eyes closed, mouths open like O's. Oddly enough, I am not frightened. Instead, I feel sorry for these pitiful, lost souls.

"Why are you wailing?" I say.

Their eyes flutter open and they look at me. My skin is prickly gooseflesh and I shiver, but I stretch my arms out to them. They fade away and disappear.

The sun was already bright through the drawn bedroom curtains next morning when I awoke. Chilled by the dream, I wanted to linger under the covers.

It was happening again. When I moved to this island, I hoped it wouldn't follow me. But it did-- my ability to have premonitions. It would always be a part of me. It was the way I *knew* this island cottage would be our home. Had I conjured up that shard on the kitchen windowsill the first time we saw the cottage?

My mother used to call these incidents "strong hunches" but it was more than that. She had the same "strong hunches" and she told me it was a burden to know about things before they happened and I should ignore them when they did. But how could I stop something that was part of me, like my height or the way my hands were shaped? That's why I saw the ghosts in my dream. They had a message for me. I hoped this was the first and only time I would see them. I had never told *anyone* about them. Not even Max. I wanted a normal life on this island with a normal community.

The clock showed it was ten, and I was famished. The smell of coffee wafted in the air.

I got up, put on my robe and went downstairs to find a pot of coffee being kept hot. God bless Max. As I poured some into a mug, I saw breakfast laid out for me on a tray--a bowl of oatmeal with carved banana slices shaped like pinwheels. Max never misses a chance to garnish.

I took the tray and coffee to the back porch and set it on the wicker table next to Max and sat in the other wicker chair. He was reading the latest copy of "Garnishing Today."

"Welcome back to the world," He put the magazine down and peered at me over his glasses. "What happened to you last night?"

"Missed dinner, didn't I?"

He chuckled. "Thought it best to let you sleep it off. Yesterday afternoon, I saw you through the window walking around the garden and the next minute you were gone. Then about an hour later, you staggered back into the house, up the stairs and fell into bed without changing."

"I went over to meet our neighbor next door." I took a sip.

"Oh?" Max took off his reading glasses. "What's she like? Should we be worried?"

I told Max about Fern, her house, Tansy and the garden. "Fern's mental capacity is a bit off, more like a little girl's than a grown woman's."

"So we have a neighbor with dementia?"

"No, that's not it. More like she's always been that way."

"Why's she living by herself on an island? Doesn't she need help getting along? Shouldn't she be in a nursing home?"

"Obviously not. It seems like she's been here a long time and she's getting along fine. From what I can tell, she lives a simple life and never leaves home. Her needs seem few and she says she gets food and supplies from the mainland. She says two people come by to see her now and again. Maybe the safety of the island is perfect for her lifestyle. She'll be a great neighbor. "

"As long as she doesn't make too much noise."

I laughed. "I don't think she's likely to give loud parties."

I told him about the brownies and tea.

Max raised his eyebrow. "A secret recipe given to her mother in Paris in the nineteen twenties ?" He grinned. "I'd stay away from her baking."

"Or not."

We laughed.

"By the way," I said, "How did I get undressed if, as you said, I fell into bed with my clothes on?"

"My dear, it's not the first time I undressed you." He twirled his moustache and leered at me. "Nor will it be the last,"

"I hope not."

In spite of our close moment, I did not tell Max about my dream, not wanting to taint my hopes of Martini Cove Island with doubt and negativity. During all our years of marriage, I had been able to keep this secret from Max and I would continue to do so. Nothing had happened. It was just a dream.

As I scraped the last bit of cereal from the bowl, I said, "You'll like Fern. She's nutty but sweet."

Max nodded. "There's always one nut in every community."

* * * *

Later that morning, still in my robe, I was sitting in the living room in front of a fire, with Truffle by my side. The chill of last night's experience and the sympathy I had felt for the two wispy ghosts were still with me. I was trying to shake it off with another cup of hot coffee and Mozart on the stereo when the doorbell rang. Neighbors?

I would have to get it. Max would never interrupt the arranging of his tool collection to answer a doorbell. I got up, ran fingers through my hair and retied the belt on my robe. I wanted to meet neighbors, but they were not catching me at my best.

When I opened the door, a man and a woman were standing on the other side of the threshold. Then I noticed another man who was hunched over so much that all I could see at first were the few grey hairs sprouting from the top of his head. When he looked up I saw black-framed glasses with thick lenses and a smile revealing long, yellowish teeth. In one hand he held a worn leather briefcase and in the other a leash attached to a large, snarling dog.

Truffle ran under the couch.

"Howdy, howdy," said the hunched man. He put the briefcase

down and held out a hand wearing fingerless gloves. "Sven Tinkin."

I bent over and shook his hand. "Sylvia Saltwater."

"My colleagues and myself," Sven said, "are The Martini Cove Island Committee for Good Taste, and an informal, *ad hoc* if you will, Welcome Wagon." Sven scratched the dog's pointed ear. "This is Sweetheart, a good citizen of Martini Cove Island, and he is my bery, bery best friend, aren't you, baby?" Sweetheart's bloodshot eyes narrowed and his snarl turned into a yawn.

The skinny woman next to him wore a flowered cotton housedress--and oversized sunglasses. Her greasy hair was parted on the side and fastened with a barrette. Around her neck glittered a thin chain with a gold pendant shaped like a life preserver. She nudged Sven. "Git on with it!" she said in a hillbilly Southern drawl.

"I beg forgiveness." Sven tried to grab her hand to kiss it, but she pulled away. Clearly flustered, he turned back to me. "Let me introduce my colleagues. This is our own Erhleen Frigh."

"Howdy," she said. I think she was trying to smile, but the corners of her mouth turned down instead of up, looking more like a grimace.

"Last but never least, let me introduce the venerable Fermin Lawsom." Sven put his hand on the other man's arm but Lawsom shook it off.

Fermin Lawsom had a wide grin showing false teeth. He wore a white shirt and a white silk kerchief around his neck. His white hair formed a wedge, reminding me of the famous portrait of George Washington.

"We are charmed to welcome you to our glorious community," he said, while making a sweeping gesture with his hand. When it rested on the knot in the kerchief, a gold ring that looked like a life preserver flashed tiny diamonds that spelled "Shit."

I was finally meeting my neighbors, but I was glad Max was busy. He is a snob and can be blunt. I felt this would have been one of those times. He might have slammed the door in their faces. Squaring my shoulders, I told myself it was going to be all right. Since these people live in a premier community, naturally they must be premier people, despite first impressions.

When I invited them in for coffee and cookies, they needed no urging. I asked Sven to leave Sweetheart outside and tie him to the porch railing. He grumbled, but did. Inside, I told them to make themselves comfortable and I'd be right back.

As I passed Max's study, I saw he wasn't there, nor was he in the kitchen. Maybe he had gone for a walk? Just as well.

When I returned to the living room with the tray, Sven and Fermin jumped back from the table where I keep mail. Obviously, the letters had been shuffled. A vase was upside down on the mantel. Erhleen was missing, but before I had a chance to ask where she was, she walked down the stairs.

"Just a bitty trip to the powder room." She was tugging at her pendant. "Thought you wouldn't mind."

"Of course not," I said. "Please sit." They sat in a row on the couch.

I poured the coffee. My guests slurped it up and ate the cookies. When the last crumb was eaten, Sven licked his fingers, opened his briefcase and took out a thin book bound in brown leatherette. He held it out with both hands, bowing over it. "This is the most precious gift you will ever receive at Martini Cove Island."

Bowing back, I took it from him. "Thank you so much." I hoped I was respectful enough. Stamped in gold on the front was the same life preserver motif with *The Martini Cove Island Rules for Harmonious Living* printed under it.

Sven brushed an eyebrow with his fingertip. "I, myself, am the chief architect of these rules."

Erhleen choked, spilling coffee on the Oriental rug. "How's that?" she bellowed. "Who's the chief architect?"

Beads of sweat sprang to Sven's forehead. "Pardon me... Er...of course...our beloved, venerable Colonel Frigh is the chief architect." He wiped his forehead with the back of his hand. "Only under his strict and wise supervision could we now have this glorious guide to community living... Of course... I was merely the scribe writing down his words of wise guidance."

"That's better," Erhleen said.

"I...I...didn't mean to offend," Sven said.

"Goodness gracious." Fermin slammed down his cup. "Let's get on with it, people. Mumsey is expecting me home for lunch and she worries when I'm late."

After buckling up his briefcase, Sven said, "Our task is done, Mrs. Saltwater. You and your husband, whom we hope to meet soon, have the rules for happy living at Martini Cove Island. Follow them to the letter and you will fit right into our premier community."

I opened the leatherette cover and saw there were only two pages, five short paragraphs on each.

"Ten rules?" I said.

"Just ten," Fermin said, and giggled. "Colonel Frigh has combed through them and the committee approved them. Ten rules take care of everything most satisfactorily." He glanced at Erhleen, as if for approval.

Erhleen sniffed.

I hugged the book to my chest. "My husband and I will certainly study the rules. Retiring was a big decision and we wanted to make sure it was in the best possible community. I can't tell you how thrilled we are to be living here. Let me assure you we will do everything to be good neighbors."

Erhleen nodded. "Our neighbors would lie under a bus for each other."

Fermin mumbled. "Hope it never comes to that." He tugged at his kerchief and stood up. "I *must* be going. Mumsey will be ever so cross."

"Can't keep Mumsey waiting," Erhleen said, under her breath.

They rose and I opened the front door.

"You will be superbly happy here," Sven said as he untied Sweetheart.

"I know we will," I said and waved as they walked away and got into their golf cart. I closed the door, leaned my back against it and let out a deep breath. I was glad Max had not been here to meet The

Committee. Just then he came down the stairs.

Startled, I said, "I thought you had gone out. Finished arranging the collection? How does it look?"

"Don't change the subject." Max banged the flat of his hand against the newel post. "You know what that woman did? She went through the medicine chest and then made a quick search through a drawer in the bedroom bureau."

Acting casual, I picked up the tray. "She was probably looking for aspirins."

"In the sock drawer?"

I walked into the kitchen pretending not to hear.

CHAPTER 4

I would not let The Committee or this incident stand in the way of my happiness. I knew Max was skeptical about Martini Cove Island all along, but soon he would see how right this community was for us. I settled into the wing chair while Max sat on the couch.

"Let's take a look at the rules." I tapped the book with my reading glasses. "This is just what I wanted--rules for getting along with our neighbors."

"So far I'm not impressed by the neighbors. I may never have lived in a premier community, but isn't it rude to go through other people's things?"

"I agree, dear, but there was probably a good reason for their behavior."

"Sure, like wanting to know our private business just because they felt like it."

I read the rules out loud.

> "One. Even though we may heap vitriol on our neighbors behind their backs, and let's face it, we all do it, let's keep it to the privacy of our own homes. When you meet a neighbor in public, smile and wave to them as if you meant it. The friendly "Howdy" is suggested or if you are feeling expansive, "Howdy, howdy" is always nice. It is rude, especially in public, during The Colonel's speeches and during edicts set forth by The Committee for Good Taste, to make snide personal comments. So, at all costs, let's be civil, no matter

how we feel about a neighbor or an issue. Never get mad, but if you must, get even."

Max let out a low whistle. "So far, so good."

"Just listen."

> "Two. Color shows our state of mind. It is best to plant flowers that are pastel. It is preferred that all residents wear clothes of pastel hues. The Committee for Good Taste tries to be as impartial and pastel as possible whatever the issue. That way we can make emotionless decisions without letting our hearts get in the way. At times these decisions may seem harsh to those that don't realize what a huge responsibility The Committee has. Letting our hearts rule instead of our heads is risky at best. Let's all follow The Committee's example and think with our heads instead of our hearts."

"Yes, indeed," Max said. "Let's not let our hearts get in the way. I'll throw away my meditation cushion. You may want to burn your leopard print dressing gown and wear something striking like Erhleen's housedress."

I slammed the book down. "Max, if you don't shut up and listen, I'll never talk to you again."

He gestured zipping his lips.

> "Three. At Martini Cove Island, invitations for dinner to neighbors are often given and they are given from the heart. (Yes, there IS an exception to every rule.) Think twice about refusing. Our potlucks are the gathering of friends for company and to promote the ideals of love and peace. Make sure your food contributions reflect this."

I looked over my glasses at Max.

He was staring at the ceiling. "Go on."

"Four. Being good Americans, we recognize the privilege of freedom of speech, but at Martini Cove Island we feel that controversy is so unpleasant. We ask you not to question or criticize our leaders, especially the President of the Association, The Colonel and any member of The Committee for Good Taste. Understand them to be hard working members of our intimate family having no personal agenda other than to serve the whole. Be assured they always know what's best for all of us. Controversy can be so painful and unattractive. Try not to think for yourself but be led whenever possible. Harmony is everything. Occasionally, our leaders have to sacrifice the wishes of one resident for the good of the whole community.

"Five. We ask you to understand that for your protection and so that The Committee for Good Taste can get things done, you look the other way when you see any or all of The Committee members walking around your property. Even though they may seem to be snooping when you see them peeking in your windows or going through your personal possessions, be assured this is not the case. Ever vigilant, they never do anything with malice in mind. They are, instead, insuring our peaceful way of living with the quality control and tranquility we all want. How they do it is up to them. They are to be trusted without question.

"Six. The Committee never permits foul smells, loud noises, inappropriate sights or haranguing of our neighbors in public.

"Seven. Because we are a discreet and premier community, please wrap all liquor bottles in brown paper bags before they are disposed of in the garbage. This is to save our children from the negative influence of such sights by our occasional overindulgence.

"Eight. Pets have always been part of a gracious society and Martini Cove Island is no exception. However, we do ask you to limit your choice of such to one small dog per family. The dog is always to be leashed when outside. We ask that any accidents the dog may have be the personal responsibility of the owner. The Committee frowns on keeping cats because they are too independent and on birds because they are messy and carry diseases.

"Nine. Please be aware of our small community's limited ability to entertain guests. If you have to have company from the mainland, please submit a written request to The Committee no less than five (5) days prior to their arrival. Please provide all names of guests, addresses, ages, and fingerprints. This is not optional. Describe as closely as possible what you intend to do with your guests. This involves the use of any common property: beaches, swimming pool, barbecue pits, etc. and times of day they will be used. Please also estimate the number of flushes for each guest as we do live on a rocky island and waste percolates slowly. These rules are not meant to discourage visitors. The Committee is merely striving to ensure our homeowners of the premier community they were promised. No matter how much we love our guests, please remember they are NOT members of our premier community.

"Ten. Last, but not least, remember the most important motto in our belief system, which to us is NOT a cliché: WHAT GOES AROUND COMES AROUND. Please bear in mind The Committee's morals, friendliness and impartiality as an example. And above all, never tell anyone what you really think."

I closed the book, put it back on the coffee table, took off my glasses, and rested my head on the back of the chair. The silence between Max and me was as appetizing as curdled béchamel. I stole a glance at him. He was looking into the fireplace and twiddling his moustache furiously. The blaze in his eyes was fiercer than the fire.

"In other words," he said after a long silence, "these rules are asking us to be hypocrites, cowards and conformists. Plus, they make no sense at all."

"I know these rules sound...bad," I said. I tried to think of something positive to say about them. "But underneath it all, it still means that the leaders of the community want things to go well. The grounds look great, landscaping impeccable. Things seem well organized."

"At what price?"

"I don't know," I said. I held my hands together, pleading. "We've only been here a short while and we've only met a few people. You just can't have a premier community without *some* good people in it. We just haven't met them yet. Let's give Martini Cove Island a chance, shall we? Maybe we could give a party?"

Max winced. "I don't want to squelch your enthusiasm but I'm tired after the activity of closing the business and packing and moving and all. I just don't feel like having people in our home yet until we've had a chance to really settle in. All right?"

"Of course, dear," I said, but I felt deflated. I wanted to start making friends. "We'll give a big party, only for the nice people and only when you're ready."

Max laughed without mirth and threw his hands up. "Someday we'll give a party, but none of those committee members better come near this house." He pretended to hold a sword, "If they do, I intend to stave them off with my Japanese pickle slicer."

We chuckled. But I was afraid.

CHAPTER 5

The rule about pastel clothing was hard to obey. My clothes had always been black with a dash of brilliant color--a red scarf, a periwinkle blue belt, multicolored pins designed by Max. But I was willing to compromise. I had been an outsider all my life, now I wanted to fit in. In deference to the rules, I bought a mint green jacket for walks with Truffle and a pink ribbon encircled my wide brimmed straw painting hat. However, I would not give up my favorite leopard print tights.

On a bright morning not long after The Committee for Good Taste had paid its visit, I took a walk with Truffle, on a leash of course. I held it in one hand and carried my painting supplies with the other, humming as I walked. Finally, after all these years there was enough time to paint. Hooray!

We climbed the gentle incline of the cliff overlooking the cove. When we reached the top, I took my sunglasses off to see the true colors of everything. Sunlight dappled the rust carpet of fragrant pine needles under my feet. Newly sprouted ferns showed lime green fronds. On the beach breakers rolled and crashed, fashioning foamy lace mantels on silver blue waves. White boats, glowing with reflected sun, bobbed in the water at the marina. Dark green pine trees and striped birches danced in the wind. The air felt fresh on my face and I could taste the sea's saltiness on my lips. Everything invigorated my soul.

An island this serene and breathtaking would surely foster serenity in its residents. Thinking about The Committee for Good Taste, I concluded they were probably better people than they seemed at first. I never was good at first impressions.

I tied Truffle to one of the birches and threw down a lap blanket for him. I unfolded the small portable chair, sat down and opened the paint box, set up the easel, folded back the cover flap of the watercolor pad, unscrewed the jar of water and squeezed paints onto a ceramic palette. Two hours later, the sun was overhead and it was lunchtime. I had finished four small paintings, each more competent than the last. What fun!

Satisfied with the beginning of my watercolor career, I packed up, put the paintings into a tie string portfolio, and headed home.

As we passed by the green surrounded by the condos, I noticed a man in dirty khaki work clothes working in a garden, shoveling mulch from a wheelbarrow. I could smell the manure in the mulch mingling with the scent of the cheap cigar he was smoking. Wasn't there a rule about unpleasant odors in The Martini Cove Island Rules for Harmonious Living? Oh, well. I needed the gardener's help.

"Excuse me, sir," I said.

No reply.

"Excuse me."

He stopped, stuck his shovel into the mulch and slowly turned toward me. He was small and skinny with a withered apple doll face. With one arm resting on the handle of the shovel, he pushed his stained cap back and took several puffs of the smelly cigar, while his gaze roamed insolently over me. In the same Southern hillbilly drawl as Erhleen's, he said, "What can I do for you, sugar?"

I thought the use of the word "sugar," that he pronounced as "sugah," was presumptuous for one in his position.

"I'm Sylvia Saltwater. My husband and I recently moved here." I thought about offering my hand, but when I glanced at his mulch coated, tobacco stained hands, I thought better of it. He did not offer his name but continued sucking on the cigar and staring. "We bought the...ah...little cottage in the middle of the island. As...ah...you can imagine, there's a lot of work to be done in the garden."

His stare made me uncomfortable.

"I'm wondering if you're available to...ah...schedule a time for mulching, trimming, that sort of thing. At your convenience, of course."

He continued staring and puffing. Suddenly, he smiled and I wished he hadn't. What teeth he had left were yellow and brown. His smile was the kind that never reached his tiny, sunken eyes.

"I do whatever I can for my friends and kin." He flicked an ash. "I hope I can count on you to be one of my friends."

A strange, inappropriate request from a gardener, I thought, but I did need his help and I wanted to be on good terms with everyone, including the gardener.

"Why, yes, of course. I do want to be everyone's friend at Martini Cove. We live over there, by--"

"I know where you lives," he said, and winked. "I'll fit you into my schedule, sugar. Once you are my friend, you stay my friend. Ah, hah. You can count on me."

"Thank you."

I made a mental note to question The Committee for Good Taste about this rude and presumptuous gardener. Working as he did for a premier community, he did not act professional. Max and I had always set high standards for our employees and told them where to draw the line and not become too friendly with the clients. And what about those noxious fumes from his cheap cigar? Shouldn't that be reported?

Truffle was pulling his leash. I walked away but could still feel the gardener's stare boring into my back. I turned to see if he were still scrutinizing me. He was, and now he had hooked his thumbs into the belt of his pants and was rocking back and forth on his heels.

"Truffle," I said under my breath, "help isn't what it used to be."

CHAPTER 6

After we'd lived on the island for a month, Max and I were huddling on the windy upper deck of the ferry going back to Martini Cove Island from the city. We needed winter jackets, even though it was already May. A couple was sitting next to us.

It was obvious that the man was in his cups. As he looked at me, his eyes crossed and uncrossed. "Howdy, there," he said, slurring his words. "I'm Lester Prown, owner of Prown's Funeral Home at Martini Cove Island. Here's my card."

"Thank you," I said and read it. *The gentle passing into the eternal everlasting--Prown's Funeral Home. We truly care.* Since there were only eighty residents on the island, he probably did not work much.

I introduced Max and myself.

"This here's the wife, Veeda," he said, and pointed to the woman dressed in a white jacket, white slacks and white shoes. She looked as warm and friendly as a snowball. "She's a high school nurse."

I smiled.

She didn't smile back.

Lester said, surprising us, "Come for dinner Friday night?"

Veeda shot him a dark look.

Max poked me in the back, probably as excited about Lester's invitation as Veeda was.

"We'd love to." I ignored Max and Veeda. I certainly wasn't going to pass up my first dinner invitation. "We'll bring an appetizer."

I thought I heard Max groan but dismissed it as the wind.

Later, when I scribbled the invitation on the calendar, I noticed it would be on Friday the thirteenth.

* * * *

Max had been grumpy since, but on Friday evening just before we were due at the Prown's, he was in the kitchen humming "La Cucaracha." Wearing white latex food preparation gloves, as he always did when working, he placed bowls of salsa, corn chips and decorative bunches of red chili peppers around the brim of a Mexican sombrero. Arranging food was a tonic to him.

"Glad you're in a better mood," I said.

"It might be an interesting evening after all." He stepped back to admire his work and peeled off his gloves. "Funeral homes are usually lovely old houses. I have always wondered about ancient Egyptian mummification practices. Perhaps Lester could give us some insights."

I winced.

"What's the matter, my dear?" Max looked at me, wide-eyed.

I played with the fringe of my scarf. "What if...um...they serve...um...*meat*? I've never been to a funeral home for dinner. I hope they don't serve meat."

Max put his hands on his hips. "Sylvia Saltwater! How very unsophisticated of you. Besides, there have been no deaths at Martini Cove Island for several years, according to Lester."

"Haven't you ever heard of freezers?"

Max picked up the sombrero, and said, "*You* got us into this. Now put on your coat and let's go."

We followed Lester's directions and walked past the condos on the green and down a deserted road, under tall pines, gravel crunching beneath our shoes. Rounding a bend, we stopped and stared. My jaw dropped. In front of us stood two side-by-side, white doublewide trailers. Over the left, a hot pink neon sign read, "Prown's Funeral Home" with the slogan, about the passing and eternal everlasting. The "p" in "passing" had burned out. The sign changed from pink to purple, dark blue, green, light green, yellow, orange, to pink. I looked at Max, watching the color changes reflected on his face.

"Did The Committee for Good Taste approve this?" he said. "If they did, I'd like to know why. Not exactly a lovely old home, is it?"

We walked to the trailer on the right, which we presumed was the residence. Car tires turned inside out and painted white, containing white petunias, added a decorative touch. Max pointed to the tires. "Seems to be Veeda's signature color."

Lester must have been watching from the small round window in the door because it swung open. There he stood, drink in hand, swaying in the doorway seeming as inebriated as the first time we met.

"Welcome," he said, again slurring his words. He gestured us in, his glass slopping over. "I'll just flick the sign off. No use wasting electricity when business is slow."

We climbed the three metal slats and entered the trailer. Max had to tip the sombrero sideways to get it through the narrow door. As soon as I stepped inside, the smell of cooking meat punched my nose.

White metal cabinets, white shag rugs and a long metal table surrounded by a white leatherette banquette made up the combined living and dining area. One white upholstered easy chair stood to the side.

"Have a little bevy before dinner?" Lester said.

"Thank you," Max said. His face was unreadable to anyone except me and I didn't like what I read. "I'd love a bevy. Do you have white wine?"

"Red wine, white wine, pink wine. You name it, we got it." Lester winked.

He turned to the wall stacked with wood crates painted white. I'd never seen such a well-stocked bar with liquor I'd never heard of--*Fire Water Scotch*, *Life Giving Gin*. The labels looked like they'd been rubbed from tombstones. I feared that bottles of formaldehyde might be lurking among the liquor.

"White, please," I said in a small voice, while trying not to take deep breaths. The overpowering smell of cooking meat made me feel faint.

"I like to ferment my own wine and distill my own liquor. Got a lot of space when business is slow," Lester said, and pointed his thumb toward the funeral trailer. He unscrewed a jug of white wine with no label at all, filled two plastic cups and handed them to us.

Max must have been desperate for a drink because he tossed the wine down in one gulp. He turned red, gagged and coughed.

"My kind of man." Lester grabbed Max's glass and refilled it.

I took a sip. I won't even try to describe the taste but I thought of asking Lester for a jug of the wine. My copper pans had stains I can't remove. I doubted, though, Max would use it on his antique tools.

Wearing white jeans and a white sweater, Veeda sauntered in through a narrow hallway. Her bare feet showed white painted toenails.

"What's your pleasure, Bunnykins?" Lester slurred.

"White wine." She didn't greet us, but headed straight for the banquet and sat down. "Max, you take the easy chair."

I slid behind the table and sat on the banquette next to her, since that was my only option. Lester sat on the other side of me. Max didn't hesitate to take the easy chair with a fluffy pillow on the seat. When he sat, we heard a loud "pfrrrt," like passing gas.

That really broke Lester and Veeda up. Her loud "Fwah, fwah, fwah's" filled the trailer.

Max sat without moving, a thoughtful expression on his face. Slowly he stood, just enough to reach for the corner of the pillow with his thumb and forefinger, and pulled it out.

"Look, Sylvia." He held it up, "a whoopee cushion. How droll. I didn't know they still made these." He dropped it on the floor beside him and sat back down.

Lester, still laughing, jumped up to refill Max's glass. "Hey, buddy." He slapped Max on the back, spilling wine on Max's sleeve. "You're a good sport."

Having a great time at Max's expense must have whetted their appetites. They attacked the sombrero with gusto leaving trails of salsa on the table.

When Lester was stuffed with salsa and chips and more wine, he leaned back, sighed and burped.

I was determined to make the best of this evening. "Lester," I said, "tell me about life at Martini Cove Island."

He rested his salsa-stained sleeve behind my back. I leaned forward.

"Bunnykins and I were the second family to move here. Of course, the Colonel and Erhleen came first. They attracted people like them: a nice crowd, family oriented, down-to-earth folks. The Colonel set the tone for the community--nothing fancy about him or his family. And most of us are like that. Of course, we do have our crazies, too. Can't help it in a community, but Colonel Frigh makes sure they don't get a chance to make it an asylum again."

He slapped me on the back and they both laughed uproariously. "Just some Martini Cove Island humor," he added, and wiped a tear from his eye. "So lucky to have the Colonel. You never met the developers of Martini Cove Island, did you? 'Course not." He cleared his throat. "What a couple of stuck-ups they were."

Veeda pursed her lips, stuck her nose up in the air and waved her hand like the Queen of England. "Too good for anyone."

"Tell us about them," I said.

Lester looked at me with bloodshot eyes, as if contemplating what exactly to say. I could almost hear the wheels of his alcohol-oiled mind churning, trying to think. He leaned back, taking a casual pose. As he put his arm around the back of my seat again his hand brushed my shoulder, lingering there longer than necessary. I shrank away. Unfortunately, the more I inched away from him, the closer I got to Veeda. I was trapped. Max had suffered momentary humiliation, but now had the luxury of sitting by himself.

Lester waved his hand in a dismissive gesture. "Hardly remember them. Some la-di-da people from the city who thought they could run this island. A while after the Colonel came, they disappeared, turned tail and ran. Never heard from them again.

Cowards. Couldn't deal with a strong leader like the Colonel.

"At the same time, a lot of money went missing from association funds. We figured they stole the money, changed their names and are now living far away in a warm country. Right, Bunnykins?"

Bunnykins nodded. "They were a regular little prince and princess." She snorted. All her mirth sounds were unpleasant. "But I could see right through them, yes siree, I sure could because I'm a plain person from plain stock just like the Colonel and Erhleen. Don't like fancy people with fancy airs. That prince and princess told us we couldn't live in a mobile home in this here community. Imagine! All my people have always lived in mobile homes. It's a proud family tradition. The Colonel understood that when he took over Martini Cove Island. We don't have to live in a cottage or condo, wouldn't feel right."

"The Colonel sounds pretty special," I said.

She nodded. "The Colonel makes sure that every member of his family, kin or extended, gets what they deserve. You are considered kin if you work with him to make Martini Cove Island a family place. He doesn't like it when you go against him, and he'll set you straight."

"Lucky for us," Lester said, "getting a real leader like the Colonel. Always knows the right thing to do." He tried to put his elbow on the table but it slipped off. "Bunnykins, is dinner ready yet?"

"I'll check."

Max ran his hand lightly over the metal dining table. "An unusual piece."

"Genuine antique." Lester slapped his hand against it. "Autopsy table I found here at the abandoned loony bin. Cleaned it up like new. Different, hah?"

Max snatched his hand away. Maybe it was just the light, but I could swear he turned slightly green. Or perhaps it was just the cheap wine. He was getting a lot of refills.

"We've never eaten from an autopsy table, have we Sylvia?"

"No, dear," I said, "but remember the plastic surgeon's party you insisted on catering? The doctor who was fascinated with jungle culture? We had to hide his shrunken head collection before the guests arrived."

Max gave me a dark look. Maybe Lester would have laughed if he had been able to focus on the conversation.

Just then Veeda came back, carrying a large bowl. She set it down on the table. "My famous goulash. Specialty of the house."

I almost fainted.

Max rubbed his hands together and said, "We love goulash, don't we, dear?"

Veeda slapped a serving on my plate.

I pushed it around with my fork to make it seem like I was eating. I felt sick.

Lester and Veeda were too busy slurping theirs down to notice.

Max ate all of his.

After the goulash, Max and I got another surprise. Lester said, "We are invited to Slick and Wanda Shaloe's house for dessert. They're swell folks and our best friends."

At least I wouldn't have to smell cooked meat anymore. And thank goodness, Max never asked Lester about ancient Egyptian mummification practices.

After dinner, I helped Veeda clean up, not because I wanted to ingratiate myself with her, but to avoid having to dodge Lester's hands. I have never seen anyone scrub dishes the way she did. She washed each plate three times, scouring with a plastic scrub and hot water. She gave me a clean white towel to dry each with. I guessed she just couldn't stop being a nurse. At least I would not be getting sick from bacteria in her kitchen.

We held on to our seats as we rode to the condos in their golf cart. Lester took the corners fast and found all the lumps and dips on the sand road.

I watched Max, whose eyes were closed. Evidently, the cheap wine had taken its toll. When we stopped in front of one of the condos, he opened his eyes and sighed.

I mouthed to him soundlessly, "It will be over soon."

He mouthed back, "I hope so."

We stood in front of a door, Lester leaning into the bell. The doormat had writing on it that said, *"Entrez vous."*

When the door opened, there stood a woman wearing form fitting pink tights and a low cut pink top stretched over large breasts, with a quarter sized diamond and gold pendant nestled between them. Streaked blond hair in a ponytail and pink high heels completed the look, not good for a woman in her fifties who was forty pounds overweight.

"Bone swear," she said, through candy pink lips.

I realized she was saying, *"Bon soir."*

"I'm Wanda, *intray vuz.*"

The living room furniture was upholstered in pink, with lace-edged, heart-shaped pillows dotting the sofas. Pink rugs depicting scenes of Paris were scattered on the floor. Two black wrought iron lamps shaped like the Eiffel Tower, with pink shades, flanked the couch. Obviously, pink was to Wanda what white was to Veeda.

Slick, her husband, a mousy man with thinning brown hair and black-rimmed glasses, shook our hands. When he smiled he showed pointy rat-like teeth.

Max headed for one of the easy chairs but just before he sat, he took off the pillow and dropped it on the floor. He plopped down, a sure sign that he was drunk, and closed his eyes.

Slick and Lester left for the kitchen to get after dinner drinks. Ignoring us, Veeda and Wanda sat down on the couch and started talking and giggling like teenagers.

I examined the living room. Over the fireplace mantel hung an abstract portrait of a woman, head in profile, eyes frontal, one on her forehead and one on her chin. I got up to get a better look.

Wanda broke from her conversation with Veeda. "That's an original. Wait 'til you see this!" She sauntered to the mantel. *"Observay vuz."* She flicked on a switch. The eyes in the portrait lit up in red. Stepping back, she looked at it lovingly. "We bought it in Vegas, an original Pablo Peekasew. You know, the famous painter."

She pointed to the name in the corner.

Max's eyes fluttered open, "Exquisite."

Neither he nor I mentioned Pablo's last name is spelled P-i-c-a-s-s-o.

Max steepled his fingers. "I'm familiar with his Blue Period. But I didn't know he had a Black Velvet Period."

Her blank stare told us she didn't know what he was talking about.

I wanted to kill Max.

Just then, Lester and Slick came back from the kitchen, Slick carrying a tray of liqueurs and Lester an assortment of glasses. They put their offerings down on the coffee table.

"*Excuzem-moi,*" said Wanda, rhyming "*moi*" with "coy." "I'll just get the petit snacks." She tapped her way to the kitchen.

I had to give Slick this much. He had a better selection of liquor than Lester.

Max snapped back to consciousness when Slick asked him what his pleasure was.

"A double Courvoisier," Max said without hesitation.

Slick poured a liberal amount into a brandy snifter and set it on the coffee table. "*Merci beaucoup,*" Max said.

I didn't think I could hold alcohol after the detestable wine, but some Benedictine might help me get through the rest of the evening.

Wanda came back carrying a tray that she set on the coffee table. She bent over in front of Max, exposing more of her breasts. She looked up at him, probably expecting a look of approval and appeared disappointed when his eyes were closed.

Maybe Wanda had heard the French eat cheese for dessert. The tray was filled with crackers and cheese squeezed from a can. I shuddered at the thought of Max's reaction when he opened his eyes.

By now I was pretty hungry having eaten neither the salsa and chips nor the goulash, and having drunk too much. Even squeezed cheese looked good. I took a cracker and popped it in my mouth. Then another and another. As I ate, I noticed the photo at the bottom of the tray. I had already uncovered an eye and brown hair. I put my reading glasses on, while stuffing more crackers into my mouth. I uncovered a large building with a sign that said, "Watergate." In front of it stood a smiling younger, thinner Wanda with brown hair, and a grinning younger Slick with mutton-chop sideburns. Slick was pointing at the man next to him, who was looking over his shoulder with narrowed eyes. I leaned forward. Could it be? Yes. It was Richard Nixon with a blob of squeezed cheese on the end of his nose.

I looked at Max. He was watching the tray, too, with the intensity of an archeologist at a dig.

After I worked the sticky cheese off the roof of my mouth with my tongue, I swiveled the tray around to Max. "Look."

Max put on his glasses. "Is that who I think it is?"

Slick had one elbow propped on the mantel and a brandy glass in hand. "Yes, that's Dick. The picture was taken when Wanda and I were in Washington at a Young Republicans meeting."

Everyone looked at Max, but he had closed his eyes again. They looked at me.

"Nice picture," I said.

Max was snoring.

"Time to go home," I said, while getting up.

Max jumped up immediately. "Yes. Still fatigued from the move."

Fatigued from the move, my ass. It was that cheap wine topped off by cognac.

"You can't go yet," Slick said, "We haven't had a chance to chat."

Before we could object, Slick had refilled our glasses. We sank back into our seats. What the heck. One more wouldn't matter.

"Just a few minutes," I said.

"Have some more *horse duvers.*" Wanda passed out cocktail napkins with the same photo as the tray.

"Great misunderstood statesman." Slick shook his head as he smiled at the photo on his napkin.

"That's right," Lester said, "like Colonel Frigh."

"You think highly of the Colonel, don't you?" I said, addressing Slick.

"If it weren't for the Colonel's down to earth, old fashioned common sense and know-how," Slick said, and jabbed the air with his forefinger to make his point, "Martini Cove Island would be a mess. Everyone would want to express opinions. We can't have that. Everybody needs to be on the same page and The Colonel puts us there." He slammed fist into palm.

Wanda moved to her husband's side and put a hand on his thigh, rubbing up and down, giggling. "Slick is a convert but he wasn't always. He used to think he could lead the community better than the Colonel when he ran for President of the Board, but the Colonel showed him the error of his ways. Didn't he Slicky?"

Slick's face turned red. "Did you have to bring that up?"

Lester laughed.

Veeda snorted.

"What happened?" Max said.

I didn't think Max had been paying attention but he was sober enough to needle Slick.

Veeda snorted again and wiped a tear from her eye. "It went like this." She leaned forward. She seemed only too happy to bring up the incident that had embarrassed her good friend, Slick.

"A few years ago, the community had to elect a new president. The original developer, who was the first president, and his wife had disappeared." Veeda stopped long enough to pour herself another drink and wiggle comfortably into the pink couch.

"He and his wife were terrible leaders. Soft and liberal. There was speculation about their sudden disappearance, too. Most folks believed they had embezzled funds from the association because thousands were missing from the treasury. A lot of homeowners were plenty mad. We believe they might have fled to a warm country, changed their identities and are now drinking cocktails with umbrellas in them.

"We needed a new president, so Slick announced he would run. After all, he had been president of the Young Republicans' Club. The

Colonel didn't like that at all because *he* wanted to be president and as we know now, he *does* know best. One night, a Port-A-Potty was left on the lawn in front of Slick and Wanda's unit, with a note on it that said, 'If you try to become president, your life will be down this.'" A fit of giggles overtook Veeda.

They all laughed, but I saw a bead of sweat on Slick's upper lip.

"Of course," Wanda said hastily, coming to Slick's defense, "the Colonel being a wonderful man, stepped down as president after a few months. He said he could do more good behind the scenes. Then, Slick, running unopposed and endorsed by the Colonel, won. He has done a marvelous job since." She smiled at him and patted his cheek.

"Most folks," Veeda continued, "were sure that the Colonel had left the Port-A-Potty." She slapped her thigh. "He has the best sense of humor."

"The Colonel is a good man." Slick wiped sweat from his upper lip with a napkin.

"Some misunderstand him," Lester said. "Great leaders like Dick and the Colonel are always misunderstood."

"Can't wait to meet him," I said. "He must be an extraordinary person."

Max had slumped to one side and was snoring again.

"My husband seems all done in. We should go," I said.

Max shot to his feet. "Thank you for an unforgettable evening."

"Thank you," I also stood, ready to go.

"We must do this again soon," Lester said.

"Let's go for a sail," Slick said. "We own that forty-five-foot beauty down at the marina, the *Screw Vous.* The name was Wanda's idea." He smiled at her with pride, and clipped her playfully on the chin.

Wanda giggled and lowered her eyes.

Max said, "I can't wait."

We shook hands and thanked them, but refused a ride home, saying that it was only a five-minute walk.

The night was brisk and clear. Stars blinked above, a sliver of waxing moon cast faint light on everything. I shone the beam from a small flashlight on the path. Max was walking fine, not weaving as I thought he might after all the cheap wine and cognac. Nothing indicated the sleepy, alcohol induced stupor he had been in a short while ago.

"What a night!" He burrowed his fists deep into the pockets of his jacket. "Veeda's proud family tradition is living in trailers, *Life Giving Gin*, an old autopsy table used for dining, a fifty-year-old pink teenager, a living room that looked like the inside of a Pepto-Bismol bottle, an original Peekasew. Dick Nixon on paper napkins, for heaven's sake! Did you notice Slick's pointy rodent teeth? He probably chews electric wires for fun."

That did it. I burst into tears. We stopped walking and immediately Max folded me into his arms.

"Don't cry, my dear," he said, while rocking me.

I howled into the collar of his jacket, "I'm so disappointed. I had such hopes for making good friends here."

Max stroked my hair. He could make me feel better, no matter how bad I felt. I dug into my jacket pocket and found an old tissue.

"Let's not give up quite yet," Max said. "Remember the strange people we've encountered throughout the years? The party we catered at the funeral home for the rich widow's deceased husband? She was so happy he was dead that she wanted us to tie black balloons to his coffin. And don't forget the woman who had a party for her fifteen cats and wanted me to pipe cat food from a pastry bag? "

"She said your cat food canapés looked better than the ones her caterer made for her last human party."

"You weren't disappointed not to become their friends."

"But they weren't our neighbors."

"I promise we'll make friends, my dear. We just need to find better people."

"Thank you for that." I blew into the tissue. Then I took a good look at him. He was as sober as if he had never drunk that horrid wine. "I thought you were drunk, what with all those refills at Lester's and your nodding off at Slick's."

He laughed. "Let's put it this way: that whoopee cushion will never work again."

"You didn't!" I laughed.

He nodded. "When their heads were tilted back to laugh at their fine joke, I poured the wine into the cushion. It's probably eaten through the floor of the trailer by now."

"Thanks for being a good sport," I said and kissed him. "I appreciate your understanding how much I want this community."

Max took my hand and we walked home.

After we got through the door and Truffle had finished jumping up and down, Max said, "How about a nightcap, my dear? To clear the palate?"

I was pretty tired by now but sitting by a fire with Max, Truffle on my lap, was too tempting to pass up. "Just one."

I put on classical guitar music and curled up on the couch while Max fixed the drinks in the kitchen.

When he returned, he said he had invented a new drink for us to commemorate our first dinner with neighbors. He had mixed brandy, liqueur, some of this and some of that, and topped it off with ginger beer. They were quite good and we sat there for a long time, not talking, watching the fire and sipping.

The best part of the evening was Max's concoction of the *F-13*.

CHAPTER 7

A couple of weeks after that night, I was leafing through a book of marine watercolor paintings, but I couldn't keep my mind on it. My thoughts kept drifting to our new neighbors.

We had assumed that in a premier community like Martini Cove Island, everyone would be classy. That was not true of Lester, Veeda, Slick, Wanda, and even The Committee for Good Taste. They were people without style and grace, the qualities Max and I strove for in our work and lives. Even simple-minded Fern was more like the people we'd hope to meet. What can I say other than that I was disappointed?

Meanwhile, I decided to pay Fern another visit. Although she was strange in many ways, she was delightful, too. Her house, although shabby, and garden were uplifting, and I enjoyed her company. I would make muffins to take. Her brownies were delicious but I didn't need more of those.

As I was taking the muffins out of the oven, Max came into the kitchen, sniffing. "Do I get a sample?" He reached for a bit of muffin that had dropped to the counter.

This was a good a time for Max to meet her. "Only if you come with me to pay a neighborly call."

His mouth was open to pop the bit in but his hand stopped in mid-air.

"Not to those people we were with the other night?"

"No."

"Don't know anybody else here," he said, while chewing the bit, "unless you just pack the muffins up and decide to knock on any door."

"I know one other person."

He stopped chewing. "Our dotty neighbor?"

"She's not just dotty; she's also sweet. I think you might like her, and we really should pay a neighborly call together."

Max sighed. "Okay."

"We'll stay a few minutes."

"Promise?"

"Be brave." I lined a basket with a napkin and stacked the muffins in.

As we stood by Fern's front door, I whispered to Max to stay out of sight for the time being and I knocked.

Fern opened the door a crack and peeked out. "I know you," she said. "You live next door. You liked my brownies."

"Yes, I did." I felt Max poke me and I jabbed him with my elbow. I held the basket up and lifted the napkin, the fragrance of the muffins wafting out. "I baked you something. My husband Max wants to meet you, too. He's right here. May we come in?"

Her eyes were wide and frightened. "Is it safe?"

"He wants to be your friend, too."

She stuck her head out and looked at Max. "Handsome, isn't he?"

"I think so."

"All right. Come in." She stepped back to let us pass, and then quickly shut the door.

Max said, "May I shake your hand?"

Fern looked at me.

I nodded.

He held her hand lightly. "Pleased to meet you."

Fern smiled shyly and curtsied. "Would you like some tea?"

"That would be lovely," he said.

After she left for the kitchen, Max looked around. Although shabby, the tasteful furniture and carpets were as neat and clean as last time. Bouquets of fresh flowers made the room cheerful. "Pleasant."

Hooray! Finally Max had something nice to say about a neighbor.

He looked at the photos and held up the one of Fern and her parents with Gertrude and Alice. He turned to me and raised an eyebrow.

I nodded. "Yes, that's who you think they are."

Fern came back with a tray and saw Max looking at the photos.

"You like them?" she said.

"Fascinating."

We sat at the table and Fern said, "I did so enjoy Paris with my parents." She sighed and poured the tea. "It's nice of you to visit again. When were you here last time? Yesterday?"

I glanced at Max. "A couple of weeks ago," I said. "We wonder if we can bring you something from the city?"

"No, thank you." She sipped her tea and nibbled at a muffin, staring into space.

Finally, she said, "I miss her, you know."

"Your mother?" I said.

She shook her head. "The lady who used to live in your house."

I was excited since I wanted to know as much as I could find out about it. "You knew someone who lived in my house?"

"They lived there, you know, the pretty bluebird and the wolf."

Glancing at Max, I saw his teacup poised mid-way to his lips.

I sat on the edge of my seat. "Who are the pretty blue bird and the wolf? What are their real names? How long ago did they live there? Why did they leave?"

She wrinkled her forehead. "I don't like to remember sad things." Looking behind her as if someone might be listening, she said, "Mustn't tell." She put a finger to her lips.

"Why?"

Fern shrank into herself and called for Tansy who jumped into her lap.

"Sorry if I upset you."

She stroked Tansy's long fur. "The buzzards swallowed them up," she whispered, and tears welled in her eyes. "Will the buzzards swallow me, too?"

"Of course not, dear." I leaned over and touched her thin arm. "If you need help, we're right next door."

"Promise?" Her eyes were wide and innocent.

"Promise," I said.

"So do I," Max said, and his gaze was soft as he looked at her.

Fern pulled a lace-edged handkerchief from her sleeve to wipe a tear. The fragile old lady entered my heart at that moment, and I felt responsible for her. For the first time at Martini Cove, I thought about what I could give to someone, rather than what they could give me. I had someone to watch out for besides Max and Truffle. I wanted to protect Fern and I also wanted to find out more about the pretty bluebird, the wolf and the buzzards who had swallowed them up.

When we got back to our house, I said to Max, "So, is Fern just a dotty old woman?"

After twiddling his moustache, he said, "She's child-like, but sweet, honest, without guile. Considering the people we've met here and most of the people I've worked with, she's a refreshing change--not the worst neighbor we could have. She keeps to herself and makes no noise. What better neighbor? When the time is right, we'll ask how she came to live at Martini Cove."

Max looked out his study window in the direction of Fern's house. He turned to me. "Who do you think are the pretty bluebird, the wolf and the buzzards?"

"I haven't a clue."

That night I dreamed again.

I'm at the bottom of the ocean where it's cold and dark. I see the columns of smoke turn into the ghostly figures of the man and woman. As I walk toward them, I see the sadness in their eyes.

"Betrayed," the woman whispers. "Betrayed, betrayed, betrayed."
"How can I help?" I ask.
They fade away.

CHAPTER 8

One Tuesday, when Max was shopping in town, I sat on the back porch working on a watercolor of the sun shimmering through the leaves behind the house. Birds sang, mourning doves cooed, the air felt crisp.

Truffle suddenly lifted his head and leaped off the porch toward a woman who was walking around the corner of the house. She had short gray hair and was wearing a lime green pantsuit. Lime green? At Martini Cove Island?

"Yoo hoo, y'all," she said, and waved.

Truffle jumped onto the woman's legs.

"Here, boy!" I called hurrying down the porch steps.

The woman bent to pet him. "Honey, I don't mind that bitty dog," she said in a refined Southern accent, not like Erhleen's. "And don't worry. I won't report you to The Committee for Good Taste for having an unleashed dog!" She winked.

I picked him up and tucked him under my arm.

"Sorry to come into your yard unannounced," she said, "but no one answered the doorbell. I took a chance and walked around back, hoping I'd find someone home. I am your neighbor, Butterfly Bordereau." She touched one of two enormous earrings shaped like butterflies. "My husband, Haywood, and I just got back from a trip down South visiting relatives, and I came over the minute I heard you had moved in."

"I'm Sylvia Salt..."

"Of course, we know your names and that you were renovating

this lovely cottage, and I just couldn't wait to meet you." She had a broad, warm smile, but razor sharp brown eyes that I suspected did not miss much.

I invited her to sit on the porch. Truffle jumped into her lap and she petted him until he was settled.

"I just adore meeting new residents," Butterfly said, "especially here on the island. Makes me feel like we still have a chance to get some good neighbors."

My voice quavered as I said, "Don't you like our neighbors?"

"Well, honey, do you?" She pierced me with a look that defied me to lie.

I squirmed. "I suppose I should lie, but I think you would know."

"Aha."

Maybe it was because Truffle liked her. Maybe it was because she wasn't wearing pastel. Maybe it was because I needed a friend. I decided to confide in her. "I really don't like anyone here yet. Oh, except for you, of course, and our neighbor Fern." I sighed. "I want to like my neighbors, but..."

"I know." Her glance swept the porch and she looked over both shoulders. "Honey, it's like this." She leaned toward me and circled a finger near her temple. "Most of the residents are s-t-r-a-n-g-e." She paused, seeming to search for the right words. "How can I say this without sounding like a snob, but they have no *class,* no graciousness manners or appreciation for the niceties of life." She paused and leaned back, never taking her eyes off me.

"Unfortunately, that's what I think, too."

She clapped her hands. "I just knew we would be on the same page the moment I saw you were wearing animal print tights." She made a helpless gesture with her hands. "When Haywood and I moved here more than a year ago, we were open- minded. We tried to appreciate the differences between our neighbors and ourselves and thought we could thrive together, being that we live in this here premier community. But, uh uh. After attending many pot luck dinners and living together on this weensy island, I have definitely changed my mind. As Haywood Bordereau says time and again, 'If you ain't got class, whatever else you got don't matter.' Have you met the Colonel?"

"Not yet."

"You will, honey. I have observed that, although he is not the president of the association, he is the leader here. Either you do as the Colonel does or you are... Ah...ha...yes, ma'am, you are O-U-T. Unfortunately, or fortunately--I don't know which--Haywood and I are definitely *not* in agreement with the way the Colonel looks at life."

She scratched behind Truffle's ear. "I just love dogs and I had a number of them, all fluffy white ones. But I wouldn't want one here. Too much fighting about them, too many rules, and nobody pays attention to the rules anyhow." She looked at her large-faced watch. "Goodness, I have rattled on so, I haven't given you a chance to tell me about yourself. Where are you from and what brought you here?"

I told her about Max, *Presentation Is Everything* and our retirement.

"Then you are celebrities." She smiled and put a hand over her heart. "My, my, my."

I blushed.

She asked to see the house, so I gave her a tour. She commented about everything.

I couldn't get a word in.

At the front door, before leaving, she said, "What do you think about Martini Cove Island, other than the people?"

"This island is the most gorgeous place I have ever seen or lived in. Its beauty breaks my heart."

She nodded. "Exactly. It was divine providence that brought me here, surely it was. I was meant to live here. I can never, ever leave. But I'm not so sure about Haywood." She checked her watch again. "Look at the time. How I chatter on. Come by for cocktails this Friday and we'll meet the husbands. Around four?"

I said we'd love to and we'd bring the appetizers. I knew Max was having garnishing withdrawals.

She was gone as quickly as she had come. I liked Butterfly and hoped I would like Haywood, too. Max had to like them. He just had to.

* * * *

Max accepted the news of the Bordereau's invitation with equanimity. If nothing else, I think he was pleased at having a chance to concoct hors d'oeuvres again.

"They are from the South," I said," and she's charming in a Southern belle sort of way."

"As luck would have it, I bought a can of okra today. Thought it might be good in soup, but would work for appetizers, too."

Good! He was interested.

"This invitation *has* to be better than the last," I said.

"There's no place to go but up."

That Friday, I decided to wear a black cocktail dress Max had always liked on me. I set it off, to honor the occasion, with an enamel pin Max had designed, a peach with a butterfly sitting on it.

In the kitchen, Max was busy piping deviled Smithfield ham into miniature grilled Portobello mushroom caps, but when he saw me, he stopped to wolf whistle.

"Thank you, dear." I picked up one of the caps and brought it to my lips. He snatched it away and put it back on the tray.

"Sorry," he said. "You'll ruin the symmetry."

That was Max's way of saying he thought I was getting fat. I decided not to mention his paunch.

Max had arranged the mushroom caps, sweet potato puffs and mini okra quiches on a silver tray to resemble a Colonial Williamsburg garden maze. My finger hovered slightly above the small morsels as I traced a path to the rose bush crafted from cabbage leaves and grape tomatoes.

"You did it again," I said. "There's no limit to your genius."

Max sniffed and looked lovingly at the tray.

As we put on our raincoats, Truffle, sated with quantities of ham, snored under the kitchen table.

It was chilly that afternoon and dark gray clouds threatened rain as we walked to the Bordereau's cottage. Max carried the tray, with toothpicks tenting plastic wrap over the canapés. Along the way, I said "Howdy!" to several people. We passed the members of The Committee for Good Taste huddled together and pointing to the roof of a house. Sven was taking notes, scribbling furiously in a thick notebook. Obviously, they were on Committee business. They noticed us, waved, and said in chorus, "Howdy!"

"Howdy!" I replied and waved back.

Max nodded in their direction.

"Say 'Howdy!' It's the rule," I said in a harsh whisper.

Max whispered back, "Be reasonable. I can't say 'Howdy!' with my hands full."

As we passed, The Committee eyed the tray and I could read the bubbles over their heads: "Where are they going? What's on that tray?" I think I saw drool at the corner of Sven's mouth.

As we walked on, I could feel their glares boring into our backs. After we turned a corner I looked back, but they weren't following.

I had passed the Bordereau's cottage on my walks before I knew who lived there and had admired the small white house with an antebellum flair--the columns, the ferns, the white wrought iron furniture on the front porch. So far, so good. It beat the Prown trailer.

I rang the front doorbell and heard chimes inside playing the first two bars of the theme from "Gone with the Wind."

Max's eyebrows shot up.

A man answered the door. He had a grizzly grey beard with no moustache that gave him a sea captain's look. "Y'all come on in now," he said in the same Southern accent as Butterfly's and we made introductions. Then he noticed the tray. "That's a mighty fine presentation, sir, sure enough. Your work I presume? Mrs. Bordereau told me you are a well-known caterer." He took the tray from Max and placed it carefully on the coffee table in the living room.

Max looked pleased. Score one for Haywood.

The living room with a polished hardwood floor scattered with Oriental carpets, boasted antique tables, chairs, and divans covered in light blue satin. Oil portraits from the nineteenth century bearing likenesses to Butterfly and Haywood hung on the egg yolk colored walls. White shutters covered the windows and ferns on carved wood pedestals carried out the Southern theme.

A gracious winding staircase with an ornate banister dominated the room. I expected Scarlett O'Hara to come sweeping down but instead, I saw Butterfly poised at the top, waiting to make a grand entrance.

When she saw that we had noticed her, she floated down. "Welcome to our home," she said, and graciously extended her arms. She was wearing a red pantsuit and a pair of large gold drop earrings, but I imagined her in a frilly hoop skirt and broad brimmed hat, with finger curls peeking out at the side. As she swooped toward us, I swear I saw her curtsey, although she probably didn't.

Max looked enchanted.

When she noticed Max's tray, she exclaimed, hands fluttering to her heart "It looks just like the maze garden in Colonial Williamsburg."

Max's face shone and he winked at me.

Haywood, after inviting us to sit, offered drinks. When he brought out the bottle of wine, we saw that it was an excellent vintage from a well-known vintner. He poured a glass for Max first and said, "Sir, I invite you to drink the devil off the bottle."

Max looked at him, puzzled.

"It's a Southern expression that means it's the first drink out of the bottle and you will ensure that we all don't get drunk."

Max laughed. "Anything to help." He downed the first sip.

"You'll get used to our Southern expressions," said Butterfly. "Now fill the ladies up, sir. We're drier than a cotton ball." She passed out small porcelain plates with scalloped edges and embroidered napkins with a fancy script "B" in the corner.

I knew Max was taking it in and all was well.

"I just can't wait any longer," Butterfly said. "May I try one of these scrumptious looking quiches?"

"Of course," said Max. "They're okra."

Butterfly's eyes widened. "Okra is my favorite vegetable and under-appreciated by Northerners. This is a treat." She popped one into her mouth and closed her eyes. "I died and went to heaven. Reminds me of my mama's garden in the summer. It was my job to pick the okra."

"Damn!" said Haywood. "That's one mighty fine okra quiche."

They also loved the mushroom caps with Smithfield ham and the sweet potato puffs. Max was beaming.

After heaping her plate, Butterfly leaned toward Max. "Please tell us about your interesting profession. I never met anyone in your line of work. I know now--" She gestured toward the half empty tray. "--why you were extremely successful."

Max blushed, lowered his eyes, and launched into anecdotes. He told them about studying in Japan, how we started *Presentation Is Everything,* catering for The White House, and his Five Golden Radish Awards. They listened intently and laughed in all the right places. I had seldom heard Max so talkative. Finally, he lifted his hands in an "I've talked enough" gesture.

"Please tell us about yourselves," Max said. "What was your profession?"

"I was in the boat designing business," Hayward said, and stroked his beard.

That explained the nautical look.

Max said, "Fascinating."

Haywood nodded. "Yes, it surely was. I had some intriguing challenges. Fulfilling millionaires' dreams is not an easy job. Lots of ego involved, but rewarding when you get it right. As a matter of fact, I designed the yacht for two of our residents, Sky and Lucia Somerport. I'm proud of that one, a fifty-four-foot sailing vessel. Didn't have to do much designing, though, just followed their sketches, designed by instinct from years of sailing and love of the sea. They call her *The Golden Fleece*. She's sleek, fast, comfortable. Perhaps they'll invite us for a sail sometime."

"Surely, they will," said Butterfly. "They are generous and gracious to a fault. Sky and Lucia are perceived as snobs by most of the residents, but they're not. They hate pretension. It's something pretentious people don't understand." She winked at me. "I believe you will like them. We are all on the same page."

"How so?" I said.

Butterfly and Haywood glanced at each other, and I noticed her exuberance was replaced by sadness. She strained to see out the front windows before she continued. In a low voice, she said, "All is not right at Martini Cove Island. No sir."

I followed her gaze, but saw only bars of twilight sky through the shutter slats.

Max and I leaned forward.

"When we moved here four years ago," she said, "we thought we were in a democratically run homeowner's association. But no. Colonel Frigh has taken over, sure enough."

Max's was twiddling his moustache. I reached for another quiche. Haywood stroked his beard.

Butterfly adjusted an earring. "After you've been here a while, you'll see how it works. I don't want to spoil your expectations about Martini Cove Island, but after people move here, I can tell whether they admire Colonel Frigh or not."

"What happens?" I stuffed a sweet potato puff into my mouth.

"It's complicated, but here's the gist. The Colonel and Erhleen want more than anything to get you into their family, as they call their community. Now, I think family and community are noble institutions, but Haywood and I believe it's important *how* you create them."

Max interjected, "Of course. Sylvia and I know presentation is everything."

"Not these people," Haywood said. "Their methods are ugly

enough to stop an eight-day clock."

"That's enough, Haywood Bordereau." Butterfly crossed her ankles and leaned back. "Oh, I just know we are going to be great friends."

"Please," I said, "tell us more about Colonel Frigh. We understand from other residents that he's terrific."

"Those other residents wouldn't happen to be Slick and Wanda, Lester and Veeda, and The Committee for Good Taste, would they?" Haywood said.

I nodded and reached for a mushroom cap.

"The Colonel's admirers," said Haywood, and cast a look at Butterfly. "We don't think much of them ourselves."

She shook her head.

"The Colonel has bullying ways, and--" Haywood sipped wine. "--there's a secret Butterfly and I know about the Colonel and Erhleen."

Haywood leaned forward. "What I am about to tell you is part truth, part conjecture and part myth. But I don't--and I reckon no one knows--where one leaves off and the other begins."

I reached for another mushroom cap and took a large gulp of wine.

"Butterfly and I had lived at Martini Cove Island for one peaceful year before the Frighs moved in. We knew at once who they were. Their family is notorious in the South. Over the years, many stories circulated about them. Some say their original name was Fright but they dropped the 't'. Now it rhymes with 'pie' and sounds homey-like."

Max reached for the bottle, something he would ordinarily never do to a host, and filled his own glass.

Haywood continued. "It all began in the mid 1800's with the first Colonel Frigh, who was the most successful slave trader in the South, operating out of Savannah. He was an excellent craftsman and builder, using his fine abilities to train slaves as carpenters to build small towns. He named them Frigh Town 1, Frigh Town 2 and so on, five in all. He appointed himself and family members to places of power: mayors, administrators and such.

"Soon, the family members became very rich, and felt much obliged to the old man. However, if any of the family went against his wishes, and occasionally someone did, they would simply disappear. The old man told everyone that the person had gone out West to seek new adventures. Curiously, though, the relative in question was never heard from again. According to rumor, the old man's wife, Grammy Sweet Pea, would notice a fresh notch on the handle of her husband's hammer after each one of these disappearances. Sweet Pea, of course, never questioned her husband."

Haywood paused and held up the wine bottle. "Refills?"

We held our glasses out.

"The Emancipation Proclamation was the biggest blow the Frigh Family ever suffered, because his free labor force was gone. The old man managed to limp along on the profits generated by the original Frigh Towns, but he never built others. The residents eventually frowned on the methods used to build them and moved out, so they became ghost towns. The defeat the old man felt went deep into the core of his being."

Haywood paused and stroked his beard. "Now here is the most intriguing and mysterious part of the story."

If we edged any closer to Haywood, we would fall off our chairs.

I was reaching for yet another mushroom cap when I caught Max's eye. His eyebrows were raised so high they almost reached his hairline. Too polite to correct me in public, he was looking at the trail of crumbs between the tray and me that dotted the previously clean rug. I put the mushroom cap down.

Haywood continued. "The old man sank deep into a depression of enormous proportions. Most of the day, he sat in his woodworking shop, blinds drawn, drinking great quantities of moonshine, which, in all likelihood, aggravated his mental state even more. At night, it was rumored, he visited former female slaves who were too intimidated to defend themselves. It was downright embarrassing to Grammy Sweet Pea, whose greatest goal had been to become a fine lady. There was no reasoning with him, so Sweet Pea decided to take matters into her own hands."

Haywood rose to pour more wine, but the bottle was empty. "Be right back," he said. He returned with a freshly opened bottle and refilled glasses.

Max took a handkerchief from his pocket and wiped his brow.

"It gets better," Butterfly said, with a nod.

Great.

"In January of 1888, without the old man's knowledge, Sweet Pea called a meeting of the Frigh relatives. She put to them the facts of his true mental condition. Alarmed, his loving family decided to send him to London, a place he had been wanting to visit for years. They reckoned that the change of scene would do him a world of good. They arranged for passage on a ship that would get him to London in July and bring him back in November, in time for the holidays. The old man went only after the family agreed to let him take a liberal supply of moonshine. Passage was booked and the old man spent the time in London in a rented flat."

"Here comes the good part," said Butterfly, poking Haywood on the arm. "Go on. Tell it."

Haywood sighed, "I will, Mrs. Bordereau, but first you need to hush up."

"I'm hushed," said Butterfly, and wiggled deep into the chair.

"Coincidentally," Haywood continued, "at the same time Colonel Frigh was there, Jack the Ripper went on his murderous rampage. The first murder took place in August, just after the old man arrived, and the last took place at the beginning of November. Several people were suspected of the crimes, as we all know, but no one was conclusively identified as the murderer.

"Some who knew the old man, and had no love for him, said it was possible that he was Jack, given his temperament."

At that point, Max dropped a mushroom cap that bounced off his shoe and landed, deviled Smithfield ham side down, on the Oriental rug. In all the years I have known Max, I had never, ever seen him drop an hors d'oeuvre on a carpet during a party. He fell to his knees.

"I'm so terribly, terribly sorry," he said scooping up the cap and its contents. "That part really took me by surprise."

Butterfly sprinted into the kitchen and was back seconds later with paper towels. She gently pushed Max aside, giving him a towel to wipe his hands, and picked up the debris.

Haywood went on. "In the middle of November, the old man boarded a ship returning to the States. He had long since drunk his supply of moonshine but had located and bought cases of cheap stuff in London that he brought along as sustenance. Then, sudden as anything, he died four days out to sea. It was said that he had contracted cholera in London, although there were no other reported cases at the time.

"The truth was, many believe, that he assaulted the young daughters of other passengers. The fathers may have united in a conspiracy, murdered him and thrown his body overboard, ensuring that the cause of death could never be determined. Of course, Grammy Sweet Pea and the loving family tried to get an investigation started, but there was no enthusiasm on the part of the authorities to come up with a cause other than the one put forth by the passengers."

Max and I looked at each other, mouths hanging open. We didn't think there could be more to this story, but there was. We had gone through the second bottle of wine and Haywood was bringing out a third. No one objected.

"Eventually, the Frigh Towns did rid themselves of the Frigh reputation and were renamed with names familiar to all and became happy places to live. Butterfly and I even lived in one of them for a while and we were as happy as pigs knee-deep in mud with a full trough nearby."

We had to chuckle. Laughing was all we *could* do.

Haywood stopped to catch his breath before taking up his story again. "But the discontent and powerlessness felt by the old man was passed on to all succeeding generations of Frighs. Subsequently, the desire to be leader of *any* town festered in the hearts of all Frighs.

"When the present Colonel Frigh and Erhleen found Martini Cove Island, they knew they were home. The Colonel wanted to be in charge, even if it was of just a bitty island. He bullied his way in and attracted plenty of easily influenced weaklings to surround himself with. He didn't even care if he was an official head or not."

A knowing look passed between him and Butterfly.

Butterfly picked up the story. "The present Colonel has met his soul mate in Erhleen. She's his greatest asset, and unquestioningly loyal. And there's a juicy rumor about her, too." She giggled. "No one has ever seen her without sunglasses and it is said she wears them even to bed. Some say she comes from a Savannah family of vampires."

Haywood said. "You'd have to be crazy as a tumble bug to believe something like that, honey. That's just ugly talk."

"True or not." Butterfly huffed. "She created The Committee for Good Taste and chose Fermin and Sven, two of the most loyal toadies, to be her eyes and ears for the Colonel, sure enough."

Haywood sighed and said, "Whether all the rumors are true or not, one thing is sure. This used to be a peaceful community before the Frighs moved in and attracted like-minded friends. For the longest time, we prayed something would make them leave. But now, as time goes on and there's more of them and fewer of us, we hold scant hope." He chuckled. "Privately, we've even called this Pinocchio Island because so many liars live here."

We were silent. What could be said?

Max twiddled.

Haywood stroked.

Butterfly played with her earrings.

I felt sick.

Haywood said, "Whoa, friends. Please remember this is part truth, part conjecture and part myth. Just wanted you to know what we know. I have not told the story of the Frighs to anyone here except our friends Sky and Lucia. I don't really like spreading unpleasant stories about people, but wanted to share this with y'all, since you seem to be like minded."

I looked down at my lap. We had made a big emotional

investment by moving here. I wasn't giving up my dream yet. I needed more time and proof.

I said, "We really appreciate your sharing this story with us, but I need to judge for myself. Martini Cove Island seems well kept, so surely there's something good about the leadership."

Max heaved a big sigh.

Butterfly nodded but didn't smile. "Yes, the lawns are mowed, the trees trimmed, the porches painted." Then brightening, she said, "We have rattled on so. Of course, you need to judge for yourself, bless your heart." She patted my hand.

"It's just... Well...you see..." I fumbled, and twisted my napkin. "I love it here. It's everything I dreamed about having--the beauty of the island, the time to paint, the community. I want to live the rest of my life here."

Butterfly looked like she was faking a smile. "I know how you feel. This is still a young community." She shrugged. "Who knows? It will probably right itself with time. Come now, let's talk of other things."

I'm sure we were all still thinking about Haywood's story, but I wanted to know about Fern, too. I was happy to change the subject.

"You know, my next door neighbor, don't you?" I said.

"Fern? Of course," said Butterfly.

"A lovely person," I said, "although childlike. Must be in her late eighties? What do you know about her?"

Butterfly seemed happy to talk about something else, too. "Fern Delamer--" She looked at me hard for a reaction. "--was a resident of Welcomer."

I took that bit of information in stride because we were working on our third bottle. After an evening of truth and myth about the Colonel, Erhleen and Jack the Ripper, heck, what difference did one more crazy neighbor make? At least Fern was gentle and sweet.

"Fern has a hatful of money, sure enough," she continued. "There's no family left, just lawyers who see to it that she gets what she needs."

"If she has so much money, how come she lives so poorly?" I said.

"I don't rightly know, but she does not have the capacity to question, she just accepts. Either the lawyers are dishonest or just banjo string tight. However, she does seem happy enough. Either way, it's none of anyone's business, as long as she gets what she needs. We look in on her."

"We?" I said.

"Haywood, Sky, Lucia and me. Fern calls me the butterfly, Lucia, the swan, Sky, the lion with white hair and Mr. Bordereau, the raccoon. She can't remember real names."

Ah, hah! Now I understood Fern's nicknames.

"Are you legally bound to help Fern?" I said.

"No, indeed, but we all feel *morally* bound to help a neighbor who has limited means of helping herself."

"That's good of you."

"Aren't we all our brother's keepers?" Haywood said.

We were all tipsy as the evening was winding down. My thoughts swirled. It was all I could take in for now. I think the Bordereaus probably felt the same.

Max was saying his good-byes to Butterfly as Haywood helped me on with my coat. It was dark and the porch lights were on. Through the half open shutters, I thought I saw something shiny like the top of a bald head.

I whispered to Haywood, "Someone's out there."

He immediately jerked the door open and stepped outside, but we saw no one.

"I think the wine and tonight's stories got to me," I said, embarrassed. "Just my imagination."

"Probably not," he said. "Sven has been known to listen at people's doors and peek in windows. A hard worker for The Committee. He's as busy as a cat covering it up. Thinks he's an intellectual because he knows a lot of facts, but the truth is, in the common sense department, he's dumber than a stump."

CHAPTER 9

I was convinced Max believed every word Haywood and Butterfly had said. Not wanting shadows of doubt cast over living on the island, I prayed that all would be well. People with differing beliefs could live together harmoniously on a small island, couldn't they?

Neither of us had an appetite for dinner, since we were still digesting the stories we'd heard, so we went to bed early.

Underwater again. I am cold and sad. The man and woman seem to expect me.

"Help us," the woman whispers.

Then they both fade into the dark.

"Wait!" I shout.

I felt something stroke my arm. Max's hand. He was bending over me. "Bad dream? Something troubling you?"

The nearby street lamp cast filtered light over Max's furrowed brow and showed his concern. Truffle was looking at me, too. The alarm clock showed it was three o'clock, a perfect time to share my secret with Max. I pushed myself up against the headboard and pulled the cover to my chin.

"Do you remember the night after I met Fern?"

Max chuckled. "Of course."

"And the night we visited Lester and Veeda?"

"Unfortunately, yes."

I took a deep breath. "Each time, I had dreams about underwater ghosts. A man and a woman."

"Oh?"

I described their wispy appearances and the coldness I felt. "I think something awful must have happened to them and they're asking for my help, but I don't know who they are, or *were*, or what they want."

I waited for Max to say something, but all he did was twiddle his moustache. "Are you listening?"

He sighed. "It's one thing to have a dream but really, my dear. Ghosts talking to you from the sea, asking for your help?"

I knew that tone, like he was being patient with a dimwitted child. I crossed my arms and looked him in the eye. "Have you forgotten the Manhattan incident?"

He spread his hands and let them drop. "I remember."

...We had been catering for three years in Philadelphia when we got our lucky break in New York, working an important Christmas party at the United Nations. It could make or break Max's fledgling career. He had spent months planning the hors d'oeuvres and garnishes. The job required that we, along with our small staff, work in a kitchen facility, several blocks away, and stay up all night before the event. At eight in the morning, I was so exhausted I told Max I would take a nap on the couch in the office.

I soon fell fast sleep and dreamed that our white catering van, loaded with trays of hors d' oeuvres was traveling along Second Avenue. Suddenly, a light drizzle turned to ice rain and driving conditions quickly deteriorated. At 42nd Street, a truck carrying live chickens cut in front of the van. Our driver tried to brake, but the slippery conditions caused our van to collide with the back of the chicken truck. Its back gate swung wide open. Chickens flew everywhere. Cars spun out of control. Our van's doors swung open. Trays slid out and went under wheels of passing cars. Smoked salmon pinwheels were flattened. Meatballs were crushed. Mini-pot pies were pulverized. Miraculously, no one, not even one chicken, was injured, but every last hors d'oeuvre, right down to the last fruit kebab, was ruined. Max's catering future in Manhattan would have been doomed.

I woke from that dream shouting, "Max! The driver has to avoid Second Avenue at all costs. Make him take the FDR Drive!"

Weary from the night's work, Max said crossly, "That's silly. Commercial traffic is banned from the FDR. He'll take Second Avenue." He motioned the driver to close the van doors.

I grabbed him by the arms and spun him around to face me. "How else could he go?"

He hesitated but finally said, "All right. He'll take First Avenue."

After working hard at the party, basking in our success and having been offered several more important jobs from appreciative guests, we had forgotten all about my dream. As we were relaxing in our hotel room, enjoying our triumph and drinking champagne, we turned to the local late night news when the lead story came on. It was about the truck with live chickens that had collided with a florist's truck at 42nd Street and Second Avenue. No one was hurt and the chickens survived, but every last poinsettia flower, holly berry and Christmas bow had been squashed beyond use...

I smoothed out the counterpane. "There's something about my past I've never told you." I shot him a worried look, but his face was blank. "You know my parents were decent, hard-working people." I fiddled with a corner of a pillow. "But I never told you that my mother's ancestors were from the Carpathian Mountains in Transylvania."

Max chuckled. "You mean where the Dracula legend comes from?"

I didn't laugh. "It's a mysterious part of the world, full of spirits and legends."

Max's grin faded.

"My mother's parents were respected in their community for being clairvoyant, and the villagers sought them out for advice all the time."

Max listened, but I could tell he didn't believe a word I was saying.

"My mother inherited the power, too, but she tried to suppress it. You can imagine how having second sight could drain a person, especially if visions about people are given away for free. She believed that in America where no one knew her, she could get away from her family's influence and powers to live a normal life. Encouraged by my father, they immigrated.

"But this power doesn't go away just because it isn't wanted. My mother still had visions. She believed the visions were influenced by psychic energies of the places they lived in. Getting away from her powers by moving was impossible."

Max hadn't said a word. He just lay there, looking at the ceiling.

"When I was a teenager, my mother told me this ability ran in the family. That explained so much for me, the strong hunches I had had all my life. She urged me not to use this ability because it would attract troubled souls and I would never have a normal life. I've ignored it many times, even though I've had hunches. The Manhattan incident was different because we had so much at stake." I took a breath. "I never told you, but at our wedding I had a vision of you exactly as you looked on the cover of *Garnishing Today*."

He raised his eyebrows. "Even though I didn't think about garnishing as an art expression until months later? Is that why you encouraged my career?"

I nodded. "That and I sensed your enormous talent. You would be excellent at whatever you did."

"Thank you, but go on. Tell me more about your powers."

"Maybe Martini Cove Island has some kind of energy field that's unleashing the visions about the ghosts. I feel...um...you know. I might be an earthly portal for them."

Max jumped up, put hands on hips and glared at me.

"Are you telling me you're related to Dracula?"

"Oh, for heaven's sake!" I groaned. "You haven't been listening."

"Having a dream is one thing, but wanting to help ghosts is quite another." He headed for the door. "I need a drink," he said and stomped down the stairs.

I lay there in the dark, everything swirling around in my head. Sleep was futile.

He came back to bed a while later. I feigned sleep and after a while I heard Max and Truffle snore, but I was awake all night. At sunrise, Max got up before me and went to the kitchen.

When I went down, he was looking out the window sipping coffee, his back to me. Uneasy silence filled the room. I was afraid he was going to say something sarcastic. He did.

"I am living on an island with Jack the Ripper's grandson. I've eaten off an autopsy table. My neighbor is an asylum inmate. Now I find out I'm married to Dracula's cousin." He turned to look at me. "You'll be relieved to hear I put away all the crosses."

"Max, shut up."

"I presume you don't want garlic in your coffee." He handed me a cup.

"No, darling, but how would you like a stake through your heart?"

We both stirred our coffee in grim silence. Then Max said, "Sylvia, dear, I love you, fangs and all."

I tossed my teaspoon into the sink. "And you, Max, are my very own Prince of Darkness."

CHAPTER 10

A few days later, an invitation arrived. It read, "The Martini Cove Island party animals are at it again! The Committee for Good Taste invites you to a Fourth of July potluck and talent night by the pool. Bring food and drinks to share. Plastic plates, utensils, cups and paper napkins provided."

I read it to Max as we were having cocktails. "What a generous invitation." He tossed down the last of his martini. "The guests bring everything to the party, including the entertainment, and The Committee provides the plastic. Magnanimous."

"Stop being such a snob. It's not a formal banquet. Besides, it's a perfect venue to show off your talent. Create a tray of hors d'oeuvres they will never forget. Wake them up."

"A detonated bomb wouldn't wake them up." He sighed. "Oh, all right. It'll be good practice. Don't want to forget my skills."

I was looking forward to having a chance to show off my entertaining talent, too. In the bedroom closet, I had stored the pink and white kimono I bought in Japan years ago when I took lessons in traditional dance while Max was at garnishing school. It was still in good shape. I, however, was not. All the years of late night champagne and dining with Max after work had taken their toll. I tried it on, but the ends barely touched and the obi was tight, too.

Just then, Max passed the bedroom and did a double take.

"What's this?" he said.

I hadn't counted on Max seeing me like this. I took a deep breath. "I thought I would do the Cherry Blossom Dance for the talent show."

Max's eyebrows shot up. "You mean the dance you learned in Japan thirty-five years ago?"

I didn't like the tone of his voice at all.

"Yes," I said, curtly. "That's the one." I slipped the kimono off. "I have two weeks to practice. It'll come back to me."

Max pointed. "You're wearing *that* kimono?"

"Yes. All it needs is some alteration."

"And the obi?"

"That needs adjusting, too." I turned to face him, my hand on the doorknob. "Is there anything else you'd like to comment on before you go back downstairs?"

He chuckled. "If you can't get the kimono to fit, wear it backwards, fasten it with a safety pin and throw a cape over it."

The look I gave him could have curdled crème fraise. His grin faded. "Good luck." His voice trailed off as he went downstairs.

I slammed the door shut. Now it was a personal challenge. Max wasn't the only one with talent. "Sylvia Saltwater," I said under my breath, as I folded the kimono back into the box and snapped the lid on, "you're going to dance with the stars."

Next day I went to the city and bought white brocade that would be a nice compliment to the pink. Everything would be within the Martini Cove Island color guidelines. I remembered enough about sewing from the early days of our career when I sewed the dresses I wore for the catering jobs. How did I ever find time to sew, in addition to working with Max?

I took out my old sewing machine, put my reading glasses on and went to work. For the next few days, I opened up seams and sewed panels in. When I tried the obi and kimono on, they fit perfectly.

Not wanting to practice the dance at home under Max's watchful and judgmental eye, I practiced in hidden spots on the island where I thought no one would see me. Truffle came along because he would bark if he heard anyone approach. I took a tape recorder and kept the volume low as the lutes, zithers and three-string banjos playing the Japanese music filled the calm settings. Practicing with a fan and artificial bough of cherry blossoms, I twirled, curtseyed, pivoted. My knees were stiffer than when I was young, so I modified the movements. The trees danced with me in the wind. The sea lapped gently to the rhythm of the music. The gulls laughed with me, not at me. What a glorious island. How happy I was.

One day, I was practicing on the cliff across the cove from Sky and Lucia's large cottage and had a chance to study it. An elegant sentinel above the sea, it had grey clapboards, a slate roof, paned windows, wrap-around porch and white trim. On the second floor, a balcony ran along the length of the cottage. Butterfly had pointed out the cottage to me when we had taken a walk. She'd told me that Sky himself had designed it for Lucia. They often had parties for friends from Boston and New York to which she and Haywood were always invited. On summer nights, the melodies from the piano in the living room floated over the cove.

I hoped I would meet Sky and Lucia soon, and then I could prove to Max that I was right. There were people here worth knowing. Maybe Sky and Lucia would participate in talent night and I could meet them then.

I dipped, swirled and pivoted for an hour, lost in my dance and the sweet, plaintive music. Then I collapsed on a nearby rock, out of breath. When I looked up at the cottage again, I noticed a man and a woman standing on the balcony with what looked like a tripod with a brass telescope, pointed right at me.

I gathered my things and escaped with Truffle down the narrow path away from the cliff and out of sight.

* * * *

Ever since the invitation came, Max had been absorbed in sketching designs for the canapé tray he would bring to the party. Stacks of patriotic designs piled up on his drafting table. Maybe he wanted to be a member of the community after all.

Days before the party, he invited me to look at the sketches. One design was of the Boston Tea Party. He explained that the water in the harbor would be caviar, tall ships would be constructed of brown bread and toasted spaghetti, "Indian" patriots of black olives and brown goat cheese, tea crates of pumpernickel, water foam of chopped onion.

Another design was of a Presidential Fourth of July party on the White House lawn. The President and First Lady would be carved from cream cheese and delegates from various countries would be sculpted from other kinds of cheeses--deep yellow cheddar, pale Munster and brown goat. Fireworks would be sliced from Vidalia onions and radishes.

I looked at Max. "Is there no end to your creative genius? You haven't lost your touch."

"Thank you." He reached for a third design and unfurled it with a flourish. "But this is the one I will bring to realization."

I gasped. It was a model of Martini Cove Island, topographically correct, with its cottages, condos, pool, gardens, trees, everything done intricately and to scale.

"Pure magnificence," I gushed and hugged the sketch to my chest. I laid it on a bit thick. "The neighbors will absolutely fall in love with it. After this, you will probably have to turn down offers of catering neighbors' parties. Are you ready to come out of retirement?"

He blushed. "It's good to be designing again." He turned his hands and looked at them. "God, how I've missed it. And if the neighbors are impressed, so much the better."

"They will be." I prayed they would. Tickling Max's ego was the way to his heart.

The day before the party, Max was in the kitchen cutting, slicing, scooping, scoring, carving, peeling, layering, stuffing, squeezing and sculpting. Every inch of our refrigerator and freezer were full of parts ready to be assembled into one splendid whole. He was in his white jacket and chef's hat and in his element, working all day, pausing only for a cup of tea, now and again. It was a grand time for Truffle, too, waiting for scraps from the occasional slip of a garnishing tool.

CHAPTER 11

On the morning of the party, I woke at dawn and saw that Max had not been to bed at all. I found him sitting at the kitchen table mulling over his creation. Truffle lay snoring by his feet.

"Like it?" Max didn't even look up. He beamed with pride and satisfaction, the way he always did after he had crafted something astonishing, but the weariness of a night without sleep was written on his face.

"They will love it," I said.

Max had unleashed all his expertise on this project. Rocks were fashioned from chicken liver pate, houses and condos from different crackers and cheese slices, trees and flowers from crudités, water from blue gelatin.

I put my arms around him and kissed him. "Why don't you take a nap before the party?"

He nodded and soon he was upstairs in bed, sleeping with a smile on his face.

I closed the bedroom door gently and leaned my back against it. The community would welcome us as valuable members now. They simply had to.

Just before the party, I went to the pool area alone and sat behind a bush, wanting Max and his creation to make a grand entrance without me while I watched the neighbors' delighted reactions. The American flag above me snapped in the wind on a flagpole. I was pleased to see that The Committee had decorated the pergola with red, white and blue balloons. A table that stood against the fence was draped with a red and white checked tablecloth. At least they tried to make it festive and it was. Sort of. In keeping with the Committee's rules, I wore a pink blouse, white pants, and a powder blue shoulder bag. Nestled safely in my lap was the box with the kimono, obi, fan and silk cherry bough. I sighed with delight. My first community party.

Wanda and Slick, Lester and Veeda arrived first, then the members of The Committee for Good Taste.

I recognized Erhleen's voice on the other side of the bush. "Shucks! It's just way too busy. Look at all them stars and stripes in that old flag. Makes you dizzy looking at it, waving back and forth like that. Tacky is what I'd call it. Am I right?"

Fermin's voice. "Beige would be more elegant, with one chic mauve star set off to the side."

Sven's voice. "I agree. According to retinal retention and for stress reduction, a beige flag would be more pleasing to the eye. As always, I am awed at your superior taste."

Kissing and slurping noises.

Erhleen's voice. "No need to kiss my hand every time we say something brilliant. You is always kissing my hand."

"Let me once more state how privileged I, Sven Tinkin, am to be serving in such a premier community. It was the happiest day of my life when I was chosen to join this awe-inspiring Committee. How honored I am and eternally grateful to be in your company and to be learning from you. Just last week I was thinking..."

"All right, all right," said Fermin, "we get the idea. Now let's get back to work. Erhleen, how do we get the government to change the design of the flag?"

"I don't rightly know, but if we research it enough, we could find a good Washington, D. C. contact, someone easily bribed."

Fermin snorted. "That shouldn't be too hard."

"Or," Erhleen said, "we could get a few Martini Cove names on a petition then drive down to D. C. with the Colonel. I'll make sure he takes his hammer and several Molotov cocktails."

"Hmm, that seems rather drastic," Fermin said. "Perhaps we

should just contact Martha Stewart?"

"Naw, never bother with a middle man when we have the Colonel's methods of persuasion," Erhleen said.

More kissing and slurping sounds.

"Boy, I told you to stop that," Erhleen said, "it's embarrassing."

"I weep at your strength and power." Sven sounded as if he were choking with emotion.

"Your devotion is touching," Fermin said with a sniff. "Now go and practice on your triangle or something."

"I shall record this conversation in my notebook for future reference for the important work done for the good of the community by this exalted Committee."

"You run along now and do that," Fermin said. "And there's no need to salute us every time you leave."

Sven emerged from behind the bush to where I could see him. He was scribbling in his fat notebook liberally flagged with Post-It notes.

"Thinking about it, however," Fermin continued, "maybe we wouldn't want to call attention to Martini Cove with such an issue. It's a story the media might pick up."

"Good point," said Erhleen. "We wouldn't want the authorities snooping in our business. We have bigger stakes at hand."

"We certainly do."

Bigger stakes? Whatever could that mean?

The table was now filling up with aluminum pans and plastic bowls as the guests arrived. Sven sauntered up to it, closed the notebook, put it under his arm, and tucked the pencil stub behind his ear. He glanced around furtively, lifted an edge of aluminum foil from a pan. He stuck his finger in, and then licked it before rolling his eyes upward, nodding, and carefully replacing the aluminum. After looking right and left, he appeared to be satisfied that no one had seen him.

I heard the voices again from the other side of the bush.

"That Sven is an irritating little scrap," Fermin said.

"I know," Erhleen said, "but he's useful. He'll do anything the Colonel or I tell him to do, and that makes him a mighty valuable member of the community. I have never bumped into such a nobody trying to be a somebody, except maybe for Slick and Wanda, and that makes them right valuable, too."

"As always, Erhleen, I bow to your superior survival instincts."

Erhleen chuckled a mirthless laugh. Then they walked over to join the other revelers by the pool.

I shrank back into the bushes and stayed there a while so they wouldn't suspect me of overhearing. What was this business that they didn't want the authorities to know about?

I would not tell Max about this.

I strolled casually from the other side of the bushes as Haywood and Butterfly arrived in their golf cart, with Max on the back seat holding his masterpiece. Proudly, he laid it on the table, pushed a cracker here, adjusted an olive there. He stood back, waiting for the usual rush and cries of admiration, but nobody had praise for Max's offering. People hacked into it, seeming not to notice its well-crafted beauty.

Max looked deflated. He wandered to my side, uncorked the wine I had brought, and took a swig from the bottle.

"Decorum, Max," I said. "Pour it into a plastic cup."

"Would it make any difference?"

"Cheer up, dear," I said. "I'm sure the praise will come later."

"Ah, *ha!*" He swigged from the bottle again.

I decided to distract him. "That's the gardener." I nodded in his direction.

He was presiding over the barbecue, wearing the same filthy work clothes I saw him in the other day. But now, he wore a chef's apron over them, liberally smeared with barbecue sauce. As he flipped burgers and ribs, ashes from his cigar fell onto the meat. "What's a gardener doing in a gathering of premier people?"

"He looks like a cheap car wreck," Max said, not whispering.

"Shush!" I put a finger to my lips. "Be kind. You're a Zen

student."

"Okay," he said. "I'll picture his soul as a Mercedes-Benz."

Just then, Lester wobbled over. "Howdy, little lady," he slurred, as he weaved and bobbed in front of me, his beady eyes glassy. He tried to put a hand on my shoulder.

I stepped backwards. "Happy Fourth."

He leered at me and grabbed my arm, "There's someone you should meet."

"How delightful," Max said.

Lester led us in the direction of the gardener. As we got closer, I noticed a slogan I couldn't quite make out written on the sauce-splattered apron.

"Looks like he's been working the guillotine," Max said under his breath.

Lester made a grand gesture and nearly whacked me in the jaw before I ducked. "Meet our very own Colonel Frigh."

At that instant, I deciphered the words on the apron. EAT MY MEAT!

The Colonel held out his nicotine-yellowed, barbecue sauce-covered hand for us to shake. After, we held our hands out at our sides. I felt like I had handled toxic waste..

"Hah, hah!" the Colonel laughed and winked at me. "You thought I was the gardener. Joke's on you. But I won't hold no grudge. Here, try some of these ribs. Folks say my barbecue is the best they ever ate." He slapped ribs onto paper plates and handed them to us.

It would have been the height of impoliteness to refuse. What could we do? I watched Max bite into a rib, and his expression changed as if he had just smelled a sewer. I bit in and my nose instantly poured out sweat. The sauce was hot, but the underlying taste was indescribably foul.

"Water!" I croaked, and ran to the ladies room. Max was behind me running for the men's room. The Colonel's guffaws trailed after us.

At the sink, I rinsed my mouth several times and scrubbed my hands until they were raw.

I met Max outside the bathrooms. He was leaning against the doorframe, mopping sweat with a paper towel. "Can we please go home?"

"I'll do my dance for the talent show. Then we'll leave."

"How soon will that be?" he moaned, holding his stomach.

"Soon as it's dark."

"Tonight I shall welcome the darkness."

We trudged to plastic chairs nearby. I poured two large plastic glasses full of wine to wipe out the lingering bad taste. I erased the mental note I had made to report the gardener to The Committee for Good Taste.

When it was time for the talent show, a space was cleared by the pool, with spotlights set up to create the illusion of a stage. People scraped plastic lawn chairs into a semicircle. Max and I sat away from the crowd in the shadows.

Off to the side, I noticed a man and woman sipping champagne from Waterford crystal flutes. They sat on gilt bamboo chairs on either side of a small round table draped with a white linen cloth. The woman's bright blue eyes blazed in a tanned patrician face framed by long blond hair and a fringe of bangs. Tall and slim, she wore a flowing green and blue dress, contrasting sharply with other women's tee shirts and shorts.

Dressed like a boater, the man looked distinguished in crisp white pants and navy blazer with a gold insignia on the breast pocket. Also deeply tanned, he had a shock of white, neatly trimmed hair and eyes blue as the sky. He was flashing brilliant smiles at the woman. I wondered if they could be Lucia and Sky, who had spied on me while I was practicing my dance. Now I was afraid of making a fool of myself in front of these beautiful creatures. Suddenly, I felt shy.

"Max," I whispered, "would you like to go home?"

"Before your dance? No, you worked too hard. Just do your best and have fun."

His kindness restored my confidence.

The show began. The first to perform was Lester, who slurred several offensive jokes involving racial prejudice, bodily functions and sexual aberrations, none of them funny. Even so, most of the Martini Cove Island residents roared and guffawed.

The beautiful people had to be Sky and Lucia since they paid no attention to Lester's extremely bad taste.

Haywood and Butterfly were not laughing, either, but sat quietly, red faced and embarrassed. She played with her earrings and looked at the ground. He was examining his fingernails.

Max slipped me a note he had scribbled on a paper napkin. "Remember PA?" It referred to a party we had catered at the beginning of our career, when we needed the money. It was the Condom Manufacturer's Grand Climax Party at the end of their convention. The organizers thought it would be cute to hold it at a hotel in Intercourse, Pennsylvania. The banquet facility had been decorated liberally with inflated condoms. I shuddered when I remembered and patted his hand.

Erhleen, wearing a pair of overalls printed with pastel-colored flowers, announced that she would stand on her head. After much huffing and puffing, she managed to hoist herself up. Upside down, her face turned reddish purple, still her large sunglasses stayed right in place. Symbolically, Erhleen was standing on her head for the Colonel, who applauded enthusiastically as he puffed on his cigar.

"She looks like a bug on steroids," Max whispered.

"Be kind," I whispered back.

He sighed. "Not easy."

If this was the talent at Martini Cove, I was gaining more confidence with each passing minute.

The Colonel took the stage next. He sucked on his cigar while blowing several smoke rings, each smaller than the one before. His performance was better than his barbecue sauce. The applause was deafening.

Next, Sven held up a triangle, and then launched into the history of it as a musical instrument. He used a lot of long words that were more complicated than the instrument he was describing. He said that he had studied it for two years in Dingenflugen, Switzerland, at a noted music school. Then he gave a ten-minute concert that seemed much longer, during which I heard loud snoring from several members of the audience. Lester fell out of his chair with a loud thud and stayed there. That was the extent of the Martini Cove Island performing talent. I was next and last.

Wrapped in the kimono and obi, I flipped the switch of the tape recorder. Light, melancholy Japanese music drifted through the air. After the performances I had just endured, the music was a balm. I thought only of the dance as I swirled and dipped, alternating fan and cherry blossom branch. In my imagination, I was in Japan again performing this lovely ancient dance. I remembered practicing on the beaches and cliffs of the island, birches and pines dancing with me. I felt the breezes and smelled the salty sea air as I moved.

The music ended and the audience was silent. Was it that bad? Then, I heard one person applaud, then another and another. Soon everyone was applauding as if they had enjoyed it. Max came to me and kissed me. "Well done."

"Did they like it?"

"Listen to the applause."

I flushed with pleasure and bowed to the audience still clapping. Holding my hand, Max led me back to our seats. Before we could sit, the man I thought might be Sky approached us.

He took my hand and, barely brushing it with his lips as refined Europeans do, he introduced himself as Sky. "My wife Lucia and I would be delighted if you would join us for champagne."

I looked at Max. Champagne? Meeting Sky and Lucia? Of course. He led us to Lucia.

"Wonderful, Sylvia!" Lucia said, "We thoroughly enjoyed it. And you are Max. Please join us." She made a graceful sweep with her arm. Her smile was warm and genuine. A servant in black shirt and pants brought two more gilt chairs to the table.

Up close, Sky's blue eyes looked they were carved from precious stones. I felt weak in the knees.

The servant placed two glasses of champagne in front of us. I sat back and tried to look casual, but in truth, I felt shy in front of these beautiful people.

"To Sylvia," Sky toasted.

We clinked glasses and I blushed.

"Sky and I seldom attend these potlucks." Lucia waved her hand, dismissing this one, too. "We've experienced the talent at Martini Cove. However, when we saw you dancing on the cliff the other day, we guessed you were probably rehearsing for tonight and we made an exception, and I'm glad we did. The performance was honest and well done. Such a good sport. You live up to my favorite motto: 'Be anything you want to be, but for heaven's sake, don't be boring.' Sylvia, you are anything but boring."

Sky raised his glass. "Soon, we will take you on a sail aboard *The Golden Fleece*, our sailboat." He tapped the embroidered insignia of a yacht on waves on his jacket pocket.

I put on my reading glasses to examine the insignia. "It looks just like an Azo Khan Mimoto drawing."

"I'm impressed! It is from an Azo Khan Mimoto. His painting of *The Golden Fleece* that we commissioned gives the feel of sea, wind, sky."

Azo Khan Mimoto is the famous Japanese painter, a national treasure. Max and I fell in love with his work while we were in Japan. Later, when we became successful, we bought a small limited edition print of his, all we could afford. I could just imagine what a commissioned painting must have cost.

Lucia leaned toward Max. "I have heard that you are the original creators and owners of *Presentation Is Everything*."

He smiled. "You've heard of it?"

"Not only have we heard of it but we attended several functions your company catered. We were at the Italian President's reception at the White House. We also attended functions in New York and Philadelphia. I'm sorry we never met."

"We never actually attended the functions we catered," I said. "We stayed in the kitchen but we always dressed as if we did.

Sometimes clients wanted to take pictures with us, so we came prepared."

"Sorry we missed meeting you--" Lucia spread her hands. "--but here we are at last. What brought you to Martini Cove Island?"

"Retirement and my longing for community," I replied. I felt I could be honest with her. "Other than Max and our dog Truffle, I have no family, but I'm hoping to make a family of friends here."

Lucia lifted her eyebrows, her smile fading.

"At the parties you catered," Sky said changing the subject, "the food was always superb and the garnishes sublime. Such creativity."

"I created a piece for tonight, but no one seemed to appreciate it," Max said. "I'm sure by now it's completely destroyed."

"Not surprising," Sky said. But then he brightened. "You must cater our next party."

Max's face beamed.

"Splendid idea," Lucia said. "We're fortunate to have such distinguished residents. Let's give a party soon and put you back to work."

Sky stood and said, "It was marvelous meeting you both, but now we must excuse ourselves. Big day tomorrow. We're sailing in the city's annual cup race." He turned and bowed toward me. "Thank you again, Sylvia, for that vivifying performance."

We said our good-byes and as suddenly as they had appeared, they were gone, the servant having taken the table, chairs and champagne away.

Not a trace of them was left, but I was still thinking about Sky's electrifying blue eyes. "Were they real or apparitions?" I said to Max.

"Real. One set of apparitions at Martini Cove Island is enough."

I looked around. Most of our neighbors had left. Wanda was talking to Sven, her almost bare chest at his eye level. The Colonel and Erhleen were laughing at something Fermin was saying. Veeda was bent over Lester, trying to get him up. Butterfly and Haywood were gone.

We saw the Colonel and Erhleen getting into their rusty old golf cart that was held together with bits of duct tape.

"I wonder if the painting of Dorian Gray's golf cart looked like that," Max said.

Just before we left, Sven gave us one last treat. He must have been feeling overheated after staring at Wanda's breasts because he walked over to the pool, set down his briefcase, took off his shirt and long pants. Underneath were bathing trunks that looked too big and hung low. He jumped into the pool and swam across. When he climbed the ladder to get out, his trunks, now full of water, gave way and slipped down to his ankles. On his bare butt was a tattoo of the Martini Cove Island logo.

CHAPTER 12

Next morning, I woke up late. Max and Truffle were out of the bed, so I put on my robe and went to the kitchen. A pot of coffee steamed on the counter and I poured a large mugful.

Always up before me, Max usually laid out toast or cereal, banana pinwheels or pieces of fruit carved to resemble heads of state in the news, but not this morning.

I walked to the study, then to the back porch. No Max. In the garden, on a stone bench in the shadow of pines, I saw him sitting, elbows on knees, head in hands, looking at the ground. Truffle was at his feet, looking at him with a worried expression.

I sat next to him. His gray, haggard face looked sad. In an attempt to comfort him, I put my arm around his shoulders. "What's the matter, darling?"

He shook his head. "I just can't believe it. The buffet table held six pans of macaroni and cheese without even a tomato rose on top. A pumpkin pie with no whipped cream to hide the crack. Not a single melon ball, not a strand of lettuce chiffonade. It's a premier community. I was expecting pickle fans at the very least."

"If you recall, we saw the plastic rocket sticking out of a sheet cake in the brochure." I patted his hand. "Just because people didn't decorate doesn't mean their intentions aren't good."

"Oh, I know," he said. "What really rankles, though--my stunning creation--did you see the attack? They scooped the chicken liver up like they were eating canned party dip. Don't they know art when they see it? These people have no class." He sighed. "You wouldn't even need a step stool to climb the social ladder here."

I rocked him. "It was disappointing."

"It was devastating."

"Don't take it so hard."

He grabbed my arms. "We're living with barbarians."

Truffle jumped up and growled.

"Pull yourself together, Max. Didn't we meet Sky and Lucia? They are beacons of hope. So are Butterfly and Haywood."

He let go, dropping his arms and hanging his head again. "Four people out of how many?"

I understood his despair but I wasn't giving up. There had to be more people at Martini Cove Island who appreciated pickle fans.

"That's not all." He held his rounded belly and moaned. "One bite of the Colonel's barbecue gave me diarrhea all night. I still hurt."

I reached for his hand and held it. "You will teach by example. The community will soon look at their plain, unadorned casseroles in a different light."

"Maybe, but it will take an awful lot of work."

* * * *

The next morning, we were sitting in the breakfast nook. Max still looked tired. I knew he felt better because he had carved stars from kiwi slices for my generous mound of oatmeal with cream. I dug into it with gusto while he sipped weak broth.

Wincing as he watched me devour the oatmeal, he said, "Why didn't you get sick?"

I dabbed the corner of my mouth. "I didn't swallow. That's why women carry purses, for emergencies. The purse is ruined, of course."

Silence. Then Max smacked the table with his fist. "Damn it! What was in that vile sauce?" It was not like him to swear.

"I've thought about it." On my fingers I ticked off: "Molasses, Nago Bhut Jolokia peppers--the hottest in the world--canned tomato soup, cilantro, cod liver oil-"

Max held up his hand. "Enough!" Beads of sweat popped out on his forehead. Suddenly, he shot up from the table, knocking over his chair. I thought he was going to run to the bathroom again but he didn't. He rolled up his sleeves, his eyes wild. "If the beloved Colonel can make barbecue sauce, so can I."

I was suspicious. "What are you up to?" I hoped he wasn't going to do what I thought he was going to do.

He ignored me, went to the pantry and threw open the door. He grabbed whisks, bowls, bottles, cans, boxes and measuring spoons.

Dread overtook me. Oh, no. He was going to cook. Only I know Max's darkest secret, a secret so big that if it were ever leaked, it could severely impact the garnishing industry and ruin his status forever.

The chicken liver pâté that he used for the map of Martini Cove? The sweet potato filling and pastry puffs? The filling for the mini okra quiches? The deviled Smithfield ham stuffed mushroom caps? The salsa and chips? *I* made them all, not Max.

The industry and his clients know him as a genius at assembly. Only I know he's a lousy cook. I alone have always done all the cooking. We kept that a secret from our small staff. That was quite a trick and my biggest burden. Everyone naturally assumed that since Max was a garnish master he must also be a great chef.

Max doesn't cook often, but when he does, it's a disaster. He's fascinated with ingredients and keeps adding to a dish until the whole thing turns gray. He's no good at timing either. Once he tried to make a birthday dinner for me. The roast beef shriveled and burned. The rice stuck to the bottom of the pot. He had spent too much time washing and plumping each pea individually. Thank goodness, he only tried to cook a few times. I remember each one distinctly, although I have tried hard to forget.

I went to the bedroom and lay down with a lavender pillow over my eyes. Truffle snuggled close. Probably he remembered the last time Max tried to cook, too. Huddled together, both of us fell asleep.

When I woke, I smelled something appetizing wafting from the kitchen.

Max came into the bedroom, wiping his hands on a kitchen

towel. "Dinner's ready!"

"It smells delicious," I said. Still, I was apprehensive.

Max had set the dining room table in a charming Western style with a checked cloth covering the table and red cloth napkins folded into triangles next to black pottery plates. Two steins held beer. A cactus in a blue tin coffee cup served as the centerpiece, with candles glowing around it. On a metal charger, nicely browned potatoes, onions and vegetables circled barbecued ribs. He had spent time cooking instead of garnishing and fussing.

He served us, and at the first bite, I looked at him wide-eyed. "Excellent barbecue sauce," I said with my mouth full. "How did you do it?"

"Simple. I did the opposite of everything I imagined the Colonel would do. When you are working with mediocrity, the only way is up!"

CHAPTER 13

I was working in my garden when I was startled by Fern's sudden presence beside me. I said, "What a nice surprise." I meant it. This was the first time I had seen Fern outside her cottage and garden.

All our visits had always been at her house. Sometimes I took fresh bread or a stew. Our conversations were always like the first time I'd met her. She seemed not to be able to go beyond that, but we enjoyed sitting together in quiet companionship. Max had, on occasion, helped her with mulching or carrying something heavy from one spot to another. He, too, liked the quiet visits with her. She was a perfect neighbor, hardly seen, never heard. I felt honored that she trusted me enough to come visiting.

Shy as a child, Fern held out a small terra cotta pot with a cutting from a bush. "For you," she said. "The white lilacs were so lovely this spring, I want you to have one."

Tears sprang to my eyes. "How kind of you," I said. "My mother painted a watercolor of lilacs every spring, so they are my favorite flowers. Their fragrance reminds me of her. This is a wonderful gift and more special because it's from you."

She swayed from side to side and with her arms behind her back. "You told me the story about your mother once. I remembered."

I wanted to hug her, but thought better of it.

I turned from her and looked around the garden. "Where would be the best spot to plant it?" When I turned back, she was gone.

I planted the cutting by the side of the back porch next to a patch of day lilies. I would see the first blooms year after year when I looked out the kitchen window.

* * * *

Later that morning I checked the mailbox to find a creamy vellum envelope with the insignia of *The Golden Fleece.*

I took it to Max's study and we stood together as I slit it open. The note, written in blue ink by a bold hand, read: "Please join us for champagne and lobster this Saturday at 5:00 p.m. at Fair Winds, to celebrate the full moon. Looking forward to seeing you again! Lucia" At the bottom was a phone number and a quick sketch of a sailboat.

It had been a couple of weeks since the Fourth of July party. Max and I had talked about Sky and Lucia several times, hoping we would see them again, soon.

Max said, "Do you think they would like me to make hors d' oeuvres?"

Good! He was getting into the spirit. "I think they would be delighted."

He went to the phone and dialed the number on the note. Just listening, I deduced that Max's offer was accepted with enthusiasm.

After he hung up, he said, "Lucia sends her best."

"Sounds like she's taking you up on your offer."

He nodded.

"How many people?"

"Twenty or so. Informal. I'll make something simple."

Max, making something simple?

He looked out the window, lost in thought. I could almost hear his mind at work, sketching canapés, arranging platters. Later that day, I heard him on the phone ordering jars of good caviar that would be shipped from his supplier in New York in time for the party.

When I went into the kitchen to cook dinner, the freezer door was open and Max was slipping a large plastic box full of water into it.

I said, "Are you going to carve an ice sculpture?"

"Grand idea, don't you think? I can try out that new set of Japanese ice carving tools you gave me for my last birthday. Can you make the crackers that go so well with caviar?"

"Of course." The next morning I baked a batch. I loved it when Max and I worked together.

The afternoon before the party, Max had turned the air conditioning way up. I found him in the kitchen wearing his winter coat, gloves and Persian lamb earmuffs, with the sculpting tools on the kitchen table in a neat row. He was chipping away at the block of ice. "The Flying Dutchman" blared from the stereo. He never even noticed I was in the kitchen. When Truffle started shivering, I took him outside with me.

We walked to the cliff overlooking the marina, and I watched the boats bobbing on the water. Haywood's vintage wood sailboat *Southern Belle* was there, along with Slick's *Screw Vous,* a small plastic power boat resembling an orthopedic shoe. The *Mumsey,* another bulky powerboat which could only belong to Fermin, and a few undistinguished boats with names like, *Hissy Fit, Cranky Pants,* and *Pot Luck* swayed alongside each other. I guessed at their owners. *The Golden Fleece,* the longest, tallest, and sleekest, outshone the group.

As I was working on a sketch, I saw Sky and Lucia emerge from below deck. He started adjusting dials near the steering wheel while she filled the water tank from the dock hose nearby. Graceful and swift, she climbed the tall mast to fix something on top and just as nimbly, she shinnied back down. When they had completed their chores, she went below and emerged with a bottle in a silver bucket and two champagne glasses. Sky opened the bottle and I heard the cork pop and saw it fly through the air and splash into the water. He filled their glasses. They sat close together as the sun started setting, and he said something to make her laugh.

I was so enchanted by the scene, I was startled to see how late it was and packed up my paints. With Truffle leading the way, I headed home.

Max was in the kitchen, tapping the final details into a replica of a sailboat. The sun shining through the window made it sparkle.

"Enchanting!" I said.

Max laid down the hammer and chisel and nodded without looking up. Truffle shivered again because the house was still freezing.

"Time to put the boat away," I said.

I helped Max put the disassembled boat into the freezer and turned the air conditioning off. Later, as we sat down to dinner, I thought about Sky and Lucia and brought out a bottle of champagne. "To life!" I said, and clinked his glass.

CHAPTER 14

Unafraid of breaking the Martini Cove dress code at Sky and Lucia's house, I was wearing a black skirt and a red blouse with a small enameled pin of a fruit basket Max had designed for me. He looked spiffy in a pair of gray linen slacks and a black silk shirt.

"Not exactly informal, are we?" I said.

"This is *our* idea of informal," he said, while brushing his hair.

Lucia had offered us a ride to the party in her golf cart, since she knew Max had made something special that would be difficult to carry by foot. At exactly three-thirty, she pulled up in front of our house and stepped out. She was dressed in tailored tan slacks and periwinkle blue blouse. In a few long strides, she was at our front door.

Max came out with the plastic container holding the ice sculpture.

"Hope you haven't gone to too much trouble." She eyed the container. "Can't wait to see it."

We got into the cart, Max in back with the container, me in front with Lucia, the caviar and crackers in a canvas bag. In a few moments we were driving around the lawn in the condo area. As we passed the Frighs' house, we saw people on the porch. They were holding plastic cups with drinks and eating corn dogs on sticks. Lester sat on the railing, slumped against a support beam, eyes closed, mouth open. Veeda was talking to Erhleen. Sven sat on the floor next to Erhleen looking up at her with adoring eyes. The Colonel was ogling Wanda's breasts. She giggled when he flicked ash from his cigar into her cleavage. Slick gulped his drink nervously. Fermin and Mumsey were engaged in conversation. I hadn't met the other residents who were present yet.

Sometime, I would get a chance to find out why people were mesmerized by the Colonel and I hoped it would change my mind about him.

As we passed, I waved but no one waved back.

"Odd," I said, "Didn't they see me?"

"They saw you, all right," Lucia said, "but, you're with me, and they don't like me or Sky."

"Why not?"

"Because we don't look to the Colonel or The Committee for leadership. Still, we follow their stupid rules as best we can. We were building Fair Winds when the Colonel and his bunch moved here. If they had been here first, we never would have thought about living here. Unfortunately, his group divided Martini Cove Island into factions, and now everyone who moves here has to choose sides."

"Can't we just all get along and--"

"Let's forget about it right now and just have a good time," Lucia said as she pulled into the driveway.

Fair Winds was floating in clouds of pink and white rugosa roses, with the shimmering sea beyond.

"Wow!" said Max, an expression he seldom used, but that said it all.

I squeezed Lucia's arm, smiling at her.

Sky bounded down the porch steps to greet us. "Welcome to Fair Winds."

"The house faces the east," Max said, "toward the rising sun, just like our house. According to Eastern philosophy, that's good karma."

"Never thought of it that way," Sky said. He came around and kissed me on the cheek. "Let's have a glass of champagne before the others get here."

We walked up the stairs and through the screened porch door that led to the large kitchen. White beadboard cabinets with paned glass doors lined the walls. Gleaming black granite counter tops formed a U shape around the high-end appliances. Oak bar stools invited guests to watch the cook and encourage conversation. Every wall in the dining/living room area had windows that framed the sea and the islands beyond, like paintings on the walls of a gallery.

Lucia pointed to a long mission-style table that held a stack of plates, champagne flutes, silverware, linen napkins and a bucket bursting with stargazer lilies. "I was hoping you could arrange everything. It would be such great help."

Max plunged in, assembling the ice sailboat. Sunlight from the windows twinkled through it. I opened the jars of caviar and scooped it into half the boat leaving the other half to hold the lobster. Max arranged the lilies. I fanned out the napkins and arranged silverware and plates.

"Dazzling!" Lucia clapped her hands. "I don't know how you did that."

I said, "For us it's easy. But I admire someone who can shinny up a mast."

"You saw me? When?"

"I was painting on the cliff."

"Next time, stop by for champagne."

"Deal."

"Speaking of champagne..." Sky popped open a bottle and filled glasses. "Let's drink to new friends!"

We sipped.

I looked around "Where's your servant?"

Lucia looked puzzled then laughed. "The one at the potluck? He was just a hire for the night, to tease our inelegant neighbors."

Just then a burly man in blue overalls, carrying a big brown paper bag, flung the door open. "Lobster delivery," he announced.

Lucia hugged him, and then introduced him as a friend and a local lobsterman. Behind him was his wife, a plain woman with a weathered face, but bright smile. Lucia brought out two bottles of beer for them and they sat down at the counter while Sky asked about his day. The lobsterman told us about hauling his traps. Lucia handed the bag to Max and within minutes, the mound of fresh, pink meat looked appetizing in the ice sculpture.

Other guests arrived in a group brought by water taxi from the city. We were introduced to a piano player who, after claiming his champagne, went over to the piano and started playing easy jazz. The wall behind the piano held the spirited painting by Azo Khan Mimoto. Done in blues, greens and whites, it captured *The Golden Fleece's* sleek good looks against the wildness of the sea.

We greeted Butterfly and Haywood, and met some of the firefighters in charge of the fireboat that serviced Martini Cove Island and surrounding islands.

A blonde young man, wearing a pink silk baseball jacket and sequined sunglasses, threw the door open with a flourish. "Here we are!" he said. He was carrying two Chihuahuas, one under each arm. Lucia introduced him to Max and me as "D. M. C."

"Dee-lighted to meet you!" he said. "I'd shake but my arms are full. This is Madonna." He held up the dog in a pink sun visor, pink sunglasses and pink sequined collar. "And this is Sting." Sting wore the same outfit in powder blue. D. M. C. kissed each on the nose.

"You look like interesting people," D. M. C. said, and rolled his eyes. "Unlike most Martini Cove residents."

"They are," Lucia said, and giggled. "Tell them that naughty thing Madonna once did."

"All right, darling, just for you." He transferred Madonna under the same arm with Sting, so he could hold the champagne glass.

"Once, early on when we all didn't know any better, Sky, Lucia and I went to a God awful community potluck. I had my babies tucked safely under my arm, just like now. When that Erhleen witch saw me, she accosted me and said my darlings weren't leashed and that was against Martini Cove Island rules. I pointed out to her that leashes were not necessary since I carry my babies all the time anyway, but she said rules were rules. That Sven person--" He shuddered. "--pulled out a book of tickets and slapped me with two fines on the spot.

"Erhleen said that if she or any other member of The Committee ever saw those dogs unleashed at Martini Cove Island again, she would call the city dogcatcher to come out here and throw them in the pound. With that, my darling Madonna did the only sensible thing she could. She jumped out of my arm--I just don't know *how* that happened--and bit Erhleen on the ankle. It was just a weensy peck, didn't even break the skin. Then Erhleen *really* got mad and said if she ever saw those dogs at Martini Cove Island again, leashed or unleashed, she would have them put down on the spot. Bitch! If Madonna hadn't bitten her, I would have. Of course, I took her to the vet's right away for shots. I mean Madonna, not Erhleen."

Wiping tears of laughter from her eyes, Lucia said, "Tell what you did after that."

D. M. C. sniffed. "I am a *major* contributor to an assist animal organization in New York where I live, so I have a *lot* of influence. I did the only sensible thing. I had my babies registered as assist animals. Of course, I went to the Ralph Lauren Boutique right after and had specially designed collars and leads made of butter soft leather. I don't want my babies getting chaffed." He blew kisses at them. "So whenever I see Erhleen or a member of the Committee, I snap their leads on. There's nothing she or anyone else can do about it."

Lucia said, still laughing, "Erhleen is furious, of course, but helpless."

"Honestly, darling," he said to Lucia when she refilled his glass, "I don't know how you can live in this ghastly place. Oh, the house and view are spectacular, but, honestly, those *people!* Not only are they boring, but worse; they have zero charisma. However do you do it?"

"We don't pay any attention to them. We just invite special people, like you, my love." She gave him a peck on the mouth.

"What does 'D. M. C.' stand for," Max said. "Is it a degree of some sort?"

"Oh, sweetie, aren't you too cute!" D. M. C. said. He swept Madonna and Sting away toward the piano, but paused half way, looked over his shoulder and threw Max a flirtatious look. "Darling, it stands for Devil May Care!"

After lots more champagne, lobster and caviar, the guests gathered around the piano for a sing-along.

Lucia took me aside and said, "Let me show you the rest of the house."

She grabbed an open bottle and we slipped away up the stairs, where she showed me the elegant, simply furnished guest rooms and baths, all with large paned windows and lots of sunlight. In an upstairs study, in front of French doors leading to the balcony, stood the spyglass on a tripod, the same one they'd used to watch me dance. She brushed it with her fingertips. "I'm glad we saw you that day."

"Me, too."

She gestured to two comfortable chairs facing the water and refilled our glasses.

"What is the most important thing in the world to you?" she said.

I was surprised at the question "Max, of course. Truffle, painting, our new community. "

"You hoped to find community at Martini Cove Island?"

"Yes."

She looked out the window.

"I believe love is most important," she said. "But it's good to have a circle of friends, of course."

I was silent looking out the window, too.

Butterfly peeked through the door. "Hope I am not intruding."

"Join us." Lucia waved her in.

Butterfly settled onto a window seat facing us. "I overheard what you said about a circle of friends. Lord knows, I am grateful for your friendships. But I'm sad *all* of us on this island can't be at least *friendly* to one another."

"A good community can't exist where bullies rule," Lucia said.

I watched the fiery orange sun gild the treetops and seem to sink into the ocean.

I said. "Do you think this community has a chance?"

A glance passed between them. Lucia tossed her braid to the other shoulder. "Have you heard the legend of this island?"

"You mean about The Welcomer Rest Home? Of course."

"No, that's its history. I mean before that."

I shook my head.

Lucia refilled our glasses and settled back.

"Centuries ago," she began, "Indians used the island to escape hot summers on the mainland. They loved the island and considered themselves stewards of it, taking from it only what they needed, mainly shellfish from surrounding waters. You can still see shell middens by the beaches. The island nourished their souls as well as their bodies, so they prayed often to its spirits of fish, animals, trees, flowers, and rocks. The Indians were grateful for the riches the island gave and in their own language named it 'Bounty.'"

"I do declare," Butterfly said, while playing with an earring shaped like a half moon. "This is just the loveliest legend, the first part anyway." She sighed.

Lucia continued. "Idyllic summers on the island lasted for centuries until greedy white settlers discovered it. They wanted to grab it for themselves and forced the Indians off with their muskets. The angry Indians fumed at the loss of their precious island, but what chance did they have against guns? They couldn't defend themselves with their weapons made of wood and stone, so they did the next best thing just before they left. They performed a sacred ritual, involving campfires, drumming, and praying to the Spirit of Justice."

"Prayer is very effective," Butterfly said.

Lucia shot her a glance and continued, "The ignorant settlers, never having bothered to learn the Indian language, didn't understand the importance of the ritual. They thought the Indians were just having a farewell party. Legend goes that with this ritual, the Indians put a curse on future white settlers who might try to make the island their home. The Indians knew the settlers cherished the saying, *'What goes around comes around.'* Fortunately for the

Indians, it was also their treasured slogan."

"Amen to that," Butterfly said.

Lucia frowned. "Let me finish, please."

"Sorry," Butterfly said.

"Subsequently, the settlers demeaned the island by keeping cows and bulls on it, away from the wolves on the mainland. Legend has it that the settlers started calling it Bullshit Island. It should still be called that, as far as I'm concerned," Lucia said, "considering all the bullshit the Colonel and The Committee for Good Taste generate."

We laughed, but it sounded bitter.

"What a shame," I said.

"The settlers," Lucia continued, "debauched it further by having many drunken parties here."

"Nothing has changed." Butterfly sighed.

Lucia shot Butterfly an annoyed look. "Even Cap and Fey, good people with worthy intentions, couldn't overcome the power of the Indian curse."

We sat in silence.

"Quite a legend," I said. "I'm curious, though. What do you think Cap and Fey's true intentions were?"

"I'll tell you, honey," Butterfly said. "They took an abandoned, run-down institution and an overgrown island and through their hard, hard work and talent, turned it into a glorious place to live. They had every hope that it would become a real community. Unfortunately, the Colonel and his bunch moved in, greed replacing good intentions."

"Did you know about the legend when you moved here?" I said.

They nodded.

Butterfly said, "You fall in love with a place and think its legend is romantic but not real."

"Would you still have moved here if you had heard the legend first?" Lucia said to me.

"Probably," I said.

We watched the full moon seem to rise from the sea, like a shimmering copper disc. I wasn't ready yet to tell these women about my dreams and the ghosts. It was bad enough that Max was making fun of me. I didn't want them laughing at me, too. So, I asked without being specific, "Do you think it's possible for the dead to influence the living?"

Butterfly burst out laughing. "Just ask any Southerner, honey. They live on Civil War stories: who owned and lost what plantation and whose ghosts are roaming the dilapidated family mansions."

I said, "Do you believe there *might* be visitations from beyond? "

I expected them to laugh, but they didn't. By now, the moon was our only light.

Butterfly, looked at the cove, and said in a dreamy voice, "All my life I have wanted to experience a ghostly presence in the house I was living in--a benign presence, of course, not one full of trouble--a visit from someone who had been happy living in the same house I was." She sighed. "But I never did. However, living at Martini Cove Island, and its being a former institution for people with troubled minds and all, I often felt as if it is entirely possible. Sometimes at night, when I stand on my front porch and look at the buildings where so many troubled people lived, I think I see a wisp of a white hospital gown in a window, just out of the corner of my eye. But when I turn to look, it's gone. Maybe they are tricks of moonlight. Sometimes, I feel a slight breeze past my face when there is no wind."

I thought about the shard I found on the windowsill in my house on the first visit and the breeze passing by me. I had thought it was Max opening the door, but maybe it wasn't.

"I know what you mean." Lucia nodded in Butterfly's direction. "I've often felt that way. Although our house is new, I sometimes feel a restless presence, like lost souls needing my help, but I never know what to do. There's never anything specific."

Butterfly looked surprised. "You, too?"

Lucia nodded. "When I stare at the sea just beyond the cove. I get the feeling that something terrible happened out there. I even checked with the Coast Guard, asking to see records of accidents or deaths around the island, but couldn't find anything. Yet I can't get over the feeling that something dreadful happened."

My stomach fluttered. I thought about the ghosts. Was there a connection between them and Lucia's feelings about something sinister happening near the waters of Martini Cove? My ghosts were more specific than Lucia's suspicions or Butterfly's feelings but I was not ready to share yet. I wanted to fit in, not stand out as an oddball. I changed the subject.

"Can you tell me about Fern, my neighbor?" I said. "I know she was a resident at Welcomer. How did she come to live here?"

Lucia settled her feet on a hassock. "Her family owned a mansion in the city. When she was a girl, her parents brought her to the island on summer days for picnics on the beaches off-limits to residents. Fern loved the island. When her parents realized she would always remain young in her mind, they knew they would eventually place her in Welcomer permanently. After they died, she moved into the cottage she lives in now. Fern was always functional and no trouble to the staff, so all they had to do was look in on her now and again and make sure she had the food and supplies she needed. After Welcomer closed, the lawyers saw to it that she was provided for and would never have to move. Apparently, that worked out fine."

"A lonely existence," I said, and shook my head.

"She seems content," Lucia said.

"How did you find all this out?" I said. "Surely not from Fern."

"Cap and Fey told us. They had to negotiate with her lawyers so they could go ahead with plans for condo development. Fern could stay here, and Cap and Fey would look in on her, much as we do now. She is sweet and unassuming, capable of caring for herself as long as she has deliveries from the mainland."

"It doesn't seem like she has worries. Her garden is her world. She must mulch it generously, it's so lush."

"It's no big deal getting manure rich soil around here," Lucia said, "not from a place formerly called Bullshit Island, where certain residents generate even more."

We laughed but it made me sad to hear this talk.

Butterfly frowned. "Certain people do not like Fern living here, uh uh. No, ma'am."

"Who?" I said, but I already suspected the answer.

Butterfly gave me a look as if to say, *After all we've told you, whom do you think?*

"The Colonel and friends?"

"Of course," Butterfly said. "They have been trying to figure out a way to force her off."

"What's stopping them?"

"The contracts that are keeping her here are iron clad. Her parents saw to that. Not even the Colonel can figure out a way to break them, although he's tried many times approaching the issue through different avenues: lawyers, city officials, petitions, even scaring her half to death with his gruff voice and bullying ways."

"Why do they want to get rid of her so badly? She's not visible in the community and she's not doing any harm."

"She is visible to the Colonel and The Committee for Good Taste, who think her house is a negative influence. They think that property values would be higher without her."

"Then why doesn't she just paint her house?" I said.

"I don't think she wants strangers like painters and carpenters fussing around her property," Butterfly said. "No one can force her to do anything, according to her parent's contracts."

"It's not just about the house," Lucia said. "These people have to erase all traces of Welcomer and Fern is a reminder. She was well protected when Cap and Fey were her neighbors, but since then?" She shrugged. "The four of us do the best we can."

I nearly choked on my wine. "You mean Cap and Fey were neighbors in the sense that they were living in the same community?"

"No, ma' am," said Butterfly, "they were literally next door neighbors. They lived in the very house you are occupying now."

This put another slant on the ghosts.

I said, trying to sound casual, "Do you have photos of Cap and Fey?"

Butterfly nodded. "Yes, in an old box somewhere."

"Why do you want to see a picture of them?" Lucia said.

I looked down at my glass and ran my finger around the rim. "No reason, just curious. I'd like to know all I can about my cottage."

"We didn't know them long before they disappeared," Butterfly said. "They had another residence on the mainland, but when funds for the island project ran low, they were forced to sell it and moved into their home on the island. They were so busy with the construction and selling finished units, that they never finished their own home before they went missing."

"So that's why our house was never completed," I said.

Lucia nodded. "Unfortunately, they did not know the kind of people the Colonel and Erhleen were when they sold to them. Otherwise they probably would not have let them move into this paradise." Lucia sighed. "But, getting back to Fern, there's something else about her."

"Shouldn't we be getting back to the others?" Butterfly said. "I do declare, all this sad talk is deflating."

"Just a minute," I said, "I'd like to hear."

"It's not a long story, Butterfly. You already know it," Lucia said, "and I think Sylvia should hear it. Besides, I still hear singing and champagne corks popping below."

Lucia took a breath and looked toward the sea. "A couple of years ago I was looking through the spyglass on a bright, moonlit night. I saw Fern wondering around the cliff just where the cove opens to the sea. That old-fashioned white dress of hers darting among the trees was unmistakable. She was quite distraught and I was concerned, since I had never seen her away from her house.

"Sky and I hopped onto the golf cart and drove to the cliff to see if we could help. We found her crouched, hiding behind a boulder, crying and incoherent. I held her until she had calmed down. Sky always keeps a bottle of champagne in the cooler under the golf cart seat for emergencies, so he popped one open and we insisted that she have a sip. Before long, we had finished the bottle, but we never did find out what she was doing on the cliff or why she was upset. After a few sips, she fell asleep. We wrapped her in a blanket, put her in the seat between us, and took her home.

"I don't think anyone saw us, but you never know. Sneaky Sven is ever watchful. I have tried several times since to question her about that night, but every time I bring it up, she gets so upset that I drop it. Probably we'll never know what happened."

Butterfly snorted. "The Colonel and The Committee certainly don't want her wandering around cliffs, night or day, when possible buyers could be around." She took a long pause, shook her head. "I once heard that you can determine the health of a community by how they treat their least fortunate."

"Doesn't seem too healthy to me," Lucia said with a bitter undertone. "There's another thing about that night that may be significant, though. This happened at the same time Cap and Fey disappeared along with thousands of dollars of association funds."

I let my breath out.

"When we were at the Shaloe's with Lester and Veeda," I said, "they brought up the disappearance and the missing funds."

Lucia slapped her hand against her thigh. "Those people love to link those events. Gives them another chance to tarnish Cap and Fey and forget their own shady deeds."

She grabbed the bottle. "Let's finish it off!" She poured the last of the champagne into our overflowing glasses. As she slurped the froth, she said, "Drink up, girls. I'd rather see a church burn than spill a drop of champagne."

CHAPTER 15

Downstairs the guests were gathered around the piano. A great number of empty bottles cluttered the kitchen counter. Max, Sky and Haywood were sitting in a corner of the living room, hunched forward, heads close together, deep in conversation. As I walked toward them, they stopped talking and assumed a casual air.

Sky held up a bottle "More champagne, Sylvia?"

"Um, no thanks. We don't want to overstay our welcome." I put my hands on Max's shoulders and said, "Time to go."

He glanced at his watch and stood. "Didn't know it was so late."

Just then, the pianist played a tremolo for attention. Everyone looked in the direction of the piano, where Lucia was holding up her hands for silence. "Before you go, let's show the full moon some respect." She pointed to the pianist and said, "Hit it."

The piano player launched into Van Morrison's "Moon Dance." Lucia, swinging her hips and waving her arms above her head, danced out onto the porch and gestured for us to follow. The champagne had loosened us up, and laughing, we danced out behind her in a conga line.

The moon had turned to silver and had risen high, its light streaking the water. Just then, the ferry, its windows lit, looking like a toy boat in the distance, chugged around the bend and headed toward the dock.

Lucia lifted her head high and howled like a coyote, "Ow-oooo-ahhh!"

We giggled, embarrassed, but the sound was so natural that soon we were all howling, even Max. Sting and Madonna really got into it.

When it was time for us to say good-bye to Lucia, she gave me a warm hug. She was so tall, my face pressed into her chest.

"Fair winds, Sylvia," she said.

I looked up at her and said, "What does that mean?"

"That's what sailors say when they wish each other good luck on rough waters. *'May you have fair winds and following seas.'*"

I hugged back. "Fair winds, Lucia!"

I suddenly had a premonition that ahead lay plenty of rough waters.

The Bordereaus offered us a ride home, but it was a mild night so we declined and walked instead. The moon lit the sand path, a buoy dinged in the distance, an owl hooted.

"Nice party," Max said. "Sky and Lucia aren't snobs, that's for sure. Look at their friends: a lobsterman and his wife, firefighters, a musician, an eccentric. Frankly, I was beginning to despair about the residents, but Sky and Lucia are astonishing."

"They are," I said. "I had a good time, too. By the way, what were you discussing with Haywood and Sky?"

Max laughed, but it sounded phony. "Oh, that...um... We were talking about sailing, Zen meditation, things like that."

"Sailing? You don't know anything about sailing."

"For heaven's sake! Don't you think I can have other interests besides garnishing? I've been reading about sailing and those two are experts. I asked good questions and they gave simple answers. I learned quite a lot."

I glanced at him sideways, "I never knew you were interested in sailing. When did that happen?"

"Oh, ever since we moved here. I've been reading magazines at the bookstore in the city...ah...to fill in time between grocery shopping and the ferry home."

Max was interested in *sailing?*

"Do you think we were with our community tonight?" I said.

"Perhaps."

"Everyone appreciated your ice sculpture. The food and wine were superb."

"True."

"So, what's bothering you?"

"The self-appointed community leaders: the Colonel, Erhleen and the Committee for Good Taste."

"But so what?" I said. "As long as you follow certain rules, we'll be fine."

"That's just it. There are double standards. Remember the rule about saying "Howdy!" as you pass a neighbor? When we passed the Colonel's house, you waved, but they didn't wave back. What about the Colonel's foul cigar smoke? What about a 'potluck contribution should reflect love and peace?' First of all, that doesn't even make any sense unless you're meticulous about the presentation. Shouldn't the residents be trying harder? Even deviled eggs on a deviled egg plate would be better. Don't even mention that horrible trailer the Prowns live in. Now *that* really reflects love and peace."

"You're nit-picking. We just came from a great party and you are still criticizing the community. Can't you just relax?"

He sighed. A cloud blocked out the bright moonlight and cast a shadow over his face, and at the same time, over my heart.

"All right," he said. "Let's go home. It's late and we're tired."

I stopped and turned to him, "I don't think you are giving the community leaders a chance."

"Sylvia," he said, and took my arm. "Let's just go home. We're tired. Let's talk about it in the morning."

We were silent the rest of the way home. What would it take to make him feel comfortable here? He was being so stubborn. Of course, *I* was perfectly comfortable here. Wasn't I?

* * * *

The next day, I called to thank Lucia and Sky for the party.

"Such a pleasure to have you," Lucia said. "Max's ice sculpture made the evening."

Her praise was genuine but her voice was sad and flat.

"Something wrong?" I said.

"Just silliness."

"What?"

She hesitated, then said, "I got a call from Erhleen this morning."

"What about?"

"It seems that since we didn't inform The Committee ahead of time about the party and neighbors complained about noise, we will be fined."

"That's absurd!"

"She said the Rules for Harmonious Living state plainly that we must inform The Committee about number of guests and number of flushes per guest. The thing is, we have a private water system that doesn't even connect with the island sewer system. Erhleen said she had forgotten about that and would strike that fine, but the noise fine stands."

"Who complained about noise?"

"Fermin and Mumsey were on the ferry and heard us howling."

"That lasted less than five minutes and was at nine-thirty on a Saturday night."

"As The Committee would say, 'Rules are rules.' "

"Except when it applies to them."

"It's not the fine we mind, but the stupid rules."

"So sorry it spoiled the memory of your lovely party."

"It didn't. To hell with them! We're not here for a long time. We're here for a good time."

Lucia still sounded down, though. Without thinking about it first, I said, "Let's go on a picnic, just you and me. I'll bring the food. I've never gone on a picnic with a girlfriend. Max is working on his memoirs and oblivious to the world."

"Great!" she said. "Sky is off island on business. We'll have it on the cliff below the house."

Early that afternoon I carried a basket with lunch to Lucia's house. The day was sunny, but earlier in the morning there had been a sudden windstorm. Leaves had fallen onto the road making green patterns on the sand. I noted the designs and decided to paint them later. The air smelled like earth and salt air. The wind was cool against my cheeks in the shade of the trees, but it was warm when I walked into the sun. Gulls cried overhead.

I prayed as I walked. *Please, please, let things work out for us. Let the community become a good one after all.*

When I arrived at Fair Winds, Lucia opened the screen door to the kitchen and hugged me as warmly as if she hadn't seen me in weeks. Then she picked up an insulated bottle bag and held it up for me to see, smiling coyly.

"Champagne?" I said.

"What else?"

"Let's go."

We ambled along a gravel path to the edge of the cliff where there was a patio large enough to accommodate two white Adirondack chairs and a small table. An ocean breeze kept us cool as we watched puffy white clouds dotting the cobalt sky and boats drifting on the sea.

Lucia reached into her bag and pulled out a chilled champagne bottle and two crystal glasses. We toasted to life and sipped slowly, sitting in companionable silence.

After the first glass, I asked Lucia if she were hungry.

"Famished," she said, and refilled the glasses.

After laying out silverware and cloth napkins, I placed two focaccia sandwiches, stuffed with grilled chicken, tarragon mayonnaise and slivered sun dried tomatoes, on china plates. Next to it, I mounded up a salad of spring greens, avocado slices, and chopped walnuts.

Lucia looked at the plates. "That's what's missing at Martini Cove Island. Look how appetizing this picnic is. Style and elegance make life fuller, don't they?"

"It doesn't take much." I picked up my sandwich. "Let's eat."

Lucia and I polished off the food and the bottle of champagne. I pulled out strawberries marinated in Sambuca for dessert. Lucia ate every speck and praised the lunch lavishly.

I eyed her slim figure, "You look like you hardly eat at all."

She laughed and tossed her blonde braid, "All that work on board *The Golden Fleece* keeps me fit. Besides, I don't eat lunches like this every day, and I make sure to drink *only* champagne--fewer calories than wine. That's why I drink so much of it."

We laughed and looked out to the cove as a boat, the *Screw Vous*, came around the bend and plodded through the water. I leaned forward to wave to Slick and Wanda, but they looked away.

"Those two wouldn't wave to me in a million years," Lucia said. "Thank goodness."

"Have you ever tried waving first?"

"Of course, in the beginning, but it was a lost cause. There's no good energy between us."

She opened the second bottle.

"You know the scuttlebutt about Slick and Wanda, don't you?" she said.

"Not a lot, just what they told us the time we were at their house. I know they are pretentious." I giggled. "Do you know about the painting hanging over their mantel?"

She shook her head, and I told her about the "Peekasew." Then I told her about the photo of them with Richard Nixon reproduced on the tray and napkins.

Lucia whooped with laughter. "Far be it from me to gossip, but I know a little secret about them and their relation to the Colonel."

"Do tell." I was never above a juicy bit of gossip.

"The residents of Martini Cove Island are smart, most of them," she said, "and have succeeded in business, I'll give them that much. But have you ever wondered how the Colonel could con so many people to his way of thinking?"

"I never thought about it."

"They're the kind of people who are never quite satisfied with their accomplishments, seeing their plastic glasses half empty instead of half full. They came to this premier community to be somebodies. The Colonel is especially sneaky and mean, but not stupid. He has a way of influencing people to his side. I don't really know quite how, but he makes sure the most needful residents have a position of importance, if you can call it that, in the community. Take Slick for instance."

"Oh?"

"The Colonel made sure Slick was elected president."

"I thought the Colonel was president."

"He was until a short while ago, when the Colonel probably thought he could do more "work" for the community behind the scenes. Besides, something else influenced him."

"What?"

"Slick had struggled for years to be somebody. He almost made it, not only by shady dealings, but because Wanda wasn't above doing a favor for any of the men Slick had dealings with."

My mouth fell open. "Do you mean what I think you mean?"

She nodded.

"Yuck!"

"When Wanda and Slick came to Martini Cove, Wanda, it is rumored, did the same favor for the Colonel."

"Double yuck!"

"It is said that the Colonel hadn't enjoyed this kind of favor for many years because he was turned off by Erhleen's wearing sunglasses to bed, and by those rumors of her being descended from vampires and all. After that, Slick had 'cart blank' as Wanda would say. She used her knowledge of French whenever and as often as she was asked to by Slick. Wanda wanted to get ahead just as much as her husband. She was one woman who was driven hard and put away wet."

We were laughing so much that Lucia had a hard time continuing her story.

"Of course, Wanda was proud of being the wife of the president. She had vanity plates made for her pink French car that read, 'Madam' as in the wife of the president of France, she thought. Considering it's Wanda, the word has a whole different meaning. She also had a silhouette of the Eiffel Tower, proud and erect, painted on the trunk."

I sprayed a mouthful of champagne.

"Soon after, she bought a diamond pendant on a gold chain and told everyone that Slick was one husband who truly appreciated his wife's talents."

We laughed until we had to cross our legs to keep from peeing in our pants.

"There was talk," Lucia said, while wiping tears from her eyes, "that Slick had put the *Screw Vous* up for sale to pay for the pendant, but that never happened. Suddenly, though, all the residents were slapped with special assessments for maintenance equipment he claimed the island needed. It was odd, but the price of the snowplow they bought came nowhere near the amount they collected in assessments. When questioned, Slick said the rest of the money would be kept for emergencies, should they arise."

"But probably went for Wanda's pendant?"

Lucia shrugged. "The Colonel and Slick have kept certain secrets from the residents, saying it's business that need not be discussed with them because, after all, the Colonel knows what's best for the community."

"Did you make this up?" I said.

She lifted her sunglasses and looked at me. "Do you think I could make something like this up? After all, who has more fun than people?"

CHAPTER 16

A couple of weeks later, I was in my studio working on a painting when Lucia called and invited us for a sail aboard *The Golden Fleece* that weekend. I thanked her and hung up, but my stomach was doing flip-flops and I broke into a sweat.

Still clutching my paintbrush, I hurried down the stairs yelling, "MAAX!"

He bolted out of his study, pen in hand. "Good God! What is it?"

"We've been invited for a sail aboard *The Golden Fleece*."

"Great," Max said.

"It's not!"

"It's not?"

"I don't know a thing about sailing."

"Neither do I."

"What will we have to do?" I gripped the brush so hard, it nearly snapped.

"I don't know."

"I thought you knew about sailing."

"I said I leafed through some magazines but I don't *really* know anything about sailing. Calm yourself, my dear. Sky and Lucia are gracious hosts who want our company, not our sailing expertise."

I slumped onto the couch, hugging a pillow to my chest. "What should I wear?" Rocking back and forth, my heart was racing. "I'll have to wear shorts, won't I? I can't wear shorts. I'd die if they saw me in shorts."

"Then wear slacks."

"Oh, sure. It's easy for you to say. Just wear slacks. No one wears slacks to go sailing in the summer."

"How do you know?"

"Every sportswear catalog shows women wearing shorts when they go sailing."

"Why don't you break the rules?"

I couldn't think of a good answer. I'd have to find another excuse not to go on the boat. "My knees," I said. "They're not what they used to be."

"I'm not what I used to be either. Sky and Lucia were younger once, too."

"You didn't see her climbing that mast."

"I'm positive they won't ask you to climb the mast."

I was almost in tears. "If I bend over, I'll look fat."

"Darling, you'll look fat anyway."

I was going to throw the pillow at him, but saw that teasing look in his eyes.

He bent over and kissed me. "You will look appropriate and pretty. Relax. We're going to have fun. They want your company. Isn't that how we got to know them in the first place, through you? They admire your spunk."

"They think I have spunk?"

"Yes, and they still want to be your friends."

Max and I spent the next day in the city shopping for sailing clothes. I finally settled on a pair of black slacks, a white blouse and a tan cotton sweater I could tie around my shoulders. A pair of aviator sunglasses and small gold earrings shaped like anchors finished off the look.

When I came down the stairs on the day of the sail, Max wolf-whistled and said, "What the well-dressed woman wears on a sail."

I gave him a look. "Don't push it."

Ready for the adventure, Max wore a pair of tan slacks and a white cotton sweater. But then we both looked down at our brand new beige canvas deck shoes.

"Do they make us look like greenhorns?" I said.

"No. They make us look like retired greenhorns."

Sunny and windy, the day was perfect for a sail. As we walked to the marina, Max carried a canvas bag with fine cheeses and homemade chutney and crackers that would go well with the champagne we were sure to have. Overhead, gulls laughed, perhaps making fun of our sailing clothes.

At the pier, only *The Golden Fleece*, a sleek vessel with a dark blue hull and white and natural wood trim, was still docked. Her tall, graceful mast, sails furled, swayed with the waves. I laughed.

"What are you thinking?" Max said.

I threw my head back and looked up at the sun. "Just happy," I said. "Aren't you?"

"You know me. Always skeptical."

"Not today," I said. "Let's enjoy the day and our new friends."

When we reached the boat, we saw Lucia wearing a pair of tan slacks, a white and beige striped sweater and brand new canvas deck shoes. She waved. "Ahoy, mates."

I sighed with relief.

"Permission to come aboard, ma'am." Max saluted.

Lucia saluted back. "Permission granted."

I turned to Max. "Where did you learn that?"

"From Sky and Haywood. And that's my entire knowledge of sailing." He took my arm, "Let's board the boat, shall we?"

I looked at the swaying boat. It was high tide and the deck was way above the dock. Oh, dear. How would I ever be able to climb aboard?

Lucia must have read my mind because in the next second, she hopped on the dock, pulled the boat closer with a rope and placed a two-step wooden ladder in front of me.

She offered her hand. "Let me help."

"Thank you." I gripped her hand. "I'm afraid I'm not very nautical."

"You'll get the hang of it," she said, as she guided me up.

I had my doubts, but I managed to hoist myself onto the deck. The boat was rocking, and I hunched over and clutched at anything that would keep me from tumbling into the water. Just then, Sky's head popped out of the hatch. My rear end was inches from his face. The only thing more embarrassing at that moment would have been to pass gas.

Looking over my shoulder I could see he was holding a bottle in one hand and four glasses upside down by their stems in the other.

"Welcome, Sylvia!" he said, his voice hearty and welcoming. "Have a glass of champagne."

Fine idea, but I still hadn't figured out how to sit down. "I don't know what to do." I felt the clumsiest I'd ever been.

"Put your left foot onto the cushion," Sky said. "That's it. Bring the other leg around. Just sit down. Well done."

The next thing I knew, Max was sitting beside me and I was holding a glass of champagne. I noticed the glass was plastic. Plastic?

Lucia must have seen my puzzled expression. "We only use plastic aboard--no breakage on rough seas."

Max had given Lucia the snacks we brought. She said we would enjoy the feast after a tour of the cabin and after some sailing.

The ladder going down into what they referred to as "the hatch," went straight down to the cabin. Would I have to climb down that? I shuddered.

When we had finished the bottle, it was time for the tour. Happy I had some champagne under my belt, I paused at the edge of the hatch.

"One step at a time," Lucia said, "and hold on with both hands."

As I took the first step, a powerboat roared by and *The Golden Fleece* rolled side to side. I hugged the ladder hard with both arms as I rocked back and forth with the boat. *Oh, God!*

"Steady as she goes," Lucia said. "Doing great."

Step by step, after an eternity, my foot touched the cabin floor. The saloon--as Lucia referred to the cabin--was surprisingly big. She pointed out that the banquettes covered with dark blue cushions and sea green throw pillows could be used for sitting or sleeping. The table to one side unfolded large enough to seat eight people. Many plaques, trophies, and photos of boats and sailors, hung on the varnished teak walls.

Lucia pointed to a brass plate that read, "Days spent at sea will not count against mortal time." She said, "That means we will have loads of good times aboard, even if we're just docked at the marina."

I smiled at her.

Sky sat down in a leather-covered swivel chair in front of a section of dials and controls and explained it was his command panel. He could sail the ship without ever going up top to the steering wheel.

The galley had storage cabinets, granite counter tops, a stove, microwave, refrigerator, freezer, and wine rack. At the front of the boat, the master cabin had a private head, a combination toilet/ sink/ shower. At the back of the boat, two smaller cabins were connected to a similar head. Lucia pointed. "These will be yours when we do an overnight."

An overnight?

"Someday, we'll take the boat on a long cruise," Sky said, "down to the Caribbean and the coast of Mexico. How would you like that, Sylvia?"

There were many reasons why that would be hard for me. But Max surprised me.

"Sounds like a grand idea." He rubbed his hands together. "A real adventure."

Was this Max Saltwater's clone?

I insisted on going last when we climbed back up the ladder. Sky took charge of the wheel. and Lucia untied the lines and tossed the fenders into the boat. We motored out of the mooring and cut through the water out to sea. When we were well away from land,

Lucia untied lines and Sky pushed buttons. The sail spun out of its cocoon, filling with wind.

Sky donned his cap and sunglasses and, suddenly, looked years younger. I tried not to stare, but every once in a while he caught me watching him and flashed a brilliant smile.

Lucia kicked off her deck shoes and jumped barefooted, agile as a monkey, using her hands and feet at the same time, working the sail, knowing exactly what to do when, grabbing the correct rope to pull, sensing the right time to tie and untie.

Max was leaning back on the cushions, hands linked behind his head, sunglasses reflecting sky and clouds.

We passed small islands along our route, where powerboats and sailboats were anchored in coves and inlets. I listened to sails flapping and the swish of the water. Once in a while, the boat tilted and salty sea spray cooled my face. Wind played with my hair. I pulled the sweater on against the chill. Joy tickled my stomach.

After a while, when we were in sight of a small, rocky island, Sky slowed the boat and turned it into the wind, sails furled again with the push of a button. He maneuvered the boat close to the island. Lucia weighed anchor. "Thorn Island," she said, "the perfect spot for lunch."

Scrubby bushes and a dead, thorny, tree were the only vegetation. We had passed more attractive islands along the way and I wondered why they picked this unattractive, weather-beaten island to stop.

"It's not the prettiest island in the bay," she said, "but a dear friend of ours owns it. His and ours are the only boats that have permanent mooring rights. When it's blazing hot, we anchor here and swim nude."

I was glad today was chilly.

"Let's have lunch," Lucia said, and disappeared down the hatch.

"I'll help." Max followed her.

Oh, no. I was alone with Sky. I hoped Max wouldn't take a long time garnishing.

"Hurry up," I yelled after them. "I'm starved!" Immediately, I wanted to bite my tongue. Did I sound like a fat lady waiting for her next meal?

"Salt air always gives me a hearty appetite, too," Sky said.

"At least, it doesn't show on you," I said.

Sky must have been flattered because he flashed another big white smile.

"Please don't do that too much." I held up a hand to shield my eyes. "My sunglasses aren't strong enough for the sun *and* your smile."

He laughed, but I think I tickled his fancy. His captain's duties were over for now and he slipped from behind the wheel and next to me, his arm resting along the top of the cushion between us, his hand near my shoulder. "You know what I like about you, Sylvia?"

I shook my head and held my breath.

"I admire your spunk."

"You mean you don't hold that against me?" I laughed.

He laughed, too. "You are unafraid to accept a challenge."

"I can say one thing for myself, I'm not afraid to be a fool."

"Intelligent fools are the only people worth knowing," he said.

I took my sunglasses off. Just then, a tiny insect flew into my eye. I tried to brush it out with my fingertip but couldn't.

"Something in your eye?" Sky said.

I nodded.

"Let me see." He slid closer, leaning over me and examining my eye. "Ah, I see it in the corner. Allow me?"

I tilted my head back. "Please."

Just as Sky was leaning over me and holding the side of my face, trying to brush the annoying bit from my eye, Max's head popped out of the hatch.

"Lunch is--"

I didn't jump back, but let Sky pick the bug out.

I thought back to Max's digs lately about me being fat. I hoped his imagination was taking over and he was jealous. Let him suffer just the tiniest bit. "Thank you so much, captain." I purred, and batted my eyelashes.

"Happy to be of service," Sky said, and saluted.

I may be fat. I may be retired. But I still had a spark and I could still flirt. Take *that* Max. Sylvia Saltwater lives!

* * * *

Lunch tasted delicious in the sea air. Although the talk was light and being on the boat was fun, I couldn't shake the sudden heavy darkness gripping me. I did not like this island and sat with my back to it. Soon, the gentle rocking of the boat, the wind, the sun and the champagne took their toll and my eyelids grew heavy. I lay my head back on the cushion and listened to the others talking, but they seemed far away.

I fell asleep and dreamed about the ghosts again--their despondent eyes, the woman's swirling hair. Hearing their heart-broken moans, I felt like I was falling. I gasped and woke up.

"You all right?" Max said.

"Sorry." I still felt groggy, and sat up. "I drifted off."

"Bad dream?" Lucia said.

I glanced at Max. He would be horrified if I mentioned the ghosts in front of Sky and Lucia, but he surprised me by saying, "Did you dream about the ghosts?"

Lucia and Sky spoke in unison, "Ghosts?"

I felt they were trustworthy, and I told them about my dreams. "I don't know why it's the same sort of dream over and over."

Sky and Lucia didn't seem as shocked as I thought they might be. Lucia snorted. "Maybe it's bad energy from the Colonel's group that's giving you mental indigestion."

I said, "Maybe we just don't understand those people. If we really try to talk to them, they might see us as the good people we are and we could work out our differences."

Nobody spoke.

Finally Lucia said, "That's sticking your head in the sand, girl. These people will never try to understand us, because they're out only for themselves and will destroy anybody who gets in their way. They see other people as their puppets." She looked me hard in the eye. "Forget it, Sylvia."

Suddenly, I felt weary. Sky opened more champagne and we watched the bright orange sunset over the water, but the joy of the day was gone.

CHAPTER 17

A few weeks after our day on *The Golden Fleece*, the doorbell rang. There stood Erhleen. Despite everything I had said about wanting to integrate into the community, I shrank back from her scowly smile. Had we broken a Martini Cove rule?

"Howdy, Erhleen," I said, "May I help you?"

When Truffle saw Erhleen, he slunk under the couch. Thank goodness Max was in the city.

"Howdy," Erhleen said. "We're inviting y'all to our annual Labor Day porch party-- nothing fancy, just friends--potluck, of course, and BYOB. The Colonel and I will provide the paper plates, paper napkins, plastic cups and utensils. We like to go all out at our parties. 'Course there'll be a family movie on the lawn after dark. No need to dress up."

I sensed that she was looking me up and down behind her sunglasses because I was wearing black slacks and a leopard print blouse.

"Everyday clothes are fine although we do like to keep up the rule about pastel colors."

"Thank you, we'd love to come. Of course," I said," we'll dress appropriately."

"Ain't nothing says community like a good potluck. No need for boring old community meetings."

When she left the porch, Truffle came to stand by me and snarled. "That's enough," I said. He lay down and looked up at me, his eyes sad. I was not looking forward to Max's reaction to this invitation.

I called Butterfly and told her about the invitation. "We'll be glad to be there with our friends."

After a short silence, she said, "If you mean us, honey, we aren't invited. I doubt that Lucia and Sky were either."

"Why not?"

"We are not in the Colonel's community."

"What about the rules. Aren't we supposed to give parties from the heart and all that? A porch party on Labor Day should be for the whole community, not just a part of it."

"It should be, but it surely is not. You don't know how hard Lucia and I tried to get the whole community together on holidays in the past. We planned barbecues, Christmas tree trimming parties, Memorial Day remembrances by the flagpole, but none of the Colonel's friends ever came. The only ones who showed up were the four of us and some of Lucia and Sky's friends from the mainland. We don't usually get invitations for their parties.

"Imagine! Everyone in the community invited except the four of us. That surely is hurtful and we felt downright bad about that until we realized we really didn't want to be with those folks, anyway. We gave up trying, heartbreaking as it was."

"What about the Fourth of July potluck we all went to? What about the brochure of Martini Cove Island with all those smiling faces?"

"Yes, I know. Erhleen invites us every once in a while when new people arrive, to make it seem as if we're one big happy family. She's calculating that way. We went because we were curious about you and hoped you'd be the kind of people who would be too smart to fall under their spell.

"It's them against us, honey. We have different standards and different reasons for making friends. Our friends are our friends because we see eye to eye, not like the Colonel and Erhleen who are working the crowd. That woman expects each person to be a picket in the fence surrounding the Colonel. Have you noticed that we do not have official community meetings? Their group has potlucks, which are their answer to what ails the community. The colonel does the dictating and they follow him like sheep."

Wanting to judge for myself, I took Butterfly's words with a grain of salt. "Would you feel as if we betrayed you if Max and I go to this party?"

Another pause. "Honey, I reckon everyone's gotta do what they gotta do. Go right on ahead to the party. But let me give you one piece of good advice: watch out. They have strong capabilities of persuasion."

"Thanks for understanding. We'll miss you."

"Have a good time," she said, and hung up.

I already knew which community Max belonged to. But I didn't want us to be outcasts like our friends. Open-minded, I would go to this potluck. There was too much at stake. Maybe we could straddle both factions? I wanted to fit in, damn it!

* * * *

Max took the news about the party with equanimity. On the day of the party, he arranged a simple plate of plain cheese on a bed of greens with no garnishes. No homemade crackers this time but a box of commercial crackers, as Max requested. Only I knew what a slap in the face that was to our hosts.

We left for the party, wearing pastel clothes and carrying the food and a bottle of wine. Max had insisted on scratching our initials on the label.

The Frighs lived in a two-story condo, formerly a ward. Haywood had told us the Colonel was a superb carpenter and I was curious about the expertise of his construction. There had to be *something* good about him.

When we arrived, the large porch was crowded with neighbors. Erhleen huddled with Fermin and Sven, who was scribbling in his notebook. When she saw us, she came over. "Welcome! It's good to have y'all in our camp--I mean, at our house."

Max winced.

The Colonel sat in a rocking chair, wearing his usual work clothes, but he was barefooted.

I sneaked a peek at his feet and wished I hadn't.

He was droning on quietly in a stream of consciousness sort of way between puffs of a foul smelling cigar. Adults and children sat at his feet. Three women, wearing pastel colored dresses with puffy sleeves and Peter Pan collars, sat cross-legged and barefoot, looking up at him, seeming to soak up every word. When I heard one of them call him "Daddy," I made the connection. The women were the three small Frighs, daughters who bore striking resemblances to their parents, even down to Erhleen's sunglasses. Surrounding them, sat lots of children in dirty play clothes.

Max leaned over and spoke from the corner of his mouth. "Refugees from the Dust Bowl?"

I shot him a withering look.

Lester was sitting on the floor, next to the Colonel's chair. His head was leaning against the side of the rocker and rocking back and forth with the chair. His eyes were closed, his mouth was hanging open. He was clutching a drink, and seemingly mesmerized by every word the Colonel uttered. But maybe he had just passed out.

A few people said "Howdy" as we passed. Max put the cheese plate on the paper-covered, grease stained table. Plastic spoons stuck out of plastic glasses.

"Erhleen has outdone herself," Max said under his breath while pouring our wine into two plastic cups.

"Try to enjoy these people's offerings," I whispered.

There were no chairs on the porch, except the Colonel's rocker. I did not want to sit at eye level with his feet so we stood, sipping wine. A young couple who had recently moved to the island, drifted over and sat by the Colonel's feet.

Mumsey caught Max by the arm and pulled him to the side of the porch. I could overhear that she was complaining about the excessive noise at Martini Cove Island, mentioning Lucia and Sky as the most recent offenders.

Max stifled several yawns.

I needed the bathroom so I asked Erhleen where it was. "Up them stairs," she said, and gestured with her thumb.

As I climbed the stairs, I admired the exquisitely crafted banister and stairs. The modernized bathroom looked true to late nineteen-hundred's architecture with its footed bathtub, beadboard wainscoting, porcelain fixtures, and brass lights. An excellent craftsman, the Colonel certainly had a way with a hammer.

When I went back downstairs, I saw a slightly ajar door in the hallway that I hadn't noticed before. I sidled over and peeked in. A small room, painted blood red, held a table with chairs around it like a conference room. Lining the walls were file cabinets.

Erhleen brushed past me and yanked the door shut. She locked it with a key dangling from a chain around her neck, next to the chain with the gold life preserver. "Tarnation! How often have I told that Sven never leave this here door open?" She grabbed my arm. "Let's get back to the party."

On the porch, Mumsey was still talking to Max, whose eyes had glazed over.

I took the empty cup from his hand, refilled it and brought it back to him.

"Bless you," he mouthed silently.

I drifted to where the Colonel sat and leaned against the porch railing. The longer I listened, the more I realized how friendly his voice sounded.

"That's right, ah hah. Nothing is more important than family. If we sticks together, nothing in this here world can harm us. We have to work together for the good of the community and the family. Y'all know that when I says family, I mean everyone in this here community that thinks like me and Erhleen. We knows what's best. Y'all knows how hard we works, keeping only the good of the community in mind at all times. Yes, it's true, sometimes we have to sacrifice someone for the good of the whole, but what does that matter? We is thinking of the best for our children and Martini Cove Island."

He held up a twig.

"See this bitty twig? Watch how easy it snaps. See? Broke plum in half. Now when I hold this bunch of twigs together and try to break it, it stays strong, same as our community if we supports each other. Yes, certain people living here, and I don't need to mention names, are poisoning our community by telling vicious lies. They is heaping vitriol on Erhleen and your Colonel by saying that all we do for the community is self-serving. No sir! They are lying liars telling lies. Mark my words, they'll all leave this paradise one by one, especially if we help them along."

Everyone was perfectly quiet and listening to his voice drone on. His voice mesmerized me. It made me think of the silkiness of chocolate icing on chocolate cake. I dismissed *what* he was saying and thought only about *how* he was saying it.

"Y'all know how many hours Erhleen spends on The Committee for Good Taste, and yet there's some that would dare criticize her and the other members. The only job this hard working group has is keeping this paradise a reality for you and your kids. Let's drive these evil-doing criticizers out!"

Rocking back and forth, talking in a monotone Southern accent, he sounded like a strong father, a man who knew how to run things. It sounded like you could lean on him when you were in trouble and he would know how to save you. Wasn't it comforting to have someone who would always make the right decisions for you? No need to think. He would think for you and you could let your mind go lazy and not worry about moral obligation. The Colonel said he knew what was moral and what wasn't. No wonder so many people looked up to him. He was the daddy to his community. Listening to him was like eating comfort food--meatloaf and mashed potatoes.

By now, Lester was asleep on the floor. The three small Frighs and their children lay at the Colonel's feet, too, dreamy expressions on their faces. Tears were rolling down the cheeks of the young couple new to Martini Cove Island as they clutched each other's hands. I slipped to the floor next to the railing leaning my head against it, closing my eyes, my mind drifting.

Suddenly, Max gripped my arm and yanked me to my feet.

I said, "Isn't he a wonderful speaker?"

"You've got to be kidding! He's talking dangerous, sentimental rubbish! He wants people to be his 'yes' men, not independent thinkers. Time to go." Forcefully, he pulled me along, gripping my arm with a force that surprised me.

"Thanks for a good time," I called to Erhleen over my shoulder.

The Colonel's soothing voice drifted after me on the evening breeze. "Y'all come back now, honey," he said, and waved.

When we had walked far enough so that no one could see us, I jerked my arm away from Max. "Thanks for spoiling everything."

He kept walking.

I grabbed his arm. "Look at me, damn it!"

He shrugged me off and walked faster. I trotted to keep up.

He kept stomping ahead without looking at me. "You're not yourself right now."

"Oh, Max! I want this community so much."

"You want community, but not *this* community."

I started to cry.

Max groaned. "Sylvia, please!"

"But...this community has everything I want."

"No it doesn't. Its beauty is only skin-deep."

We were silent the rest of the way home. At the door, Truffle seemed to stop in mid-jump. He came to me and licked my hand.

"Want a nightcap?" Max said, softening his tone.

"Definitely."

The nightcap did little to cheer me up. I felt empty and let down. Maybe this was not my community after all. That thought hurt. It hurt like hell.

CHAPTER 18

Again I dream I am underwater with the ghosts, wispy like fog, desperate, lost souls.

I say, "How can I help? Please, please tell me."

I see a flicker in the woman's eyes. She says with great difficulty, "Write."

"Okay! But... What?"

The woman makes the motion of writing with her hand. Then she fades.

"Don't go." I say.

But the fog thins. They are gone.

Next morning Max was shaking my arm to wake me up. His face grim, he held up a piece of my drawing paper with writing on it.

"What's that?" I blinked, and put my glasses on.

"Just what I was going to ask you. It's your paper and your handwriting. It was on the floor next to the bed."

I took the paper from him and read, "*SYLVIA-- ONLY YOU CAN BRING PEACE. ASK BUTTERFLY AND HAYWOOD.*"

"That's my handwriting, but I didn't write it," I said.

"If you didn't, then who did?"

"I remember dreaming about the ghosts, and the woman asking me to write something."

"Which you obviously did."

"I did *not* write that. Maybe she did."

"Don't give me more of that psychic stuff."

"Don't take that tone." I threw the paper down.

"I can't deal with this if you're going to lie." He stomped down the stairs.

"I'm not lying. Hey! Come back here!"

Truffle lay on the floor by the bed, paws over his head.

I picked up the paper again. It was my handwriting all right, but I did not remember writing it. Did I channel this message from the ghostly woman?

I went to Max's meditation shrine. He was in his kimono, twiddling his moustache. He looked up, his brow wrinkled. "You know I'm worried about you, don't you?"

That did it. I sank down on the cushion next to him, put my head against his arm, and sobbed. He put his arm around me and waited for my sobs to subside. "Tissue?" he said, and pulled a package from his kimono sleeve.

I blew my nose. "I don't feel danger from them," I said, with my face against his chest, "and it seems I'm the only one who can help."

Max looked stern.

"Do what you need to." He encircled me with his arms. "But if it looks like you're in trouble, I'll get you away from this island, even if I have to throw you into a sack and carry you off."

"About last night... Maybe we can live with the Colonel and his community as well as with our friends."

Sighing with weariness, he said, "Maybe."

Later, when we sat down to breakfast, I was happy to see Max's banana pinwheels on my oatmeal. On a linen napkin next to the bowl, lay a perfect white shell, the kind found on the island's beaches. I picked it up and saw it had left a damp spot on the napkin. "How sweet of you. Thanks for the shell."

Max looked up from tapping the top of a soft-boiled egg. "What shell?"

I held it up.

He shook his head. "I didn't put it there."

"Well, Truffle certainly didn't."

Max put down his knife, folded his arms over his chest and looked at the ceiling. "Here we go again."

"If you didn't put it here, who did?"

"The ghosts?" One eyebrow was raised.

I examined the shell and set it back down. "As the note said, it might be time to talk to Haywood and Butterfly. She once mentioned she had a photo of Cap and Fey. That might be a clue to all this."

"I'll go with you."

* * * *

Haywood answered the door and Butterfly swept down the stairs as always, making a grand entrance in a green pantsuit and large silver earrings that looked like Christmas tree bulbs. She offered iced tea with fresh mint and we settled into the living room chairs. The overhead fan whirred, and sun streamed through the slats of the shutters.

She sat back and crossed her ankles. "To what do we owe the pleasure of this visit?"

I smoothed the lace-edged napkin on my lap. "I hope you won't think I'm crazy because of what I'm about to tell you,"

Wide eyed, she and Heywood looked at each other.

"We are surely intrigued," Butterfly said. "Whatever you will tell us will be no crazier than what we have already experienced at Martini Cove Island."

I took a deep breath and said, "I have been visited by ghosts."

Haywood leaned back in his chair and let out a low whistle. "Well, butter my butt and call me a biscuit."

"Ghosts? At Martini Cove Island?" Butterfly's eyes popped. She leaned so far towards me that she almost fell out of her chair.

I told them about my dreams, the ghosts, how sad they made me feel, and about them asking for my help.

"Well, I never!" Butterfly clasped her hands together. "I just knew it. A former rest home for the mentally weary, like Welcomer, must have lots of ghosts. I, unfortunately, have never experienced any." She sniffed. "They must trust you."

"You believe me?"

"Bless your heart, darling. Course I do."

"For heaven's sake," Max said, as he clanked his glass down on the coffee table. "Not you, too?"

Haywood wagged his finger at Max. "Sir, when you come from the South, you are not shocked by such matters. We have always lived with spirits. Just think of those abandoned, moss-covered mansions with ghosts from the Civil War floating around in them. Ghosts are a Southern tradition."

I pulled the paper with the message from my pocket and handed it to Butterfly. "I dreamed about them last night, and must have channeled. That's my handwriting, but I swear I don't remember writing it."

"You mean this is a message from beyond that mentions *me*?" Butterfly read the message out loud then grasped the paper to her chest.

"Can you help?" I said. "Now would be a good time to show me the picture of Cap and Fey. It might be a clue."

"Sure enough, and I have something else to show you, the only known documentation I know of from Martini Cove Island's past. Maybe there's a clue there, somewhere." She almost skipped up the stairs. "Oh, Lord above! I just love ghosts."

Max slumped in his chair.

"Sir," Haywood said, "would you care for anything stronger than tea?"

"Got any scotch?"

Soon Max and Haywood were holding stiff shots of single malt. Butterfly fluttered back into the room holding a small, flat metal box. She cleared the coffee table and set it down.

"Before the original developers disappeared from Martini Cove Island," she said, "Fern gave me this box for safe-keeping. I'm not sure how she came by it and we'll probably never know, but she said it would be safer with us. It contains old photos of Welcomer, probably a real find. Fern does appreciate old things. Sky and Lucia know about this box and its contents, too, of course."

I wished she'd stop talking and show the contents of the box.

"Since we became trustees of the box, Haywood and I have often dreamed about starting a Welcomer museum, but you can imagine what the Colonel and his bunch might think about that idea. They do not want anyone to be reminded of Martini Cove Island's past, no sir. Someday, however, we will be rid of those people and maybe, with luck, we can start one."

Haywood scratched his beard. "Well, now, honey, starting a museum is a noble idea, but I don't hardly think there's enough photos in there to fill a whole one. Maybe a single room, if you frame them large. On second thought, we could give them to the city museum."

Butterfly shook her head. "Mr. Bordereau, we have discussed this before, and I am *not* giving these photos to any other museum. We will start one of our own right here on this bitty island, and since it's a bitty island, we could have a bitty museum."

"It will cost more than a bitty amount of cash, sure enough," Haywood said.

"Poop!" she said, and finally opened the box. She pulled pairs of white cotton gloves from her pocket and slipped a pair on. "Be careful how you handle the photos." She gave out the other pairs before handing me a worn stack of sepia and black-and-white photos.

The photos were of Welcomer around the turn of the twentieth century when it was built and might have been publicity photos taken before residents were admitted. The buildings looked new and grounds well-manicured, but sterile and barren. The stately trees now circling the green were saplings. The photos showed reception rooms furnished with functional mission style furniture and plants in old-fashioned jardinières. Clean, yet clinical looking, dining rooms were outfitted with long tables and chairs. Pictures of rooms showed white iron beds covered with white sheets and blankets. A bakery, kitchen, occupational therapy rooms, medical exam rooms, mechanical repair shops, garages, and a theater revealed Welcomer as a complete small village. Some photos showed individual cottages.

"Oh," I said, "these are similar to ours."

"All of the cottages, except yours and Fern's, and the theater were destroyed by deterioration or fire, according to Cap and Fey," Butterfly said.

I shuffled through the photos. "These would be a treasure for a museum."

She nodded. "But I wish we had some photos of the people who worked and lived here. That would give a complete sense of the place." She handed me another photo. "Do you recognize this?"

The photo showed the front of a cottage with dark painted shutters. The woods had not grown up around it, making it exposed and barren. Another photo clipped to it showed the back.

"It's ours," I said, excited. "Except for the dark shutters, it looked a lot like that when we bought it."

"Are you sure?" Haywood said.

"This photo of the back shows the large boulder near the edge of the woods. It's still there." I studied it some more. "However the photo bothers me. Something has changed." Then it struck me and I jabbed the photo with my finger. "There, at the peak of the roof, the small diamond-shaped window. There's no diamond-shaped window there now."

"I never noticed." Haywood leaned over to look. "But you are more familiar with your cottage."

"Why would it be taken out?" Butterfly said.

Max leered and made creeping motions with his fingers. "Maybe because the staff wanted to hide a resident in the attic."

"No more Scotch for you," I said, and turned back to the photo.

Butterfly handed me a color photo taken only a few years ago. It showed a handsome, gray-haired man and a pretty woman with long dark hair, both smiling, standing on the pier at Martini Cove Island. "That's Cap and Fey."

I gasped. They weren't blue and transparent but I recognized them at once. "My ghosts!"

Max choked on his scotch and coughed.

"What?" Butterfly snatched the photo back. "You sure?"

"Positive. Only, when they appear to me they have blue skin and sad expressions."

Max leaned over to look. "Those are the people who renovated the buildings on Martini Cove Island and absconded with association funds?"

"They renovated Martini Cove Island," Haywood said, "but I'm sure they never stole association funds. That's an ugly rumor the Colonel likes to spread. The truth is that the Colonel's sorry butt would not be living here if it weren't for the long hard years of work those two put in on bringing the place back to life. I never for a moment believed that they would steal from the community."

"So, if that's true," I said, "and my ghosts really *are* Cap and Fey, they might have been the victims of foul play. Maybe that's why they're trying to contact me."

I put the photo down and collapsed into my chair, "Any scotch left?"

CHAPTER 19

Knowing who the ghosts were shed light on everything. They had contacted me because we lived in their house and I was open to their energies. Why had the window in our house been removed? The answer might be relevant to their disappearance.

Excited, we all piled on Haywood's golf cart, taking the photos of our house with us.

"Ghosts!" Butterfly whooped. "This is the most exciting thing that has ever happened to me!" Her eyes shone, and even her hair looked alert. "Can't you go any faster, Haywood?"

"What do you think you'll find in the attic?" said Max. "A secret padded chamber, complete with straight jacket?"

I gave him a dirty look.

At our cottage, we hurried to the back and scrutinized the peak, searching for signs of the window, but the boards looked seamless.

As we crowded around the photo looking from it to the cottage, Haywood said, "Are you sure this photo is of *your* cottage?"

"It's ours." I pointed to the boulder in the photo and then to the one in the yard. "See? Same boulder. Let's take a look at the attic."

We hurried to the front where Truffle greeted us at the door, but we rushed past him. Max got a stepladder from the kitchen pantry, and we climbed the stairs to the bedroom. I pushed aside the clothes in the closet to expose the panel that led to the attic.

"You first." I handed Max a flashlight.

"Thanks a lot," he said, but he climbed the three steps on the stepladder. When he pulled the handle on the ceiling panel down to expose the attic ladder, it creaked and a few tufts of dust fell on his hair. He brushed them off and they fell on Haywood.

Haywood brushed his head. "Sir, do be careful."

"Sorry." Max said, while huffing for breath. At the top, he turned, sat down, and then swung his legs up. "Ah, the joys of retirement," he muttered. Then he shrieked.

"What?" I shouted.

"Lots of cobwebs but I'm okay."

Haywood went next. Thinner and more agile than Max, he quickly reached the top.

Butterfly took her shoes off and climbed the stepladder but hesitated at the unstable attic ladder. "I don't think I can do this."

"Woman," Haywood said, "you can move quicker than a striped ape when you have to. You know how much you've been wanting to see a haunted house." In one quick motion, he reached for her hand and pulled her up.

"I'm all mussed up." She smoothed her hair back.

"You look fine." Haywood rolled his eyes.

My turn. The only good thing about this was that Sky wasn't here to see me. I took it one step at a time, until Haywood and Max pulled me to the top, where I fell forward onto the attic floor. "Graceful," I said, and sat up.

The attic was high enough in the middle for us to stand if we hunched over, but it was easier to drop to our knees and crawl.

"Hot up here." Butterfly fanned herself with her hand.

"Nothing we can do about that," Haywood said. "The only window up here is fixed." He pointed to the diamond-shaped window at the front of the cottage. When he shone the flashlight beam over the walls, floor and ceiling, it revealed nothing but cobwebs.

I had read enough mystery novels to know that you can tell if a space is hollow or solid by knocking on it, so I crawled to the back wall and knocked on it.

"What are you up to, Nancy Drew?" Max said.

"Looking for a secret door," I said. "The walls sound solid. Maybe they're filled with insulation."

Haywood knocked on the wall, too, top to bottom, and then shook his head. "My boat building experience tells me this wall is hollow. Also, you can see that the height of the wall from the floor to the slant of the ceiling in the front is shorter than in the back."

"Mr. Bordereau," Butterfly said, "talk plain. What does that mean?"

"It means, Mrs. Bordereau, it's right likely there may be a small secret room at the back."

"Really? A secret room? Oh, Lordy!" Wide-eyed, Butterfly stood up and hit her head on the ceiling. She crouched back down, rubbing the top of her head.

"Dang it," Haywood said. "Don't knock yourself out. I wouldn't relish carrying you down those rickety ladders."

"Get the crowbar, Max," I said.

"Now you want me to tear our house down."

"Honestly! We're going to pry a board away to see if there's anything behind that wall, that's all."

"Glad to oblige." He climbed down the stairs. When he returned, he handed Haywood the crowbar and dusted cobwebs off his trouser legs. "I'm too old for this. Weren't we supposed to enjoy our golden years in style?"

Haywood shone the flashlight on the back wall while Max pried at the boards with the crowbar.

"Ooh," Butterfly said, while clapping her hands. "What treasure could be in there?"

Max grimaced as he tugged at a board. "A dead body."

I gripped his arm. "That's creepy. You don't really think there's a dead body in there!"

"Or maybe two. Cap and Fey." He shook my arm off. "I can't do this with your hanging on."

"You're scaring me."

"Don't worry. With the heat up here, they're probably mummies by now." He resumed board-pulling.

I looked at his face and saw the grin. I punched him.

"Ow! That hurt."

"Keep going." Butterfly wiped her forehead on her sleeve. "The sooner we see what's there, the sooner we can get back downstairs."

Max pulled and twisted until a board loosened.

Haywood shone a light into the hole.

We all looked in and gasped.

CHAPTER 20

The secret room was narrow but large enough to hold a chair, an old trunk and a small wood table on which stood a battery powered camp lamp.

Max said, "What secret thing went on up here?"

"Max, take the wall down," Butterfly said. "I'm dying to see what's in that trunk."

"Calm yourself, woman," said Haywood. "No need to take the whole wall down. Let me help."

The men took turns until they had opened a hole big enough to squeeze through. Max passed through first with the flashlight and we followed, shuffling along on our knees.

"Were Cap and Fey midgets?" Max said. "You'd have to be short to be comfortable in a space like this."

Haywood said, "Or so worried about a secret getting out that comfort was irrelevant."

I crawled to the table and turned the switch of the lamp. Dead.

Max wiggled the lock of the trunk, and then tried lifting the lid, but failed to open it. "This lock needs a key," he said, and shone the beam over the room. "Where could it be?"

"The drawer of the table?" Butterfly crawled over and yanked it open. A spider scurried out and ran across the table into the darkness. "My word." She hit her head on the ceiling again.

"Calm down," Haywood said. "You're going to give yourself one terrific headache."

"I'm so keen to find out what this is about that I'm going to explode any minute." She was rubbing her head, almost in tears.

Max shone the beam inside the drawer. "No keys," he said. "Just cobwebs and some pens."

"If we can't find the keys," said Butterfly, "why don't we just blast it open?"

Haywood frowned. "Sure enough, woman. Destroy the contents of the trunk, blast a hole in the house, and alert The Committee for Good Taste. You sure do bowl up common sense."

"Don't talk ugly," Butterfly said, huffing.

"Finding the key would be simpler," I said. "Or, could we move the trunk downstairs?"

Max tugged but it wouldn't budge. "It's incredibly heavy or bolted to the floor. We'll have to try opening it here."

"Can't we just stick a paper clip into the lock and wiggle it?" Butterfly said.

"Dear lady," Max said. "You've been watching too many crime dramas."

No one offered further suggestions.

I shone the beam over the outside wall. "Why was the back window taken out? Why the secrecy?"

Haywood ran his hand over the wall. "Aha!" he said. "Looks like the outline of a diamond-shaped window right here," he said. "These boards are relatively new."

"Doesn't explain the need for this room," I said.

Heywood frowned. "Could be tax records in there."

"Tax records?" Butterfly said. "How boring. No, it's more interesting. Love letters, that's it! Tied up with ribbons." She placed her hands over her heart.

"Or patients' charts," Haywood said.

"You're so romantic," Butterfly said.

"Or maybe more old photos of Welcomer," I offered.

"That's it." Butterfly brightened. "More photos for the museum."

"I'm curious, too," I said, "but I'm hot, cramped and my knees hurt."

"You can't give up in the middle of everything," Butterfly said.

Max said, "We can't open that trunk right now and we need to think over a cold drink. Let's take a break."

"Second the motion." Haywood rubbed his bottom.

"Phooey." Butterfly shot a longing glance at the trunk.

We crawled toward the ladder and reversed the climbing process.

* * * *

The only sound in the living room was the clinking of ice as we sat with glasses of water.

Finally Butterfly said, "More photos for my museum are up there. I feel it."

"Let's see what's in that trunk before we put up a tent and start the revival," Haywood said.

"Killjoy," Butterfly said.

I shook my head, "But why the secrecy?"

"I suspect," Haywood said, "it might have something to do with our beloved Committee or the revered Colonel."

"Think The Committee is that horrible?" I said. "They really haven't done anything terrible."

"That we know of," Haywood said.

Max, in the wing chair, was swirling his glass at a rapid rate.

"What are you thinking?" I said.

He shifted in his seat. "I was wondering…"More rapid swirling.

"What?"

"I was wondering about something Butterfly said."

"Oh?" Butterfly perked up.

"About picking the lock with a paper clip."

I said, "You've been watching too many movies, too."

"I may have a solution."

"The only way is with a key," I said.

"Maybe not. I have an idea. Might not work, but it's worth trying." He jumped up and went to his study.

Haywood and Butterfly gave me puzzled looks. I raised my eyebrows.

I recognized the sound of his unlocking the door of the garnishing tool display case. He returned and sat down holding up an intricate bronze sculpture of a dragon, about five inches in length and one inch in width. "This sculpture is really a tool." He turned it with his fingertips.

"It was crafted in eighteenth century Japan, and could be compared to a Swiss Army knife. Three unique blades are hidden in the body. Nobody would ever know they were there, so well are they integrated into the design. It needs to be pushed, twisted and pulled in certain ways to release them. The blades are the sharpest I've ever handled, so it has to be opened with extreme care."

Max pressed the head of the dragon gingerly with his fingertip and out shot a blade. He twisted and turned the dragon carefully and slowly until three paper-thin blades were out: a blade with a loop at the end, a double-pronged blade, and a curved blade.

"They look delicate," he said, "but they are the sharpest and strongest I've ever seen."

"What was it for?" Haywood said.

Max shrugged. "It might have been used for anything, I suppose. Perhaps a samurai had commissioned it to take on trips when he did battle, or he might have cut flowers for arranging ikebana."

"Why are you telling us about this?" I said.

Butterfly bounced up and down in her chair, while holding her hand up. "I know, I know. You're going to pick the lock, aren't you?"

"I'm going to try." Max carefully folded the blades and pushed them back in. "Shall we return to the attic?"

Once again we climbed the stairs and crawled through the hole into the secret room. I shone the flashlight on the lock of the trunk. Max took the dragon from his pocket. Then, gingerly, he exposed the curved blade, stuck it in the lock and wiggled it.

I looked over his shoulder. "Don't break the lock."

"Twist it more to the right, the right." Butterfly made circles with her hand.

"If that fine blade gets stuck we'll never get the damn thing open," Haywood said.

Max stopped and looked over his shoulder. "Listen, experts, feel free to try this yourselves."

I stroked his shoulder. "Max, anyone who can decorate a real hard-boiled egg to make it look like a Faberge egg commissioned by the Czar of Russia can handle this, too."

Haywood clapped Max on the back and said, "Sir, you are doing a mighty fine job."

"Thanks for the confidence," Max grumbled, and turned back to lock picking.

I could hear the delicate rattle of the blade in the lock and everyone's breathing. Then, a faint click. Max tried to open the lock but it wouldn't budge, so he switched to the loop blade and stuck it in, pulling gently. A louder click.

Everyone stopped breathing.

"You did it," Haywood said.

"Oooh goody!" Butterfly clapped her hands.

Gingerly Max closed the knife and lifted the lid as easily as if its hinges had been basted with butter.

The beam from the flashlight shone on a book covered in burgundy leather. Underneath were boxes. Butterfly reached in and handed me the book. She lifted the lid of the first box.

"Dear heavenly stars," she breathed. "Photos!"

As we sifted through them, we knew this was an important find. The photos, some of them portrait shots, were of the people at Welcomer from different time periods. On the reverse side names, places and dates were documented. The photos showed groups of caregivers in starched white uniforms, residents working at crafts and listening to a radio in a common room, enjoying a play in the theater, and employees working at various jobs. My skin prickled at later photos taken during the decline of the rest home. Vines climbed the once pristine walls of the buildings, trees grew haphazardly from caved in roofs and lawns were overgrown.

Butterfly said, "Now we have photos of the people. Just what we need for our museum. Visitors will get a real sense of the place."

"Oh, yeah," Haywood said, "the Colonel and The Committee will really love that."

Butterfly ignored him and kept shuffling through the photos.

The book's smooth cover smelled faintly of leather. I turned it over to look for a title, but there was none. I opened the book and saw handwriting, done with flourish on thick creamy vellum. A lack of foxing on the pages indicated it wasn't old.

I read the first page out loud "*Fey's Journal.*" I closed the book and shook my head.

Butterfly gasped. "Aren't you going to read it?"

"A journal is private and not meant for other eyes."

"Lordy be, Sylvia," she said. "This journal could answer our questions. We *have* to read it. In this matter, we don't have the luxury of honoring privacy." She snatched it from my hands, opened it, and shone the light on the first page. "If you're too ethical to read it, I will."

I sighed. "I suppose you're right."

"Of course I am." She flattened it out on her lap.

We sat cross-legged next to her on the floor.

She flipped through it. "Heavenly stars. This is a day to day account of the renovation of Welcomer to Martini Cove Island. Here's the first entry."

> "After ten years of planning, obtaining permits, and convincing people that Cap and I were not crazy for taking on this enormous project, we are allowed to clear the island of vegetation and debris to begin. It's been a dream for so long, I can't believe it, but, yes, we can start

to build our model paradise community! We plan to renovate floors of private rooms into condominiums, restore cottages, build a community hall for bringing people together, dig a swimming pool, and create a museum to preserve the unique history of this island, and many other proposed projects."

Butterfly jabbed her finger on the page. "There it is in black and white, Mr. Bordereau. Fey wanted a museum."

Haywood grunted. Butterfly read on.

"First, we need to clean the beaches, take away the debris from the crumbled buildings, trim the trees. Later we can restore the lawns and plant gardens. A few lots will be offered for sale, too. I pray we can sell to people who will love and care for this island the way we do and whose children will carry on the tradition long after we are gone."

Butterfly paused. "Does that sound like people who would abscond with community funds?"

"We hope to sell to honorable people who will think as we do, and hope to transform this island from a place of sadness and sorrow to an enlightened community. When people are actually living on the island, they will come to love it and become stewards of it, with such positive energy that they will break the Indian's curse, which I never personally believed in, anyway. Cap thinks I'm being idealistic but I want to prove it can be done."

"Poor woman," Haywood said. "She had no way of knowing the kind of people who would move here and what a hard row of stumps she would have to hoe."

"Sush," Butterfly said. "There's more."

Haywood rubbed his bottom again. "Let's take the journal and boxes downstairs. Sitting on this here attic floor is tougher than a one-eared alley cat."

Butterfly and I climbed down the ladders to the bedroom and Max and Haywood handed the boxes and journal to us.

In the dining room, Max peeked out the windows before drawing the curtains and closing the blinds.

"Aren't you being a bit paranoid?" I said.

"Cautious."

We sat at the table, the photos spread out. Butterfly continued reading.

> "We are worried about Fern Delamere. She has continued to live in her own cottage after the other residents of Welcomer left. The reason she has survived here this long is because of her trust fund. Her family (they are dead now) was highly connected with powerful political figures who saw to it she got what she was promised--a lifetime home on the island. Her parents had at one time suggested that they might buy the island for her, but that was not possible because it was government property and the government was not willing to sell. When Cap and I came, she was upset that her house would be taken from her and she would be displaced, but we assured her we had no such plan. Cap convinced Fern that it would be best for her to have neighbors, especially us, who could help her if she needed help."

Butterfly stopped reading and fiddled with an earring. "That's not the complete truth. They wanted to keep an eye on her because they did not want any trouble with the other residents. As nice as Cap was, when it came to this island and his project, he couldn't let go. He did see Fern as a potential threat to the Martini Cove project--a reminder of Welcomer--but I think Fey convinced him Fern would not be any trouble. Fey is--or was--the motherly type who loved taking care of people and was good to Fern."

"When Cap and Fey disappeared," I said, "you and Lucia took on the task of watching out for Fern."

"By that time," she said, "the four of us had grown fond of Fern. She is sweet and gentle, so like a child. Anyone with any heart would want to care for her."

"Unfortunately, not everyone on this island *has* a heart," Haywood said.

As Butterfly read more entries, we learned about the clearing process. Brush and trees had to be removed from the grounds. Dilapidated buildings beyond renovation had to be torn down. We learned about the architect's plans for the condo units, the cost of materials, landscaping plans, the joys and woes of supervising such a large-scale project. Page after page revealed Fey's perspective on events and the progress made.

> "Finally we sent the last of the rubble out on the garbage barge. We begin!"

Several pages later:

> "Renovation of buildings in progress. Cap is so pleased with the progress. Materials are more expensive than originally estimated, though."

The entries went on with details about construction. Butterfly skimmed through those.

> "Ready for the interiors. The old wood floors in the condos and cottages look bright and warm with new varnish. We hope the advertising pays off soon and we get buyers. I had so wanted to sell only to people we like, but I'm afraid we won't have that luxury."

After a few more pages:

> "First buyers! Butterfly and Haywood Bordereau--a charming couple from the South. They loved the island and condos at first sight.

Butterfly is enchanted by the way we renovated the wide staircases in the units. She said it reminded her of her old family mansion. I'm happy they are the first. I feel encouraged that all the buyers will be good people like them."

Butterfly stopped turning pages. A wet drop hit the vellum and smeared a word. Her tear. She quickly dabbed at it with her finger and shoved the journal away. "Oh, my," she said between soft sobs and more tears.

I put my arm around her. "What's the matter, dear?"

"That was so nice of her, to write about us like that in her journal. She is a lovely person. Or *was*, I should say, if your dream is true."

I squeezed her shoulders.

"I remember how happy Haywood and I were when we first came here." She wiped her nose with the back of her hand. There was a faraway look on her face. "I used to say I had to pinch myself to be sure I wasn't dreaming. Oh, I love it here so." Then she gnashed her teeth and made fists like a child having a tantrum. "But those awful people who came after us spoiled it all."

Hayward gave her a handkerchief he pulled out of his pocket. "Now, honey. Not Sky and Lucia. They have the same beliefs as us."

She blew into the handkerchief and wiped her nose. "That's a pitiful community--just four people." Then she nodded at Max and me, "I believe you are with us, too. You don't think the Colonel's the last word in leadership. Still, it's the others who have a community, not us. We are the outsiders."

Her brightness was gone. The wrinkles around her eyes and mouth were deep.

I folded my arms across my chest. "I'm not letting go of my dreams just yet. Maybe we haven't tried hard enough to understand them."

Haywood said, "I don't think that's the case. They have no morals. I suspect that underneath it all, the Colonel and Erhleen are meaner than a sack full of rattlesnakes."

Max sniffed and pulled up his collar. "I'd put them in jail in a minute, for making a travesty of food presentation."

"Oh, Max. You can be such a snob," I said.

Butterfly blew her nose again and pulled the journal toward her. "Let's read more."

> "Sky and Lucia Somerport, good people who love sailing, plan to build on an available lot overlooking the entrance to the cove. They showed us the architectural plans for their cottage (a modest name for a grand home) that will be an elegant beacon to those entering the cove. We have sold to excellent people so far--I keep praying."

Then Fey's entries took a dark turn.

> "What I feared most has happened. The people offering to buy condos and lots seem calculating, but Cap and I have no choice but to sell to them. Our creditors are clamoring for their returns and the way we can pay them is to sell the units and lots as soon as possible."

First mentioned in Fey's journal were the Colonel and Erhleen, then Lester and Veeda, Fermin and Mumsey, Slick and Wanda, Sven and the other people like them.

> "I begged Cap not to sell to the Colonel and Erhleen and their children. They seem sneaky. I can't put my finger on it. It's just something I feel. On the surface, they appear friendly, although common. I pray my feelings are wrong."

Butterfly shook her head, "Bless your heart, Fey, your feelings were right."

Another entry:

> "Arguments, arguments. The Colonel is trying

to set himself up as leader of Martini Cove. Cap has a fight on his hands every day, but there are so many more of them than of us--Cap and me, Sky and Lucia, Butterfly and Haywood. The Colonel wants to run for president of the association. Of course he will win. Slick also announced that he wanted to run, so the Colonel put a Port-A-Potty on the lawn in front of Slick's house. Now, that shows real class!"

Haywood said, "The Colonel was busier than a one-legged man in a butt-kicking contest. He would do anything to be leader."

"Fulfilling the old Frigh wish to be the head of anything," Max agreed.

Haywood nodded.

The next entry:

"I am outraged! Erhleen organized The Committee for Good Taste and made herself head of it. I objected strongly to this as did Cap, but she had overwhelming support at the homeowner's meeting especially from Lester and Veeda who adore the Colonel. They have simply bullied their way in and are now running the show."

"Cap and I are beside ourselves. The Committee for Good Taste has made up a rulebook called THE MARTINI COVE ISLAND RULES FOR HARMONIOUS LIVING and voted null and void the association rule book Cap and I had so carefully composed. Their rules are crazy and don't make sense and besides are bound in brown leatherette! I wanted our rule book to be bound in burgundy leather, like this journal."

Butterfly flipped the book over and ran her hand over the cover. "I do declare. That would have looked better. Makes me even madder."

"Keep reading," I said.

"Cap and the Colonel are involved in a power struggle. Most people here perceive the Colonel as a strong leader but how wrong they are! Cap is a strong leader. Without his vision, Martini Cove would not exist. The Colonel has bullied his way in and is trying to take over another man's work. That's not the same as being a strong leader. That's simply being a bully! The election for president is between Slick and the Colonel. Either way won't be good. I fear the outcome."

Butterfly said, "She was right to be afraid. The Colonel won."

"Then he put Slick in charge," said Haywood, "to show people who was boss, so he could connive under cover, mesmerizing the fools who inhabit this sorry island."

Butterfly read the last entry in the journal:

"Cap says I'm imagining things but I have the weirdest feeling that something terrible is about to happen. Cap is just too vocal about the Colonel and that ridiculous committee. What set it off was the special meeting the Colonel called to address "The Fern Delamere Problem." What problem? She is a harmless old woman who does not have many years left. The Committee says, however, that it gives Martini Cove a bad name to have a former inmate of a mental institution living here. Hah! Fern is saner than the Colonel, Erhleen, and the rest of them put together. Cap suggested we have a private meeting with the Colonel to hash things out and the Colonel agreed, as long as Lester could be there as witness. The Colonel wanted the meeting to be late night so that none of the other residents would see us together. Cap is willing to do anything for M. C. I. They are coming to our house tonight."

"That's all there is," Butterfly said, closing the journal.

"I wonder what happened next," Max said.

Haywood said, "Nothing good, seems like."

I said, "Do you think they were paid off by the Colonel, to leave Martini Cove Island?"

"Didn't seem like Cap and Fey were that kind of people, ma'am." Haywood scratched his beard. "But you never really know."

CHAPTER 21

"So much for the journal, sad as it is." Butterfly set the journal carefully aside. "Let's take a look at the photos."

I opened one box labeled *Photographs by Paul Surrey Ipswich 1911.*

"I've heard of him. He was famous for taking extraordinary photos of institutions."

"Wait!" Butterfly held my hand back. "I can't allow this. The photos are fragile and must not be treated in a casual manner. They need to be handled with white cotton gloves."

"Well, we don't have those lying about," I said, annoyed. Honestly, if it hadn't been for me, she wouldn't have known about the photos in the first place. "I appreciate your concern. I want them to be perfectly preserved, too. I don't think, though, the four of us looking through them to find a clue would cause harm. What if we wash our hands first?"

"Well, all right."

"Okay." I pushed away from the table. "Everyone to the sinks."

With washed hands, I dipped into the pile of photos and sifted through them. These, unlike the others, showed a more personal side of Welcomer.

Butterfly rubbed her hands together. "Yes, these are just what we need."

The photos showed well-cared-for residents, but depression and far away expressions marred their faces. In those times, the theory was that many ailments could be cured by continued exposure to country air, the singing of birds, trips on boats, and good, plain food.

The photos had been taken in the formal gardens surrounding the buildings with living room chairs placed to serve as outdoor furniture. The residents, dressed in good clothes and hats, were being served tea by a maid. Some photos showed bucolic gazebos with stiffly posed residents in groups facing the camera. Nurses in crisp white gowns, aprons and caps, loomed in the background, revealing these were not photos of people in country homes but taken in an institution.

Other photos showed the laborers of Welcomer. Kitchen staff with white bandanas, dark uniforms and white aprons were cutting up vegetables and stirring large pots. The bakery had large troughs for mixing dough and movable shelves with sheets of freshly baked bread. The laundry showed workers in blue jeans and aprons lifting laundry from large cylindrical washers. The pharmacy had glass counters and brown apothecary jars with hand written labels. Pharmacists, also in white uniforms, were measuring medicines on scales, with rows of boxes and jars behind them. More photos showed that Welcomer had baseball teams and basketball teams, a bowling alley, rug weaving and a hospital band.

"These are just the kind of photographs we need for the museum." Butterfly smiled broadly. "They give a sense of who the people were who lived and worked here."

"They could be quite valuable," Haywood said, "since they were taken by a famous photographer."

"Look at all the notes and dates glued to the backs. Fey's work?" I said.

Haywood nodded. "Logical."

"Sure enough, it was Fey, bless her soul." Butterfly opened the journal again. "Look at the handwriting on the backs of these photos, identical to the handwriting in the journal."

"She worked on all this in that small, hot, attic room?" Max said.

Haywood shrugged. "She was dedicated to the island and Cap's work."

The last box of photos had no notes. Haywood rubbed his chin.

"I guess she didn't have enough time to get through all of them before she disappeared."

I studied the photos slowly, absorbed into each scene, wandering around in them as if I were there. Gloom overcame me, yet I was fascinated, too. I began to feel the residents' pain, to imagine the sounds, the smells of the rest home. Looking at those haunted people became more difficult the longer I perused them.

Butterfly and Haywood were too absorbed in the photos to notice, but Max must have seen my distress. "You all right?"

"Just sad, from the energy that used to dwell here." I did not mention that I was getting the same cold feeling as when I dreamed about Cap and Fey. I sure wasn't going to tell Max about that.

Haywood was still shuffling photos. "It's a complete history of this place. Quite a find."

"And it's all mine." Butterfly spread her arms, like protective wings, over the photos, glee shining from her eyes. "I am just the luckiest woman. The museum I have been dreaming about for so long will become a reality." Then she sat up and gathered the photos into stacks. "All right, no more handling the photos. You might wrinkle them." She tapped the edges of the stacks to even them up into neat piles.

"Hold on a bitty minute." Haywood put a hand on her shoulder. "I want to spare you a lot of heartache, honey, but there isn't going to be any museum as long as the Colonel and his friends are in charge."

He carefully took the photos out of her hands and put them back in the boxes. "These people are trying to reinvent themselves here. They want everybody to think Martini Cove Island was always a playground for the elite, and never a loony bin. They are going to rewrite history, no matter how they have to do it."

Butterfly deflated. She looked older and smaller, her enthusiasm gone. She stared down at the table and her hands clenched. "I know what you are saying is true."

Suddenly Haywood pounded the table with his fist. "Tarnation! As long as the Colonel and his kin and friends remain on this island, no possibility of change exists. As long as the other residents squawk, 'I'm neutral,' and continue to be the cowards they are, not taking a stand against the Colonel's bullying ways and convincing themselves he is a good leader, no change is possible." He put his hand on Butterfly's shoulder. "I don't know, honey, maybe we should leave."

"No!" Butterfly shouted. She turned to him and clutched his sleeve. Her eyes filled with tears. "Don't ever mention leaving here, ever again. Not even in fun."

"Fun? What kind of fun are we having now? I haven't had any fun here yet, other than the few sails we had with Sky and Lucia."

Max must have felt as sorry for them as I did. He changed the subject. "The photos and journal will be safe right here, where they've always been, but we have to keep any knowledge of them from the Colonel and The Committee." He looked at Haywood. "As a precaution, could you build us a special panel to the secret room?"

Haywood sighed, but nodded. "Another fun thing to do in this fun community."

"Good," Max said. "We all agree it's best for now?"

"Poop," Butterfly said. "I was a hoppy toad's hair away from my museum."

"Maybe you're wrong." I ran fingers through my hair. "Maybe The Committee would be happy to have these precious archives."

They stared at me.

I got up from the table, "I need to talk with Fern. I think she might be able to give us a clue to Cap and Fey's whereabouts."

"Fern?" everyone said in unison.

"Just a feeling." I walked out of the house, slamming the door behind me.

* * * *

I rang Fern's doorbell and waited.

She peeked through the curtain, and then she opened the door just enough for me to squeeze through.

When she had closed the door behind me, I said, "Hello, dear.

Okay if I pay a visit?"

"Made some brownies." She swayed back and forth, her arms behind her back. "Like some?"

I could have used one of Fern's special brownies just then, but I said, "Not today, but thank you."

She stopped smiling and hung her head.

"It's nothing against your brownies. You see, I started a new diet today, no desserts. But would you brew me a cup of your mint tea?"

She smiled. "Be right back."

After she had poured the tea, I dipped the tip of my tongue in. Good. Just mint. I settled on the couch. We sat quietly in silence and sipped for a few minutes.

After a while, I said, "Do you remember the people who lived next door?"

She started playing with the edge of her napkin, and whispered, "The pretty bluebird and the wolf?"

"Dear, you know they don't live there anymore, don't you?"

"You and the silver fox live there now."

"Do you know where the bluebird and the wolf went?"

Her eyes filled with tears and big drops fell on the bodice of her dress. She twisted the tie string of her apron around and around. "Big, bad buzzards got them."

I guessed that she was telling me was that someone attacked Cap and Fey. I suspected it wasn't really buzzards.

"Don't be upset, dear, but I need you to tell me some things."

The blank stare in her eyes told me she had retreated into her own world and seemed to have forgotten I was there. She was rocking back and forth now, and I didn't want to upset her further. I don't think I would have gotten more out of her anyway, so I stood, took her hand and led her to the bed, sat her down and took off her shoes. How clean her frayed socks were. I covered her thin, fragile body with a quilt, sat on the bed and hummed a few lullabies. I felt her hand relax in mine and she was asleep.

Looking at her innocent face, I thought about the photos of the residents of Welcomer. Fern had been lucky to live in her own house. She was privileged and seemed happy enough in her own world, but what a sad life to have led. Yet, she had been able to care for her few needs quite well. Why would anyone be against having this simple, harmless soul as a neighbor?

As I was holding her hand, I felt the same sort of gloom and cold in the pit of my stomach I'd felt when I saw Cap and Fey. I had the feeling Fern was in grave danger. I locked the back door to the garden and pulled all the curtains closed.

"Don't worry, Fern dear," I whispered, as I bent over her and brushed a thin lock of hair from her forehead, "we won't let anything happen to you."

I let myself out the front door and made sure it was locked behind me.

As I was walking away from Fern's cottage, I caught a glimpse of something shiny in nearby bushes. Sven's bald head? I walked over, but saw nothing unusual. Was my imagination running wild or was Sven spying on us?

Max, Butterfly and Haywood were waiting for me, drinks in hand, when I walked into our cottage.

"Any luck?" Max handed me a glass of wine.

I told them what Fern had said about the buzzards.

"Not much, is it?" Butterfly said.

"There's something else." I told them about possibly seeing Sven spying on us.

"So what?" Haywood snickered. "All he knows is that buzzards attacked a blue bird and a wolf. That shouldn't concern The Committee."

I said, "It's a good thing Sven doesn't know that Fern speaks in metaphors. At least I don't think he does."

"Don't worry, honey," Butterfly said. "None of them have actually ever talked to Fern. They don't know a thing about how she speaks."

Max said, "Frankly, I think The Committee would be too stupid to figure it out,"

"Don't underestimate that committee." Butterfly wagged a finger. "What they lack in smarts they make up for in sheer cussedness."

I swallowed hard. "What do you think The Committee might do? Something violent?"

"Don't you trust the community, my dear?" Max said.

I felt sick. "Bad time for sarcasm, Max. It's one thing for me to hope, another to risk Fern's safety." I decided it was a good time to tell them about the conversation I had overheard between Erhleen and Fermin at the Fourth of July party, about the design of the flag and the weapons they'd take to Washington.

"A hammer, Molotov cocktails, Martha Stewart?" Max said. "These people *are* crazier than I thought. Why didn't you tell me about this before?"

I shrugged. "Giving them a chance."

Then I told them about Erhleen and Fermin deciding not to go to Washington after all because they didn't want to call attention to Martini Cove Island due to bigger issues.

Haywood drummed his fingers on the arm of his chair. "What bigger issues? Now I really can't wait to see the files in The Committee's meeting room."

Max shot him a look.

Haywood coughed and avoided Max's gaze. "Of course, we'll never see those."

What was going on between Max and Haywood? I felt my stomach tightening. "There's a more important issue right now," I said. "Fern is in real danger. I feel it."

Max said. "One of your intuitive feelings?"

"Yes."

Butterfly said, "Honey, I'm starting to trust your intuition. What should we do?"

I said, "What about hiding Fern on *The Golden Fleece*?"

Brightening again, probably at the thought of another adventure, Butterfly said, "Sky and Lucia would be glad to help. Maybe we could get her away under the pretense of a sail."

"How can we get Fern to go along with that kind of plan?" Max said.

Butterfly said, "She trusts Lucia and would do anything she told her to do." Then she chuckled. "And to help her along, maybe we could give her a little of her own medicine. Brownies."

I called Lucia and told her we needed her and Sky's help with Fern immediately and that we'd explain everything. She agreed without question.

A few minutes later, they arrived in their cart. We told them about my channeling the message from Fey, the attic, the photos, the journal, questioning Fern, the possible Sven sighting and our fears for Fern's welfare.

"Whew!" Lucia said. "You've been busy."

Sky said, "What can we do?"

"Would it be possible," I said, "for all of us to go out on a sail this afternoon with Fern?"

"Of course, dear lady." Sky smiled at me. "Glad to help."

"We have plenty of champagne and food on board," Lucia said.

I was grateful to them and hoped with all my heart that getting Fern away from Martini Cove Island would save her. From what, I was afraid to guess.

We were reluctant to leave the journal and the boxes in plain sight in the house, although it was illegal for The Committee to break in and enter. They certainly couldn't be kept in the attic, not with a big hole in the wall. The better plan was to take everything aboard *The Golden Fleece* where Sky and Lucia could see them, too.

Lucia went to Fern's house and emerged twenty minutes later carrying the fragile old woman wrapped in a blanket. She laid her gently on the back seat of the cart.

"How did you manage to get her here still asleep?" I said.

"She had awakened, and was groggy and hungry. I brought her

one of her own brownies and after a few bites she dropped off again. I thought about eating one myself, but of course, I didn't indulge." She held up a paper bag. "Might come in handy later, though, huh?"

"What about Tansy, her cat?" Butterfly said.

Lucia reached down to the floor of the cart and picked up a cat carrier. "Back in a sec," she said, and hurried into the house again. She came back with the meowing cat. "Didn't take much to get her in. I think she's pretty old."

She put the carrier on the floor of the cart by her. Sky stashed the journal and boxes underneath the cart seat and they were off, heading for the dock.

Max and I, with Truffle on my lap, rode on Butterfly and Haywood's cart. None of the residents were around, thank goodness, because it was happy hour, a sacred time, when everyone was paying homage to the setting sun and passing out in the cabins of their boats, at their homes, or at the Colonel's condo. We didn't need to worry about being seen.

At the dock, Sky parked close to the gangway. Lucia slung Fern, as light as a small canvas sail, over her shoulder, and carried her to *The Golden Fleece*. Sky had the cat carrier and followed Lucia on board, into the cabin, out of sight. We were right behind with the journal and boxes, not stopping until we were in the cabin.

I unleashed Truffle who ran to the carrier and started barking at the cat. She arched her back, hissing at him.

I said, "This may not work out at all."

"Watch this." Lucia went to the refrigerator in the galley and got a piece of cheese. She knelt down, looking Truffle in the eyes, and held out the cheese. She gestured with her hand for "stay" and "down." When he did, she rewarded him with the cheese. With the other hand, she unlocked the cat carrier and whispered quiet, soothing things to both animals. Tansy sauntered up to Truffle, licked his nose and lay down beside him, purring.

"Amazing," I said.

She put Tansy next to Fern, who was sound asleep on the bed in the aft cabin. Truffle followed and hopped on the other side. Lucia closed the door and we tiptoed away.

"She should be out for the night," I said, "if I remember correctly from my one experience with those brownies."

In the saloon, Sky was already pouring champagne. "Welcome to this impromptu party." He handed us glasses.

"Hardly a party." Butterfly shook her head, looking grim.

Sky settled into the swivel chair by the control panel. "Fill us in."

We told them about the events of the day, starting with my channeling Fey's note and ending with my possible sighting of Sven's bald, shiny head and why I felt it was important to get Fern away from Martini Cove.

"So, Sylvia, you have special powers." Sky smiled my way. "Extraordinary!"

"You *are* extraordinary." Lucia put her arm around me. "Why didn't you tell us about this gift of yours before?"

I wanted to deflect attention off myself. "Why don't we put out nibbles to go with the wine? We haven't eaten much all day."

"Great idea," said Lucia. "I'll pull some shrimp out of the freezer."

Away from the others in the galley, Lucia said to me in a low voice, "What a story. Cap and Fey appeared to you in dreams, really?"

I stopped spooning olives from a bottle and looked at her.

"You believe me, don't you?"

"Absolutely. You are one special person, Sylvia Saltwater."

Tears came into my eyes. "No one ever told me I was special except Max."

"*I'm* telling you, too, right now." Lucia hugged me.

The boat motor started up. Through the porthole, I saw we were slipping out of the dock. Soon we were heading out to open sea.

As he gunned the motor, Sky said to us over his shoulder, "Getting away from prying eyes and listening ears."

We were well away from Martini Cove Island when Sky stopped the boat and anchored it. Before we opened the boxes of photos,

Butterfly ordered us to wash our hands.

As we did, Lucia read the journal out loud, occasionally stopping to glance at the photos. "A treasure trove of vintage photos. Who could we trust them safely to?"

Butterfly's eyes narrowed and her lips formed a tight, straight line. "They're not going anywhere except into the museum we will build at Martini Cove Island."

Lucia guffawed. "I don't think our beloved neighbors would allowed that."

"My opinion exactly," Haywood said.

"Butterfly's right," Sky said. "The island needs its history. I would sponsor the creation of a museum."

"Would you?" Butterfly was fluttery again, all smiles.

"Honey," Haywood said, "dreaming about that museum is as useless as tits on a boar. You'll just go on hurting yourself with that notion. Let's just turn the photos over to the city historical society."

Butterfly put her hands on her hips and said, "I do declare, Haywood Bordereau, if you do that, I'll hit you over the head so hard, you'll be numb as a pounded thumb."

"Calm yourself, dear lady," Sky said, patting her hand. "Nothing will happen to the photos as long as they're aboard *The Golden Fleece*. Someday you might have that museum."

Max coughed hard and I saw a look pass between him, Sky and Haywood.

"Of course," Sky said clearing his throat, "that may not be for some time, not before leadership at Martini Cove changes." He held the bottle up. "More champagne?"

Lucia turned the pages of the journal until she reached the last entry. "The important question is what happened to Cap and Fey after they met with the Colonel and Lester."

Haywood stroked his beard. "It seems right likely that the Colonel and Lester could have some knowledge about their disappearance, but I don't know how anything can be proven. If we could only get into The Committee's files..."

Max spilled his glass of wine on the table.

"Watch the photos!" Butterfly scooped the journal and boxes away.

"Sorry." Max ran to get paper towels. "Of course, we can't get anywhere near those files." When he came back and was wiping up the spill, I saw he was sweating.

"Course not," Haywood said with a nervous cough. "That'd be tough as whit leather."

What *was* the matter with Max? He *never* spills anything.

Everything was safe. The photos and journal were aboard *The Golden Fleece*. We were away from Martini Cove Island. Fern was sleeping a few feet away from us. Why did I have a sense of impending doom?

Relaxing into the cushions of the settee, I took my shoes off and put my legs up. I was worn out after listening to Lucia read the journal and watching everyone sift through the photos.

Lucia looked at me and jumped up. "What we need is food."

"I'll help." I started to get up.

"You've been through enough for one day." She pushed me back on the cushions. "Max, could you help?"

"Pleasure," he said, and followed her into the galley.

A short while later, we sat down to a gourmet meal. Max had cut lemon peel into spirals and wrapped them around Lucia's juicy grilled shrimp. He had arranged individual green salads with red and yellow pepper strips and tomato wedges to resemble abstract paintings. Sourdough garlic bread studded with black olives rounded out the meal. Of course, there was more wine, and the evening turned merry after the tension of the day. It was great eating and releasing tension with laughter and wine.

We turned around and moored at the Cove for the night, too exhausted to think of another plan. Sky drew the curtains and locked the doors.

Butterfly and Haywood slept in the bunks next to Fern's room. Max and I volunteered for the berths in the saloon. We lay head to head, sleep coming more easily than I imagined.

During the night, I woke to the ship's bell chiming four times. I got up and used the head. When I came back into the saloon, I peeked through the curtains and looked toward the west, the direction of our house. The sky glowed with the rising of the sun. I looked back to the clock that showed it was five minutes after two. Something was terribly wrong.

It wasn't the sun rising at all.

"Max!" I screamed.

Everyone rushed to the saloon.

I pushed the curtains all the way back and pointed. "That glow is coming from the direction of our house."

"Good God!" Max said. "Fire!"

He pulled his shoes on and was up the companionway. Sky was on the ship's phone calling for the fireboat. Everyone hurried up the ladder, even me. We ran along the dock and up the gangway to the carts. Sky had taken the time to lock the hatch again so Fern would be safe. We waited for him as he sprinted toward us and jumped into the cart. We peeled out and rushed up the hill to our house.

I knew the island had a fire truck in an old barn but would the crew of the fireboat get here in time to save whatever was on fire?

Max's brow was furrowed and tears rimmed his eyes. I put my hand over his. "The main thing is that you and I, our friends and Truffle are safe," I said.

He brought my hand to his lips and kissed it.

As I watched the glow grow brighter, the pit of my stomach felt tight. I gripped Max's hand. "Maybe it's only the woods."

Just then, we rounded the corner of the woods by our cottage. The black silhouettes of the pines stood out in sharp contrast to the fire's orange glow. Sparks flew in all directions. I smelled the smoke and heard the crackling of burning wood. Next to the fire, we saw our cottage, safe and unharmed for the moment. It was Fern's cottage at the center of the blaze.

The outlines of windows, door and roof looked like a simple

child's drawing of a house. Fierce flames licked and spiraled upward, a column of smoke rose blocking out the stars. Suddenly, the roof collapsed into the walls of the cottage. A last whorl of fire consumed Fern's few possessions--worn furnishings, small art collection, memories and comforts of her simple harmless life. We watched the flames steal Fern's garden away, too.

Mesmerized, no one could talk, no one could move. Then, as if remembering, Max ran to the side of our house and uncoiled the garden hose. He pointed the stream of water to the woods between our cottage and Fern's. It was the only thing that could be done. Fern's cottage was gone.

I heard the fire truck's clang and saw the crew of the fireboat clinging to its sides. The captain shouted orders as they ran to a nearby hydrant, pulling a fire hose. Within seconds, the men were aiming water in a strong stream at the bottom of the blaze. They held it there until the fire died. Then they doused the last of the cottage rubble and what was left of the garden. Smoldering embers, burnt trees and bushes marked the spot where Fern's home had once stood.

Max and I clutched each other as the firemen worked to spray water on the brush around our cottage and on the roof until no sparks were left. No one spoke as we watched the men search around the rubble.

No one else from the island had come to see what the commotion was about. Wasn't that odd?

Breaking the silence, I said, "How do we tell Fern?"

Lucia shook her head, tears in her eyes.

When the work of putting out the fire was over, the captain of the fire crew approached us. He took off his hardhat and gloves and tucked them under his arm. His face was streaked with sweat and soot. "When the rubble cools, we'll search for remains. I understand one Fern Delamere lived here. Know anything about her?"

Sky stepped forward. "Fern Delamere, a woman in her eighties, a former resident of Welcomer, lived here by herself in this cottage for many years."

"Where is she at the moment?"

"Aboard my boat, *The Golden Fleece*, docked at the marina."

"I need to inform her of the condition of her house."

Sky hesitated. but Lucia spoke up, "Her mind is fragile but she's safe and sleeping at the moment. I think it would be best if we, her friends, informed her."

The captain wiped his brow with a bandana. "After dawn, we'll have to investigate further to determine the cause of the fire."

I was in a daze as Max took my arm and pulled me to our cottage. "Let's check on things inside." Our friends followed us up the front porch steps.

As I walked through the house checking the condition of everything, Max inspected his garnishing tool collection. Thankfully, all was in place and unharmed. I went to the kitchen and looked out the window where Fern's cottage had stood. Only steam and smoke rose from the ashes. Finally, the enormity or it all hit me and I cried. Lucia and Butterfly put their arms around me and the three of us stood together, hugging and sniffing.

"It's going to be awful for her." I wiped my tears with the back of my hand. "How will we ever be able to explain?"

"Poor old innocent thing," Butterfly said.

Lucia squeezed our shoulders. "We'll tell her together."

When we entered Max's study, he was already pouring single malt scotch for the men.

"God bless single malt." Haywood downed his drink and slumped into a chair.

Lucia held out three more glasses. "Don't forget the ladies."

Butterfly said, "If you weren't an alcoholic before you came to Martini Cove Island, bless your heart, you surely will become one once you get here." She knocked her entire shot back with one gulp.

* * * *

At six o'clock in the morning, the firefighters were still at the scene of the fire. The glow of the rising sun shone on the rubble, as we watched the men searching for clues and remains.

The captain strode back to where we were huddled. "Thank goodness, no human or animal remains," he said. "As to the cause, the pattern of the fire is such that it suggests it had been started with either a cigarette or a cigar, more likely, a cigar. Did Miss Delamere or any of her guests smoke?"

Sky answered. "She did not. The only people who visited her were the six of us and none of us smoke."

The information about the cause struck me as hard as the fire. I realized there was no need for the rest of the community to come see the blaze because they already knew it would happen. The only person on the island who smoked cigars had a motive in setting the fire. In that moment I understood what I had refused to believe in all the months of living here, that there were no lengths to which the Colonel and his hangers-on would not go to reach their selfish goals. The others who turned away in the face of injustice were equally guilty. I felt as sorry for myself as I did for Fern.

When we rode back to the dock, the sun shone brightly but we were totally deflated. Our feet dragged to the boat and slowly we descended to the saloon. I felt as if I could lie down on the berth and be asleep in an instant.

No one wanted to tell Fern the bad news, but finally Lucia went to the cabin where Fern slept and pushed the door open. One by one, we all filed into the cabin. Still sleeping peacefully, Fern lay on her side, the blanket tucked under her chin, looking as innocent as a trusting child. Truffle and Tansy, on either side of her, were awake and alert as if they sensed we were bringing bad news.

Lucia stood over Fern and stroked wisps of hair from her face, enough to make her wake up.

When she raised her head from the pillow, she stared around the room. "Where am I?"

Lucia sat beside her and stroked her arm. "Dear, you spent last night here aboard *The Golden Fleece*, our boat. You're safe with us."

"Tansy?" Her eyes were frantic and searching.

The cat must have recognized her name because she stretched, yawned, walked up to Fern's face, and licked it.

"There you are, my little love." Fern stroked the cat, and seemed comforted by her presence.

Lucia tossed her long braid over her shoulder. Tears welled in her eyes. Her voice was tight as if it took all her strength to control it. "Dear, I have something to tell you."

Maybe because of the way Lucia said it or from the look on her face, Fern seemed to sense something was wrong because she sank far into the pillow, staring at Lucia and holding the cat tight in her arms.

"Last night a terrible thing happened," Lucia said. "A fire...in the woods...your home was in its path. I'm so very sorry to have to tell you, your house was completely burned and your garden is destroyed. Nothing is left." She touched the old woman's cheek.

I was waiting, holding my breath, as I'm sure the others were, for Fern's reaction but there wasn't one.

She continued to stroke her cat, but it was a weak gesture. Over and over she whispered, "Tansy mustn't worry. Mustn't worry." She retreated back into her own world. The physical strength I had seen in her the first time I met her was gone.

Lucia started singing. "Hush little baby don't you cry,/Mama's gonna sing you a lullaby..."

Fern closed her eyes looking peaceful, and the cat stayed in the crook of her arm.

I felt soothed by the melody, too.

Truffle, though, must have had enough sleep, because he jumped off the bed and ran around in circles.

"Time for a walk?" I said to him.

He barked.

"Want me to take him up?" Max said.

"I'll do it. I need the air."

By this time I had gotten used to the ladder. I tucked Truffle under my arm and climbed up. I leashed him and descended the steps to the dock.

It had been quite a night. For me it was the turning point.

CHAPTER 22

In the early morning light, the dock was deserted and peaceful. The last of the sea smoke disappeared as the sun rose. Pink and gold clouds hung over the islands in the distance. Gulls cried, ripples of waves sparkled on the water, buoys dinged in the distance. The dock creaked as it swayed with the changing tide. The air smelled of seaweed and ocean.

The island was stunning. But its beauty couldn't make up for a community that was a vicious lie.

I tasted salt on my lips, not from the sea air but from my tears. I would never again pretend this was my community, would never paint another watercolor here, would not consecrate it one more time by doing so. The community was simply evil. The Colonel and his followers were self-serving at the expense of other people. Those who remained neutral were just as guilty.

Max and I had always celebrated the good things in life: the best food, the wittiest garnishes, the lushest flowers, the sweetest music. No, we were not perfect, but the world we tried to create had the best kind of energy there is. For us, it was not even about the money. It was about uplifting the world.

The Colonel and his followers had the most stunning scenery anyone in the world could have but they fouled it by greed and trying to control the uncontrollable: people with morals and simple Fern who had never done them harm. The Colonel was not a leader, just an ugly bully. If he had to sacrifice the few to achieve his goals, what the heck!

I could not understand this kind of thinking. My stomach

churned as I thought about the times I had defended those people to Max, or worse, to my own conscience. This "premier community" was a spiritual slum.

After these thoughts had rolled around in my head for a while, I realized one sickening fact- I was heartbroken.

* * * *

The fire fighters, having done a valiant job, were at the dock loading equipment back onto the fireboat. I told the captain we had informed Fern about her house and, at the moment, she was again sleeping peacefully.

I had forgotten it was Tuesday, island shopping day, when most of the residents would be going into the city on the early ferry. Leaning against the rail of the dock with my back to the water, and Truffle at my feet, I watched a parade of carts line up. It didn't matter a whit that a neighbor's cottage had burned to the ground during the night. Shopping day commenced as usual.

The residents arrived in the predictable procession I had noted on previous Tuesdays. The first to roll down the hill in their rusty golf cart were the Colonel and Erhleen. Then came Sven walking with Sweetheart on a leash beside him. Next was Veeda driving the Prown's golf cart. Inside Lester, wearing a pair of sunglasses, and with his head lolling on the back of the seat, was probably dealing with another hangover. Slick and Wanda arrived in their pink golf cart. Fermin and Mumsey came next. I haven't mentioned the others who gathered because they were uninteresting, their most remarkable trait being a blind adoration of the Colonel.

The Colonel did not get out of his cart and walk to the end of the dock to talk to the others as usual. It was the first time I had seen him without a lit cigar in his mouth. Maybe he was afraid that the fire fighters would see him smoking. Erhleen paced back and forth by their cart, staring at the ground as if trying to decide something. She then strode to stand in front of me, that strange scowl smile on her bright red face. As ever, she was wearing large black sunglasses. I couldn't see her eyes, only the reflection of myself looking worn and haggard.

"Lots of excitement last night." She was making nervous twitching gestures with hands, arms, and shoulders.

I remained silent.

"We were downright worried about those chunks of flame traveling on the wind. Sure could have set other houses on fire."

I didn't reply. She looked down at her shoes scuffing the ground with her toe, then back up at me.

Sven came rushing up to Erhleen, saluting her as always.

"Stop that saluting, hear?" Erhleen poked him in the arm.

Sven blushed and tugged at Sweetheart's leash, without even acknowledging me.

Fermin swished over. I noted he was perspiring profusely, although it was a cold morning. He pulled the kerchief from his neck to wipe his sweaty brow, the diamond "Shit" ring glinting. He did not acknowledge me, either, but said to Erhleen, "We just have to get that mess cleaned up as soon as possible. Ernest just called and said people will be coming by this weekend to look for vacation property." He nudged Erhleen and giggled. "And they're from *Hollywood*."

Erhleen twitched some more. "Hollywood! My, my, my! It's high time we got quality folks moving in."

Fermin wiped the back of his neck and frowned. "That's all we needed right now, a fire that completely destroyed a cottage. Bad publicity. The Committee must have a meeting as soon as possible to talk about debris removal, tree planting, that kind of thing."

"Wait a minute." I spat my words. My blood was boiling. "Don't you even care whether Fern is dead or alive?"

Erhleen turned red all over again. "Of course we care. We know she's fine because the fire captain didn't say anything about finding a body in the rubble. She started that fire in the first place, crazy old coot. Didn't mind a whit what a fire could do to this community's property values."

"Property values!" I shrieked. My hands clenched "You're not at all concerned about helping her, are you?"

Sven shuffled his feet then screwed up his face as if trying to figure something out. He pointed a finger at me. "Define 'help.'"

My mouth dropped open.

"I'd like to know." Fermin made a sweeping gesture with his hands before resting them on his hips, "where that Delamere woman is, anyway, so that we can talk to her about the bill for clean-up, which will be *enormous*, I'm sure. We don't want to tax the residents with special assessments. It's just like that loon to disappear without meeting her responsibilities."

Erhleen shook her head. "If her insurance doesn't take care of it, the family money will. No need to tax us innocent residents who had nothing at all to do with that fire, sure enough."

"Did you know," I said, trying hard to keep my voice from shaking, "that the probable cause of the fire, according to the captain, was a lit cigar."

Without missing a beat, Erhleen said, "I told that loon many times to quit smoking those cigars, didn't I Fermin? I'm sure the residents would sign an affidavit attesting to that."

I was speechless. So, that's the story the Colonel and The Committee would give the investigators. It would be our word against that of the majority of the residents.

Just then Max appeared at my side. He had probably heard everything. I was glad because I couldn't repeat the cruel words these people had just spewed.

With the stiffest formality I had ever heard in his voice, he said, "My dear, I believe you are finished here."

He gripped my shoulders with his arm and steered me away. I was dragging Truffle who was pulling on his leash, growling at The Committee. If let loose, he would have gone for Erhleen's throat.

"Good thing that yappy mutt's on a leash," I heard Erhleen whine to my back. "We'd have to give him a citation if he was ever to break loose, you hear?"

I yanked away from Max's grip and turned to face her. Trembling, I screamed, "Erhleen, you are a truly ugly person," and turned to walk away.

After a moment, I heard Erhleen snarl back, "And you're really fat!"

I paused, turned, stood straight and held my chin up. "True. But *I* can always lose weight."

When we were at *The Golden Fleece*, I let out a great sob.

Max continued pulling me along. "Keep moving until we get below. I heard it all. Poor darling."

His sweetness made me sob even louder. I fumbled for a tissue in my pocket and soon soaked it.

As soon as I was below and in the saloon, Max led me to a settee and I sat down, not caring how I looked or what anyone would think of me. I couldn't help it. Tears flowed free. Fern's circumstances had been the catalyst, but I was really crying about my own disappointment. The dream for community and acceptance at Martini Cove Island were gone.

The others were sitting quietly as Max recounted what had happened at the dock. Butterfly came to sit beside me, put her head on my shoulder, and started crying, too.

"Good God, woman," Haywood said. "Not you, too."

"You hush, Haywood Bordereau." Butterfly said, and sniffed.

Butterfly and I cried, arms around each other until Lucia handed us glasses of water and aspirins. "These will make you feel better."

"I'm so sorry," I said to no one in particular. I started to hiccup and held my breath, but couldn't make them go away. Max held my hand and coached me with deep breathing, but I kept hiccupping.

Lucia looked out a porthole toward the dock and said, "Oh, my God! Here comes The Committee. Looks like they're heading right for our boat."

I got up and looked out the porthole too, but no one was there. Lucia looked at me and started laughing. The scare had finally stopped the hiccups.

I had to giggle. "You mean thing."

When I had calmed down, I noticed everyone looked sad. No one said a word.

Butterfly had stopped crying and was fidgeting with the handkerchief in her lap. Sky was playing with the controls, and Lucia was looking out toward the sea. Haywood was scratching his beard as if it had fleas. At the table Max sat with head in hands.

I heard Tansy meowing plaintively from Fern's cabin.

Alarmed, I said, "What happened?" In that moment, my heart told me to suspect the worst about Fern.

I went to her cabin and looked in. She was on the bed, but instead of resting on her side as I had last seen her, she was on her back, her hands folded on her chest. Her eyes were closed and she looked paler than ever, yet more peaceful than ever. She was dead.

Since Fern had never really been an adult, she now had the sweet, innocent face of a young girl who led a life of sheltered innocence. She had gone home to mother and father. Max stood behind me and put his hands on my shoulders. "She simply fell asleep."

I stood beside the bed, stroking her cheek with the back of my fingers. "Sleep well, dear," I said. "Nothing more to worry about." Her cottage was destroyed and there was nothing left for her on this island, not even decency. Going home was the only thing she could do.

I didn't cry. I had done all my crying.

When I returned to the saloon, Sky had made coffee and the others sat silently at the table holding steaming mugs. I sat, and Lucia brought me one, too.

After a while, I said, "Did she say anything before she died?"

Lucia gulped. "Yes, Her voice was faint and we could hardly hear her, but she said, 'Tell the plump pigeon the secret is in blood walls and buzzards.' We all know she used her own made up names. Do you have any idea what that means, though?"

"Yes." I felt my cheeks turning pink. "She always called me the plump pigeon."

Sky said, "She seemed not to be able to remember people's real names. I was the lion with white hair and Lucia was the swan."

"The buzzards..." Lucia tapped on the side of her mug. "Could be The Committee. At least that's what *I* would call them."

"Or hyenas." Sky sneered.

"Bottom feeders," Max said.

I held up my hand. "Let's stick to the subject."

"But what does the 'the secret is in blood walls' mean?" Lucia said.

Her question stirred my memory. "Has anybody, other than Max and me, been to the Colonel and Erhleen's house?"

Butterfly pulled an earring and frowned. "*We* have certainly never had the pleasure."

"It wasn't much of a pleasure," Max said, stirring sugar into another cup of coffee.

"We have never been invited, either," Sky said, "but I consider that a compliment."

"I think," I said, "I know what Fern meant by 'the secret is in blood walls'. When we were invited to the Colonel's house for the Labor Day potluck, I caught a glimpse on the first floor of a room painted red. I was shocked because it made me think of blood, but I dismissed it because I was still in denial about the Colonel and his group."

Butterfly shook her head. "Heavenly stars!"

"Erhleen saw me peeking in and was quick to shut the door, locking it with a key she wears around her neck."

Haywood said, "I heard some gossip about that room once, I forget from whom. It was before the cliques formed. Might be the room used for their secret meetings."

"What was the gossip?" I said.

"They keep files in there. What kind of files, I don't know. Probably reports about citations The Committee has given out. Important stuff like how many flushes were made during Sky and Lucia's parties, whose dog was unleashed--only if it was not one of theirs, of course--things boring as a mud fence."

I leaned forward on my elbows. "Or, the files could hold a clue as to the fate of Cap and Fey."

Sky said, "Would they keep information like that around?"

"I don't know."

Max coughed and put his cup down, glancing at Sky and Haywood. "Of course it would be impossible to find out anything about that room."

"Course it would," Sky said.

"Course," Haywood echoed.

Butterfly put a finger to her cheek, "How would Fern know about the red walls in the Colonel's house?"

"Good question," I said.

"Maybe," Lucia said, "she went on more nocturnal wanderings than we knew."

I snapped my fingers. "And that's the real reason The Committee wanted to get rid of her, not just because they felt her presence lowered property values. Maybe Sven, busy little Committee member that he is, was aware of her nocturnal wanderings and reported her."

Haywood gave a long, low whistle.

I thought I couldn't feel any worse than I had at the dock. But now as the pieces of Fern's secrets fit into the puzzle, I wondered why I hadn't seen the truth about the island sooner. Of course, I had seen the truth. I just couldn't admit it.

CHAPTER 23

The next few days were a wretched blur. Sky called the fire captain to tell him of Fern's death. Within the hour, the fire crew returned to the island to take Fern to a funeral home in the city where she would be cremated, thereby making sure Prown's Funeral Home would not benefit.

Still, Lester called Sky aboard *The Golden Fleece* about it.

"What nerve!" Sky slammed the phone down.

Sky contacted the trustee of Fern's estate who said he would take care of the death certificate and legal documents. Not wanting to get involved in the funeral, the trustee left the arrangements to us.

After talking at length, we decided to hold a ceremony for her aboard *The Golden Fleece* and we would sprinkle her ashes at sea.

A few days after the fire, Haywood and Max went back to our attic. Haywood brought along his carpentry tools and wood boards and, with assistance from Max, who didn't know a thing about carpentry, he built a panel in only a few hours, staining it to blend with the existing wall. The journal and pictures would be well hidden until we decided what to do with them.

Our timing was perfect. No one on the island, not even the ever-vigilant Sven, could have heard the buzzing of Haywood's electric saw or the pounding of his hammer. The Committee had hired a cleanup crew from the city that spent many hours making a lot of noise with bulldozers, tractors and trucks, removing the ruins of Fern's house. After all, everything had to look pristine when those potential buyers from Hollywood arrived to look at property.

On a bright, crisp autumn morning, we set sail aboard *The*

Golden Fleece with Fern's ashes in an antique Chinese ginger jar from our collection. The ashes had rested on our mantel for the past week and now Lucia placed it on the table in the saloon in the middle of Max's arrangement of fragrant freesias and white lilies. Two thick white column candles glowed on either side. Not knowing what kind of music Fern liked, we chose Mozart and it played softly in the background.

On the same day, Lester and Veeda invited their friends to a potluck at their trailer. Butterfly remarked that they were actually celebrating Fern's funeral. She showed us an invitation depicting a cartoon of Fern in her old fashioned dress, googly-eyed to show she was crazy. It also showed three photos of *The Golden Fleece* getting smaller sailing into the horizon. "Going, going, gone!" was written under the photos, another appalling community milestone.

Haywood snickered. "They'll be so drunk by five o'clock they'll pass out face down in Veeda's white tire planters."

How could I ever, *ever* have thought I belonged in this vile place?

Sky turned the boat toward Thorn Island, saying it would be the most logical place for the ceremony as it would be the most private.

But I was apprehensive. "What if the ghosts try to contact me again out there?"

"What if they do?" Lucia said.

"Isn't there somewhere else we could go?" I said. The others had no idea how disturbed the ghosts made me feel.

Lucia let out a weary, irritated sigh. "Why don't we go out there and see what happens?"

We were all tired and edgy. I didn't press the point although I was hurt by Lucia's lack of sympathy.

At mid-morning, we approached the bleak landscape of Thorn Island with its single barren tree. I wasn't looking forward to another encounter with the ghosts and I still didn't know what to do for them to get the peace they pleaded for.

The sea was calm when *The Golden Fleece* anchored at the tiny island. The ship's clock chimed eight bells--noontime--and we started our ceremony. One by one, we filed to the deck. Lucia was the last to emerge, holding the blue jar in the crook of her arm. She placed it on the deck where Max had fashioned a small carpet of roses and daisy heads. None of us said much, only our good-byes to a gentle soul. If it hadn't been for us, Fern would not have had a ceremony.

Lucia stood at the edge of the boat, opened the jar, and made a wide sweep with her arm. Shimmering in the sunlight, the ashes arched over the water, and then fell into the sea. We tossed the flowers in, too, and watched them float away. The slapping of waves against the side of the boat and the cry of a distant gull marked the end of the funeral. Fern's secrets sank with her ashes into the depths of the ocean.

Butterfly sniffed and blew her nose. When I glanced at the men, their eyes looked moist and they turned away. Lucia's arms went around me, and her head nestled in the crook of my neck. She was sobbing hard. I stroked her hair, muttering, "There, now. Fern is at peace and with her parents again."

Lucia lifted her head and wiped her eyes on the sleeve of her fleecy. "You may think I'm pretty selfish, but I was crying for myself as much as for her, poor soul. Her life was simple and she was happy but Sky, well...you know he built Fair Winds for me. He put so much love into every detail and I realize now... I realize we can't continue to live there. Not with those people. It will never get any better with the likes of a brute like the Colonel running things."

Sky, his face red and eyes dark as the sea, slammed the flat of his hand onto the panel next to the steering wheel. "God damn it!" He looked at Lucia, "I can get you anything money will buy, but I can't get you decency in the place where we live."

Lucia rushed over to him and buried her face in his chest, sobbing again.

Haywood said, "I know how you feel. My bell's been rung pretty hard, too." He kicked a float so hard it flew overboard.

"Who do they think they are anyway?" Max said to no one in particular. "How do they get away with things like this?"

Haywood said, "Hell's bells! They got us by the balls."

"Haywood Bordereau!" Butterfly said. "Watch your mouth. Ladies are present."

No one spoke for a long time. Then Lucia wiped her eyes and jumped up, "They can't take everything away. How about lunch and some champagne to toast Fern?"

"Marvelous idea," Sky said, and disappeared down the hatch after Lucia.

Max and I followed, but before we even got to the hatch, we heard the pop of a cork. Below, Lucia was pulling steaks and salad fixings out of the refrigerator. I offered to help and so did Max. Before Lucia could put him to work, Sky snagged him by the arm and pulled him along. "Let's go above, mate, and have a glass in honor of Fern, just the men."

"Aye, aye, Captain."

Butterfly came down to the galley. "Well, I do believe the men want a private moment to themselves. Although why they can't talk in front of us, I'll never know."

Lucia was stabbing raw potatoes with a fork. "Men don't like to show emotion in front of women. They have drinks instead."

"You're right," Butterfly said, "but I do like being informed of everything that goes on."

Lucia began slicing tomatoes. "We find out everything that goes on eventually, anyway. So let's have some champagne ourselves and fix some victuals for the men folk."

The salt air, the relief of finally laying Fern to rest, the disappointment about Martini Cove Island, and the champagne, made us tipsy and hungry. Haywood said he was starved enough to eat the sole off his shoe. Sky said that wouldn't be necessary and grilled the steaks to perfection on the barbecue. We ate as if we hadn't been fed in days. By three o'clock, we were all ready for naps.

Butterfly and Haywood took the bunks, Haywood volunteering to take the top one, much to Butterfly's relief. A light blanket over us, Max and I lay on the bed in the aft cabin. Soon, I heard snoring from open doors. Although I tried to relax, I stayed wide-awake.

My body started to tingle and I felt Cap and Fey nearer to me than ever. It's one thing to dream about ghosts, but it's another to feel their presence while awake. I had to face the ghosts and my fear if I were ever going to be free of them. Feeling drawn to the saloon, I sensed the center of their energy there. I stumbled to the table, sat down, closed my eyes, and waited. The air in the room was freezing.

They were by my side.

I say out loud, my voice cracking, "What do you want?"

Fey says in a stronger voice than I had ever heard, *"Can't stay long...need to tell my story."*

My voice is quavering, "You are Fey Falconer."

"Yes."

"Is Cap with you?"

"Yes, but I will talk. Get paper and pen. All need to know my story."

Someone sat down beside me. Max.

"What's happening?" he said.

I put a finger to my lips. "I'm communicating with the ghosts. Get me paper and pen, quick!"

He put a pen in my hand and shoved a pad of paper toward me.

Fey speaks. I write. *"We mean no harm. All we want is justice, peace."*

I heard footsteps coming into the room. Max said quietly, "Shh! She's in a trance and talking to ghosts. Did I ever tell you she's Dracula cousin?"

Annoyed as I was at Max, I didn't open my eyes or speak, not wanting to break the connection to Fey. I heard gasps and Haywood saying, "Thunderation." Someone else whispered, "Shush."

I am writing Fey's words. I feel the others crowd behind me.

"Did you find my journal--the last entry?"

"Yes," I write.

"The Colonel and Lester came to our house late on that last night--took us out on the Colonel's boat--said they wanted to talk--to work with us--make a better community. We believed. We didn't tell anyone about the meeting--mistake--Lester drunk--passed

out--Colonel--mean scowl on his face said, *"I'm running Martini Cove Island now. Democracy...bah! Elections...bah! Museums and culture...bah! You love and peace shit people don't know leadership. People is like children--need a strong daddy. Me.*

"Betrayal was full as the moon that night. Colonel pulled hammer out--whack, whack, whack--over Cap's head...whack, whack, whack--my head--our souls left our bodies. But Cap and I know Fern saw it all--reason they wanted to get rid of her."

When I wrote this, I heard the collective gasp behind me.

"Colonel headed for Thorn Island, dumped our bodies overboard."

She pauses, sniffing. "The files--Committee for Good Taste--look there--secrets."

"Damn it!" I heard Sky say.

"Shush," someone else said.

My eyes still closed and concentrating hard to keep Fey's voice in my mind, I write, "You are the restless undead."

"Yes," Fey says. *"You are our portal on earthly plane--your special powers--our voice for justice--only you."*

Although this was grueling for me, I was proud of myself. Dracula's cousin, indeed!

Fey's voice comes again, softer. *"Weary--need rest--need to expose evil people--want Martini Cove Island to succeed."* Her voice fades. *"Have to go."*

A breeze rushes past me although the portholes are closed. Fey and Cap are gone. It is warm in the saloon again.

I collapsed against the back of the bench, exhausted, the tingling in my body subsiding little by little until total calm spread through me. I opened my eyes.

The others, eyes round with wonder, watched me. Nobody spoke for a long time.

Finally breaking the silence, Butterfly said, "I do declare, how come they didn't channel through me? I would just love to experience a ghostly presence."

"Believe me," I said, while breathing hard and shaking my head, "you don't want to have the ability to channel ghosts. It's frightening and exhausting."

Haywood put his arm around her. "Honey, you've always said you wanted to experience ghosts that were not troubled. These ghosts are as troubled as ghosts can get."

Butterfly, pouting, turned and looked out a porthole.

"Max," I said, "there's no point in holding back now. I want to tell our friends about my background."

Max groaned.

Ignoring him I said. "It's about my family. I'm not altogether unfamiliar in dealing with the supernatural."

The others looked puzzled except for Max who was holding his head in his hands.

Lucia chuckled. "I knew you weren't boring."

"Thank you, but I never felt in an enviable position because of my powers."

"Powers?" Haywood said.

I riffled through the pad of writing I had just done.

"Cap and Fey visited me several times in dreams because of something special I was born with. It's sort of a gift, you might say, inherited from my ancestors who were from Transylvania."

Everyone gasped, except for Max, who was twiddling his moustache and staring into space.

"In the small town where my parents lived, Mother was known for her powers of divination and intuition. The people of nearby villages came to her for help when someone in their family was sick and they wanted a cure. Some wanted her to foretell their futures. My mother never accepted payment for helping because she believed her gift should be freely given. What people didn't realize was how much energy it took out of her."

Lucia said, "Does it take a lot out of you, too?"

I wrung my hands. "It's scary and exhausting and I truly wish I didn't have the power. But--" I threw my hands up.

Lucia sat down beside me and shoved a mug of hot tea to me. "Sorry I was cross with you before about coming to Thorn Island. I had no idea."

I smiled at her, clutching the mug with both hands. "My parents left that town, wanting to become anonymous. They immigrated to America, where I was born. Mother kept the power a secret, hoping it hadn't passed on to me. But when I was six, something happened that she couldn't ignore.

"One day during school, I had a vision about my teacher in a car accident. I pretended my homework was too hard and asked if she would stay to help after school. When Mother came to pick me up, she looked shaken and told us a tree fell on the corner by the school during a sudden windstorm. The tree was in my teacher's path on the way home and could have crushed her car.

"When I recounted my vision to Mother, she revealed the power in her family and told me to ignore it if I ever experienced it again. Being a child, I thought that if Mother said I could, I could. I lived in denial for many years, but when it comes up, there is no ignoring it."

"Whoa!" Sky said. "Do you realize how crazy this sounds?"

Lucia put her hand on Sky's arm. "It's not crazy. It's what Sylvia is."

Sky blushed. "Sorry. Didn't mean to offend."

I said, "You know I didn't make this up. You experienced it with your own eyes this afternoon."

Haywood frowned. "Never underestimate the strange goings on in homeowner associations."

CHAPTER 24

The men huddled together at one end of the deck. Lucia and I were at the other, watching the orange and purple sunset. I couldn't hear the men, but since Max had said they liked to talk about sailing, I assumed that's what they were doing.

Butterfly, looking as pale as a ghost and wrapped in a blanket, came up from below to join us. "Well, I never," she said. "I still can't believe the ghosts visited you and not me."

I touched her hand. "Believe me, it's no fun being in the middle of this."

"Maybe they'll come back sometime just for you," Lucia raised her voice so the men could hear. "Who's for more champagne?"

Haywood called back, "How about a single malt?"

Lucia disappeared down the hatch and came back with the bottle and fresh glasses. We all sat together, watching the sky turn from lavender to star-studded periwinkle.

I sighed and pulled my sweater on. "What's next?"

Max said, "We know the truth as told to you by ghosts. If we tried to tell the authorities about this, who would believe us?"

I gasped. "Surely after all Cap and Fey--and I--went through, how could you doubt we're not genuine? We *have* to tell the police."

Max looked me in the eye. "We believe you, but asking the police to believe this improbable story? Hah! What would I say?"

"'My wife has recently had visions in which spirits appear, who look like Cap and Fey Falconer, the developers of Martini Cove Island. We were on *The Golden Fleece*, anchored near Thorn Island, when they appeared to her again, and this time they spoke to her. She wrote down everything they told her, that they were murdered by Colonel Frigh, using the legendary Frigh hammer. The murder was probably witnessed by Lester Prown, but he may have been in a drunken stupor and not actually have been a witness to the murder. Because recently deceased Fern Delamere, a long-time resident of Welcomer, also witnessed the murder, we believe The Committee for Good Taste burned her house down.'

"My dear, I don't think so."

I could see Max's point. "Okay, so what *do* we do?"

Max glanced in Sky and Haywood's direction but they were ignoring him. He made a helpless gesture and said, "Let's think about it for a few days."

"A few days?" I ran my fingers through my hair. "And wait for the ghosts with their blue skins and hollow eyes to visit me again and ask why nothing has been done yet to get them justice? No, thank you."

"We need some hard evidence," Lucia said.

The boat was rocking gently from side to side. I got up and paced, and realized that I had developed sea legs.

"What about the red room in the Colonel's house?" I said. "Fey mentioned the files. Might be something there to incriminate the Colonel."

Lucia said, "Like a hammer with two fresh notches?"

Haywood swatted at a flying insect with his cap, "I don't think that's a good idea. Remember that the Colonel is probably still in possession of that hammer. I believe he wouldn't hesitate hitting anybody else over the head with it either."

Max nodded. "Haywood's right. We have to think about this more before we act."

Sky cleared his throat. "Let's think about it until we have a solid plan. Sorry, Sylvia. None of us want you to suffer unwanted ghostly visitations, but we have to think about this a lot more. If we don't know what to do, it's best to do nothing for the time being."

I threw my hands in the air. They were right.

"For now, I think we should get a good night's sleep," Sky said. He switched on some lights and started the engine. "It's been a long day and I for one would like to sleep in my own bed tonight. Let's head for home, Lucia."

With that, Lucia weighed anchor, Sky took up the helm and turned on the running lights. We were already heading away from Thorn Island. That alone made me feel better.

* * * *

The Golden Fleece slid into its berth at the marina. As Butterfly had predicted, no one was around, probably having passed out on Lester's lawn, celebrating Fern's departure. The other boats lay sluggish in their slips.

We helped Lucia and Sky clean up, locked the boat, and headed toward the golf carts. Haywood and Butterfly waved as they drove up the hill away from us. Sky and Lucia gave us a ride home.

At our cottage, I said, "Thanks for giving Fern such a nice send off."

"She was a good person and a neighbor." Lucia shook her head, "and should have been better cared for by the community. Isn't there a saying that goes, 'Do onto others as you would have them do unto you?'"

Sky laughed. "Yes, but we are talking about a homeowner association. That rule doesn't apply."

"I could write a book of Martini Cove Island homeowner association rules myself." She ticked them off on her fingers. "1) Always think of yourself first. 2) Your neighbors are guilty of all accusations until proven innocent and then question that. 3) The biggest loudmouth and bully in the community rules, however mean and stupid he/she is. 4) If The Committee can find a way to keep assessments down, even if it means screwing your neighbor, they should go right ahead and do it because it's about money, the hell with morals. 5) Do what you have to..."

Sky grasped Lucia's hand in his own. "That's enough, darling. You are ravishing, smarter than most, a skilled sailor, a moral human being. Bitterness does not become you."

Lucia slumped on the seat.

Sky made a wide sweep with the cart and turned it around. Before waving to us, he called over his shoulder, "Frankly, my dears, this is the only shit box I've ever lived in."

We laughed and they disappeared into the night. I looked up and saw the full moon rising from behind the silhouettes of pines. Lifting my head, I did the only thing that would make me feel better. "Ow--ooo--aahh!" I howled.

Max howled right along with me. Truffle must have heard us because he howled inside the house. How I had missed him all day!

Inside we found Truffle jumping up and down, happy to see us. Max poured us brandy and tossed Truffle a biscuit, while I lit kindling in the fireplace. As we three sat together looking at the flames, the sweetness of wood smoke filled the room.

I swirled the brandy in my glass. "Now that we know what kind of place this is, what next? Where should we go?"

Max looked at me, eyes intense. "You're heartbroken aren't you, my dear?"

Tears filled my eyes while I scratched behind Truffle's ear. "This is such a glorious place, the most picturesque place I've ever lived, yet I've never been as unhappy in my life as I am now." I swiped at the tears. "You know what's strange, though? I'm not angry with the Colonel or Erhleen or Lester or Sven or any of them, I just feel sorry for them. They have so much and all they can think about is themselves and how to get more."

Max stared into the fire. "In Buddhism, it's called a 'poverty mentality,' having much but never being happy with it."

"Exactly. Take the Colonel. He has a splendid condo, lives on a gorgeous island, doesn't have to work anymore, but still he couldn't leave Fern alone. What did she ever do to him? Visitors never even noticed her, yet he had to get rid of her."

"Bullies like him are so insecure they have to get rid of anyone who threatens their beliefs. He bullies by exclusion, by threats, by doing whatever he can to protect his fragile ego."

I threw my hands up. "And people just stand by and watch, thereby supporting him. They even believe he is a leader. How can they be so blind?"

"Even you were almost seduced."

I nodded. "On the surface it looked inviting. A big supportive family in a gorgeous setting."

Max was twiddling his moustache again.

"What are you thinking?"

He sighed. "Oh, nothing. Just going over the events of this strange day."

Truffle looked at me and I bent down to kiss the top of his head. "This community is like a seductive lover. You are obsessed with him but you know he is cheating on you. You see only how handsome he is, but you know he's not good for you. If you're smart, you'll leave him and not look back."

Max nodded. "God knows, the beauty of the place seduced me, too, but the dinner with Lester and Veeda should have tipped us off. Hearing the stories about the Colonel, Slick, and Jack the Ripper should have cinched it. I was hoping things would get better, but...they didn't." He sighed. "How would you feel about looking for a new home?"

I blinked rapidly to hold back fresh tears. "Seems to be the only option." After draining my glass and stifling a yawn, I said, "Wow, am I tired. I'm going to bed. Aren't you going to finish your drink?"

"It's not late. A little antique tool polishing will help relax me." He looked at his drink. "Didn't want this brandy after all. Want it?"

"Well, since it's poured, okay."

Max kissed my cheek. "Good night." He gave me his drink and left.

Maybe because I downed the brandy in two gulps, I swayed a little when I stood, feeling tipsy for the first time all day even though I had drunk my share of champagne. I stumbled up the stairs to the bedroom with Truffle right behind me. Too tired to brush my teeth or wash my face, I was barely able to take my clothes off and fall into bed. Sleep soon enveloped me.

No dreams about the ghosts that night, thank goodness. Maybe they had used up their energy contacting me during the visit aboard *The Golden Fleece*. Maybe they had accomplished what they needed to do. Whatever the reason, I was grateful that they didn't show up.

CHAPTER 25

I got up late the next morning, refreshed rather than groggy. Max was in the kitchen, humming and carving a kiwi into a heart. I watched him pierce it with a toothpick and spear it into a grapefruit half for me.

"How sweet." I headed right for the coffee.

"How did you sleep?"

"Like the dead." I made a face. "Bad joke."

Max had set the table with a white linen tablecloth and napkins and set out my favorite blue willow dishes. The coffee, a blend of hazelnut and Mountain Blue, was Max's *piece de resistance*. He may not know how to cook but he makes the world's best coffee. He sat opposite me and rubbed his hands together before taking a toasted piece of my homemade bread, smearing it liberally with butter and damson plum preserve, and eating it with gusto.

He seemed to have forgotten last night's sad talk. "You're in a good mood this morning." I helped myself to the toast.

Max pointed toward the window with the jam spoon. "Just look out there. The start of a whole new day."

I glanced out the window. Red, yellow and orange leaves on the trees danced in the wind. He was right. It was the start of a new day, a day when we would be thinking of living somewhere else, where there was no island, no rocky beaches with shells, no sound of bell buoys. I sighed and chewed on the toast.

Max covered my hand with his and said, "You don't mind too much about the island, do you?"

"No, not as long as we're together."

After checking the kitchen clock, he said, "I do have to leave you for a while today, though. Sky and Haywood are going to a boat show in the city and they've invited me. Lunch will be part of the day, too. You'll be all right?"

"Sure." But the truth was I would miss him, especially today. "I still can't figure out your sudden interest in boats."

He shot me a quick sideways look. "Well, er, that is... I was thinking of spending some time on boats."

"Are you planning to invite me on a cruise?"

"Maybe." He glanced at the clock again. "It's getting late. Let's talk later." He gave me a quick peck, grabbed a jacket and was out the door.

Max's only interests had always been garnishing and decorating. Boat show? My, my. How things do change.

I went to the window and looked at the site where Fern's cottage had stood. Quick to erase any sign of Fern, the association had employed landscapers to work double time planting saplings and ground cover on the site. The only sound or movement on that lonely spot was the wind rustling through the small trees. No signs of Fern or her house were left.

I ran my hand over the cool, smooth slate kitchen counters, opened and closed the door of the pantry, looked out each window, touched the mantel in the living room. Upstairs, I went into my studio and tidied the art supplies and books. I untied the Italian portfolio holding my paintings and leafed through them. These were scenes I knew so well: the cliffs, water and vegetation of the island. All were reminders of the joy I'd once felt here, and they would be personal memories of the island I had been in love with.

I sat down at the drafting table. Truffle lay and put his head on my feet. I knew I had to spill my grief otherwise it would stay with me and haunt me for the rest of my life. I crossed my arms over the table and put my head down, and sobbed for a long, long time.

* * * *

I was lying on the bed in the late afternoon, when I heard Max come in through the front door. Truffle jumped off the bed and raced to greet him. I was exhausted from crying. Hoping that the swelling had gone down, I took the teabags off my eyes and went into the living room.

When Max saw me, his expression was a mixture of concern and uncertainty. "How are you?"

I went to him and put my head in the crook of his neck. "I missed you."

"Me too." He stroked my hair.

"How was the boat show?"

"What boat show?" He held me at arm's length and looked at me, brow furrowed. "Ah, the boat show."

He paused a moment. "I have something to tell you." He took my hand, led me to the couch. Looking directly into my eyes, he said, "There was no boat show."

"So, what were you doing in the city?"

He got up and stood with his hands behind his back and looked into the fireplace even though there was no fire. Then he turned to face me. "Sky, Haywood and I arranged for a package to be delivered."

"What package?"

"You remember last night when I gave you my brandy?"

"Of course."

"I didn't want you to wake up in the middle of the night to find me gone."

I sat at attention.

"The truth is, I slipped a sleeping pill into that brandy."

I crossed my arms. "So, you wanted to knock me out."

"Wanted to make sure you were asleep."

"Are you seeing another woman?"

He did a double take. "Another woman? One is all I can handle, thank you very much."

"It should be. So, why was it necessary to drug me?"

"I didn't drug you. I just didn't want you to wake up."

My eyes widened. "What did you do?"

"Sky, Haywood and I did a dangerous thing last night. Dangerous, but necessary."

I jumped up. "If you don't spill it immediately, Max Saltwater, you will be in more danger right here with me than you were last night."

He sighed, leaned against the fireplace mantle and began his infernal moustache twiddling. "Last night the other residents were celebrating Fern's departure from the island, right? That presented a perfect opportunity for Sky, Haywood and me to slip down to Lester's trailer and we saw what we hoped to see. The merrymakers were drunk and sleeping on the lawn." He snickered. "Premier community, indeed! But that gave us free rein to do what we did next."

"Which was?" I said, tight lipped.

"We drove to the Colonel's condo and found the front door unlocked, as we hoped we might. All the lights were off, so we assumed no one was home. We went in."

"Are you crazy? You could be arrested for breaking and entering. Did you touch anything? Did you leave fingerprints?"

Max shook his head. "We wore food preparation gloves."

"Thank God!"

"We tried to open the door of the red room to get to The Committee's files but that door was locked, so I picked the lock with the help of the dragon sculpture tools."

"You didn't."

"I did, and opened the lock." In spite of everything, he looked proud of himself.

I threw my hands into the air. "Do you know how illegal this is?"

He nodded. "Once we were in, I used the tool again to pick open the lock on the file cabinet."

"You're getting pretty good at picking locks."

"Maybe I could take it up as a second career."

"Not funny. What then?"

"We took out the files. Of course, we didn't read them there. No telling when the Colonel or Erhleen might have shown up. Sky photographed them, though."

"When did you read them?"

"Later. Sky knows someone who developed the photos for us, no questions asked, and will deliver them anonymously in a package to the police in a couple of days. I'll tell you about them later but rest assured, the information in them will change the face of this community."

"Why can't you tell me now."

"Trust me. Later."

"Did you find the Frigh hammer, too?"

"We didn't have enough time to go through everything. There's just enough time for us to pack our most valuable things and put the rest in storage."

"Wait a minute! What are you saying?"

"We committed a crime by breaking and entering, but let me assure you what the police will read in those files about our neighbors is way more criminal than anything the three of us did. Nevertheless I suggest we leave the island as fast as possible."

I couldn't help admire Max for such a bold act. "Mild mannered, high minded, Zen practitioner, master garnishing guru Max Saltwater, a wanted criminal. Was it worth it?"

Max stood straight and raised his chin. "We may have committed a crime, but that sorry bunch will be exposed to avenge Fern's death. You bet it was worth it."

I put my arms around him and said, "You did the right thing."

"I was hoping you'd say that." He untangled my arms. "Pack your most precious possessions. What are they, anyway?"

"If we're going on the lam, then Truffle, the jewelry you

designed for me, my paintings and my art supplies. And you?"

"The antique garnishing tools, of course, and the first draft of my memoir. We only have a couple of days to pack. We'll put the rest in storage."

"Where you go, Truffle and I will go. By the way, where are we going?"

* * * *

Before the police could have received the envelope, we had packed and were ready to leave the island on board *The Golden Fleece*. Sky and Lucia had also packed and, like us, had hired the same moving and storage company to put the entire contents of their home into storage. Max and I did not put our house on the market but we knew we would never live on the island again.

The community must have known that we were planning to leave when they saw the moving trucks at our homes. We let word get out that we were going to take an indefinite cruise aboard *The Golden Fleece*.

As we were packing, the doorbell rang.

I peeked through the curtain of the door window and saw the top of Sven's bald head. I whispered, "Do you think The Committee found out about the break in?"

Max whispered back, "If they had, they would have already left the island."

While Sven was tying Sweetheart to the porch rail, I opened the door.

"Sven. What a surprise. What can I do for you?"

His broad smile exposed most of his long yellow teeth. While rocking on his heels and clasping his fingerless gloved hands in front of him, he said, "On behalf of The Committee, may I inquire, are you leaving our glorious community for good?"

I put on my unhappiest face and said, "Yes. My husband and I can no longer stay in this community. We find that we have nothing in common with our neighbors. It's a sad day for us."

Sven was almost jumping up and down for joy. "On behalf of The Committee for Good Taste and your neighbors, we bid you a fond farewell."

"How gracious."

He almost skipped down the stairs taking Sweetheart with him and hurried, I'm sure, to the Colonel's house to give him the wonderful news.

Later that day, when I was taking Truffle for his last walk on the island, I saw flyers stapled to trees announcing a spontaneous potluck. I never got so many smiles and waves from the residents and suspected it was because of our imminent departure. Erhleen even managed a scowly smile. The Colonel waved when he passed me in his rusty golf cart. They wouldn't have been so jubilant if they had known what was coming.

Butterfly and Haywood had decided, after an agonizing discussion with the four of us, to stay on the island. "Even if they suspect anything," Haywood said, "I don't think anyone will be able to prove who engineered the break-in. They have a lot more to lose than we do, so we'll be fine."

Butterfly said she would never let the Colonel or The Committee evict her. Not even Haywood would be able to pry her loose from her home. She would rather buy a shotgun and hole up in her house.

Haywood said he wasn't buying any shotgun.

Butterfly had said, "God damn it all to hell! I'm staying on this island and building my museum. Fuck them!"

Pretty strong language for a genteel Southern Belle. Haywood didn't dare argue.

We decided to leave the photos of Welcomer and Fey's journal right where they were, safely behind the wall in our attic, since the Colonel and The Committee did not have an inkling that they even existed. Haywood had a key to our house and could get them when the time was right.

Although the Colonel and The Committee would undoubtedly have their suspicions as to how the police came by copies of their files, they would not have any evidence, thanks to the gloves and to the dragon sculpture which only we knew was a tool that could open files and locks. Max assured me once again that the disclosures about the residents would far overshadow the way they came to the police. Some people might even applaud the people who were brave enough to expose the worst homeowners association in America.

Working quickly to pack with the help of the movers, two days after the break-in, the four of us left Martini Cove Island on board *The Golden Fleece* before dawn on an overcast, drizzly day. Truffle was with us, of course. We left Tansy with Butterfly and Haywood.

I wanted to be on deck when we pulled out of the cove for the last time. In my quiet way, I wanted to say good-bye to painting on the beaches, the boats, our cottage, my hope for community, my lost dream. As Sky and Lucia were busy with the boat, Max came to my side and put his arm around me. "Sorry it worked out like this, especially for you."

I looked down at the swirling water. "You know what really disappoints me? As much as anything else that happened?"

"What?"

"It might sound silly but--" I ran my hand across the rail. "--I'll never see Fern's lilac in bloom, the one she gave me in honor of my mother." I was determined not to cry. "Well, Mr. Saltwater, what next?"

He looked out to sea in the direction the boat was heading. "Let it unfold."

CHAPTER 26

Now was the perfect time for Sky and Lucia to make a long sail along the coast of America as they had wanted to do for a long time. Always gracious and generous hosts, they gave us the aft cabin and me the bunk cabin to use as my studio. The setup was ideal. The bunks would serve as shelves to hold art supplies and the rest of the space would hold the drafting table. Since Max and I didn't like a free ride, we offered to work for our keep. At first they protested, but they finally accepted, since they had many boating friends and anticipated giving lots of parties in ports along the way. Max was to be their party planner and chef.

At that point, we had to confess Max's darkest secret, his lack of cooking ability, except for his barbecue sauce, of course. They agreed to the deception. Max would keep his reputation intact. I would cook, as I always had, and would not mind since I wanted to repay their generosity. Max would be in charge of planning, flower arranging and garnishing. Buoyed by this new job, his spirits soared.

Lucia frequently sent out for food when we were docked, and she cooked, too, understanding how important painting was to me. What a friend.

Enjoying his unlimited budget, Max sketched new designs for garnishes and flower arrangements he would use at parties.

When we were approaching Key West, D. M. C. called aboard. He asked to speak to Max. "Darling, when I heard you were here, I couldn't believe my good luck. I'm wild to have you cater a birthday party for Sting and Madonna and their close personal dog friends. As you know, nothing's too good for my puppies. Make it extra special."

Max suggested flowers, balloons, dog bone party favors, colorful cone hats with elastic bands and sirloin cubes lightly seared served in individual baskets of pommes frites. As party favors, gift certificates for pet massage and pedicures with nail polish.

"Fabulous!" D. M. C. said.

We all had a great time at the party, especially Truffle.

When we sailed to Tulum, the Mayan ruin on the Yucatan Peninsula overlooking the Caribbean, Sky asked Max to plan an anniversary party for Lucia. Among other guests, he invited the Governor of Yucatán, who was an old boating friend, to dine under a palapa built especially for the occasion. Sky said he wanted the party to be held there, because the color of the sea was the same as the color of Lucia's eyes.

When Max told me that, I felt jealous. "What do the color of my eyes remind you of?" I looked at him through my lashes.

Max studied me for a moment and then said, "Sylvia, you are more to me than the color of your eyes. You are my mountain."

That was sweet. Oh, well. So I wasn't a goddess of love, but Max could count on me. That was nice, too.

Max was happier than I had seen him since we sold *Presentation Is Everything* and he loved carving four banana pinwheels for our breakfasts every morning.

* * * *

A few weeks after the anniversary party, a call came through from Haywood. He told us to tune in the U. S. news on the boat's satellite TV. He had just seen a preview of the lead story, but he wouldn't tell us what it was. "Let it be a surprise," he had said.

As we gathered around the TV, we mused what the story Haywood was so secretive about might be.

Sky said, "How about, 'Exposure of Wrong Doing at Premier Community on Small Island.'"

"Let's pray," Lucia said with a snicker.

I said, "I hope it's not about searching for wanted criminals on board a yacht in the Caribbean."

"Haywood would have told us if that were it," Max said. "How about 'Island Community Fined for Non Observance of Basic Food Garnishing.' "

I said, "Max, you are the quintessential snob."

"Thank goodness." Lucia laughed wickedly.

Sky had already popped open the champagne when the TV anchor's image came on. "Tonight, in news so bizarre we will devote all our air time to it, we bring you a big story from a small place, Martini Cove Island, located off the coast of North America."

"Holy mackerel." Sky said, as he spilled champagne on his sleeve.

"Shh," Lucia said.

The anchor continued. "A package sent anonymously to local police launched a chain of events leading to the arrest of criminals and extortionists long sought by the FBI and Interpol. The investigation of a suspicious burning of an island cottage, belonging to one Fern Delamere, a resident of the community, seems to have sparked the events, following forensic investigation proving that a cigar started the fire."

Our mouths dropped open.

The TV image broke from the anchor to footage taken from a helicopter of the burned spot where Fern's cottage had stood. The burn mark had not been as visible from the ground because of the quick work The Committee performed for the benefit of the potential buyers from Hollywood. But from the air, the spot was clearly visible.

The anchor went on. "The Martini Cove Island development, advertised as a premier community, had until the 1950's, been known as Welcomer Rest Home for the Treatment of Ennui and Melancholia. After it was abandoned, it fell into disrepair until developers, Cap and Fey Falconer, created this striking community."

The TV panned along the condos ringed around the green.

"After selling most of the units, the Falconers mysteriously vanished under suspicious circumstances. Most island residents believed that the Falconers embezzled association funds and disappeared with them. The whereabouts of the developers and the missing money has remained an unsolved mystery for the past several years. Now new aspects of the story surfaced."

An image of the front of the Colonel's condo appeared on the screen.

"Recently, from an anonymous source the local police received copies of files that had been kept at the association office of The Committee for Good Taste, the enforcer of rules for the association. The revelation of the contents of the files led to the arrest of several prominent pillars of the community, among them officers of the association."

"I'll be damned," Sky said.

Lucia threw her hands up and yelled, "Yahoo!"

Max and I were speechless.

The anchor's image came on again. "Interpol is investigating one Fermin Lawsom, who has been living at Martini Cove Island for several years. It is alleged that Lawsom's former name is Adolf George. Mr. George had owned a lucrative condom manufacturing business in the United States in the 1970's and had opened a distributing branch in India. Eagerly awaited, the products were snapped up because of the innovative Mehendi designs appearing on the shafts of the product when fully in use. The first batch of condoms were cheaply produced in a small third world country, and had a ninety percent breakage rate that caused the population of India to soar nine months later.

"The Indian government sued the manager in charge of the Indian distributing branch. In turn, the manager tried to sue Adolf George who, unbeknownst to the manager, had disappeared to Martini Cove Island, changed his name to Fermin Lawsom and became a member of The Committee for Good Taste."

The TV showed a clip of Fermin being led to the police boat in handcuffs, head bowed against the bright lights of TV cameras mouthing the word "Mumsey" over and over.

Lucia laughed. "Was Mumsey in on it?"

The anchor continued, "Revealed in the files were also the practices of one Lester Prown, a resident and owner of the Prown Funeral Home on the island. Prown, a consistent imbiber of alcohol, has allegedly, on several occasions, mistakenly embalmed his customers with gin instead of embalming fluid."

Lucia hooted.

"One former customer, Chester Goodhue, complained to Mr. Prown at his mother's funeral, that she smelled strongly of gin."

The image of a man in his sixties, gray hair parted in the middle, came on the screen. "Mother was a religious person," he said. "She never drank a single drop of spirits. But at the funeral, several members of Mother's church expressed shock and dismay when they smelled liquor while paying respects at the coffin. I asked Mr. Prown to admit to any error he might have made while embalming her such as filling her with gin instead of formaldehyde but Mr. Prown would not confess to an error nor did he offer me a refund. I dropped the matter because Mother and I are God-fearing folk and I did not want to make a fuss. But I'm mighty shook up about the whole thing since I heard of Mr. Prown's arrest."

The anchor's image came on again. "Prown apparently got away with several mistakes. In another incident, one Elma Klutz asked for her husband's body, which had been treated for burial at Prown's Funeral Home, to be exhumed. It was discovered that Mr. Klutz had not been alone in his coffin. Another body, a woman's, was found in the same casket, lying next to Mr. Klutz. A test on the body revealed it is the missing first Mrs. Prown, who disappeared at the same time Mr. Klutz died."

Mrs. Klutz said in an interview, "You mean my Irwin has been sleeping with another woman for the past five years?"

"Lester Prown is now charged with murder, as well as defrauding his customers."

The image on TV showed Lester, in a not unfamiliar state of inebriation, being led away in handcuffs by two police officers trying to hold him up and keep him walking.

Max said, "I wonder if they'll let him keep his whoopee cushion in prison."

The anchor continued. "Lester Prown's common-law wife, Veeda, is also under investigation. The police allege she is the same Veeda Prown who went by the name of Veeda Blank, a school nurse, who several years ago escaped arrest in another state for fondling young boys during routine school medical exams. At the time of her husband's arrest, she was working at a public school in the city across the bay from the island. Since then suspicions about her past arose. She was dismissed immediately and is now under investigation."

An image of Veeda flashed on the screen. She was in a white uniform, head bowed, being led away in handcuffs from the school's infirmary by a female police officer.

After another sip of champagne, Lucia said, "I guess she'll have to change her signature color to orange."

The anchor continued, "Slick Shaloe, the Martini Cove association president, has been accused of stealing association funds and with them purchasing a Tiffany diamond pendant for his wife, Wanda. The Falconers have been cleared of the association fund theft, and their disappearance and possible murder is linked to prominent members of the community."

A clip of Slick and Wanda, escorted by police, showed Slick sweating profusely and Wanda posing for the cameras as if she were a Hollywood starlet on the red carpet. In the bright lights, her blond hair showed inches of dark roots. She was wearing a snug pink top and pink tights, and unfortunately, the camera added several more pounds. She was not wearing the Tiffany diamond pendant.

Max smirked. "Wait until the authorities discover that the 'Peekasew' was stolen from the Louvre."

Back to the anchor. "You may wonder how these seemingly separate events and personalities are related. In a twist to this complicated story, the authorities are pointing to two persons known as Colonel Frigh and his wife Erhleen, prominent members of the Martini Cove Island community."

The screen flashed a clip of the Colonel in handcuffs. He was weeping as he was being led from the island's dock onto the police boat. Erhleen tried to shield her face from the camera with a blue windbreaker, but those huge sunglasses and her bright red face remained visible.

The anchor said, "Police revealed that in her position as head of The Martini Cove Island Committee for Good Taste, Erhleen Frigh kept files on these individuals and allegedly was blackmailing them. If they toed the line for her and the Colonel, their sordid backgrounds would not be revealed. Thus the Colonel was able to easily set himself up as the unofficial leader of this small island community. An inside source quoted the Colonel as saying about his wife, 'She's as full of mean as a tick on a dog.'"

The anchor continued. "Our investigative reporters uncovered the facts of Erhleen Frigh's heritage. Contrary to legend, it is her ancestry, not the Colonel's, which has been traced back to old Buford Frigh, who built the Frigh towns on slave labor in the Old South. The same Frigh ancestor was a suspect in the famous London Jack the Ripper murders of the late nineteenth century. Unfortunately his departure from London and his death soon thereafter on the vessel returning to the States halted further investigation, since none of his fellow passengers were willing to speak of the incident.

"Erhleen Frigh's husband, known at this time only as the Colonel, has been implicated in the murder of Cap and Fey Falconer. It is also alleged Lester Prown was an accomplice. Evidence implies the Colonel caused the fire at Fern Delamere's cottage, since he is the only person on the island who smokes cigars."

Lucia snapped her fingers. "That proves what Sylvia channeled from Fey was true."

"Only if the police find the hammer," Sky said.

Erhleen's face came on the screen. She was on the police boat as it prepared to pull away from the dock, but she had enough time to whine into a microphone held by a reporter. "I came to this island and fell in love with its beaches and forests and wanted to live here forever. What's wrong with that?"

Lucia said, "As if the rest of us didn't. How do you spell 'sociopath'?"

The anchor was on again. "Investigators have informally dubbed this bizarre circle of alleged criminals 'The Pinocchio Island Ring.'"

Lucia snickered. "Bet you Haywood let 'Pinocchio Island' slip to the reporters and they ran with it."

Subsequent newscasts revealed that the Colonel, hoping for a plea bargain, confessed to the murders of Cap and Fey, but tried to shift the blame for everything that went wrong on Erhleen. "She made me do it," the Colonel wailed into the camera. "She planned it all. It was always her."

The authorities recovered Cap and Fey's bodies, near Thorn Island. They searched the Colonel's house and found the famous Frigh hammer in an inlaid box with two fresh notches gouged on the handle. DNA found on the hammerhead matched the DNA of Cap and Fey. Blunt trauma marks on the skulls proved, beyond a doubt, the hammer was the murder weapon.

The Colonel, Erhleen, and Lester, an accessory, were charged with murder, even though Erhleen had planned it all. The authorities did not offer a plea bargain.

Sven was never implicated in any of the crimes; however, the information he kept in a fat notebook painted a grim picture of The Committee and the Colonel. Sven did not want to stay in a community that had no leader and where he would not be told what to do. Without the Colonel, Erhleen and The Committee, it just wasn't the same. Haywood told us Sven had gone back to Dingenflugen to study the triangle some more.

With glee, Haywood kept us informed of the aftershocks. The crimes committed by the pillars of the Martini Cove Island community were numerous and heinous. The island was now infamous. Inquiring reporters dug up the story of the Indians' curse and that was all it took for the tabloid shows to make a field day out of Martini Cove Island's woes. It was no longer the quiet place it had once seemed.

The meek residents, who were not guilty of wrongdoing but without the courage to think for themselves or the morals to speak up against the bullies, left. Property values dropped sharply.

Haywood, instead of panicking about dropped property values, waited until they hit rock bottom and bought up quite a few of the condos. He felt certain, he said, that when the story of the island and the Pinocchio Ring became yesterday's news, potential buyers would once again see only the beauty of the island.

Butterfly loved the commotion and gave several interviews on TV, revealing that she and Haywood were looking into funding the Martini Cove Island Museum. It was safe for Haywood to bring out the photos that had been guarded in the attic of our house. After the police scrutinized Fey's journal for evidence in the murder, they turned it over to Butterfly for the archives.

One day, Butterfly called us as we were idling aboard the boat off the coast of South America. "You'll just never guess what happened."

I could picture her jumping up and down, earrings bobbing.

"The trustee of Fern's estate just called to inform us Fern had left her estate and the land her house had stood on for the museum. Her will stated the best times of her life were the ones she and her parents had spent in museums and she wanted the island to have one, too."

Sky said, "Are the photos and the journal enough material to fill an entire museum?"

"Haywood and I thought so at first, but no, they aren't. They will be hung in a special museum room. We approached the trustee with the idea of using the money to create a place of spirituality and naming it The Fern Delamere Wellness Center. I would be in charge of all the programs, of course. We would offer meditation, chi gung, yoga, therapists, spiritual leaders, what have you. We convinced the trustee that a wellness center would be more in keeping with Fern's spirit than too many reminders of a rest home."

The police were baffled about the instrument used to pick the locks at the Colonel's condo. No evidence of who sent the files to the police was ever found, although there must have been plenty of speculation. The results of the break-in were so spectacular, and the authorities so grateful, this aspect of the story became a minor concern and was, in time, forgotten. Max, Haywood and Sky never had to answer to the authorities for housebreaking.

CHAPTER 27

Max and I, Sky and Lucia, had our fill of island living. We planned to keep our properties and sell them someday, at tidy profits if we were lucky. Still, I pondered what might have been.

One evening as I was sitting on the bow of the boat, watching the orange and gold sunset, I became weepy. Lucia sat next to me, put her arm around my shoulders, and asked what I was thinking.

I wiped away a tear "The island, of course. It was glorious, everything any artist could hope for. Everywhere I looked there was another scene I wanted to paint. It was every fantasy I had about living by the sea. I'm sorry it's over."

Lucia was quiet for a while and when I looked at her, I saw she was crying, too. She said, "I remember a quote I read once. It might be helpful. 'Don't cry because it's over; smile because it happened.'"

I nodded and blew my nose. "You know what I realized?"

"What?"

"Community is different from what I had imagined before we moved to the island. It's not the number of people who live together in a certain place. It's the people who care about and support each other. It doesn't matter if they live close to each other or are thousands of miles apart. They're still community. You and I, Max and Sky, Butterfly and Haywood will always be community. So, in an unexpected way Martini Cove Island gave me a community after all."

She squeezed my shoulders and we sat together until the sun had set completely and the sky was alive with stars. Suddenly we both pointed to the same spot at the same time and said, "There's Orion."

Lucia said, "I always thought of Orion as my constellation."

"So did I."

"Let's make a pact." She took my hand. "As long as Orion exists, and you and I are friends, we can look up at him, no matter how far apart we are, and we'll be reminded we're connected."

Later, when we no longer lived close to each other, I would remember that moment and knew that once our hearts had made the pact, it was unbreakable.

* * * *

Not long after, while I was painting in my cabin, I thought about my life and all the crazy, wonderful experiences Max and I had in the business. I thought about my childhood, my special powers, how I helped Cap and Fey, and how rich people at Martini Cove Island could have led such impoverished lives. Max and I never had the money that most of them have. Out of ordinary items--cabbages, carrots, radishes, broccoli--Max had crafted sculptures that delighted people and tickled their imaginations. I made delicious food. Together, we made many people happy.

The residents of Martini Cove took one of the most gorgeous places in the world and turned it into a moral slum.

Sky and Lucia often stayed in hotels or visited friends in different ports where we docked. Those were the best times to cobble together a manuscript of memoirs. I described characters and incidents from Martini Cove Island. I doubt that anyone will believe my story, but how could I have made any of this up?

I painted a picture of Fair Winds, not from a photo, but from how I remembered it. Full of energy, it captured the spirit of the home they had created and had to leave. I proudly presented it to them one night after they had been gone a few days.

They were surprised and both fought back tears.

"Oh, Sylvia," was all Lucia said.

They hugged me for a long time.

Truffle lived happily on board for most of the time we spent on the boat, but eventually he became a senior and one day crossed over the Rainbow Bridge. At first Max and I thought we might bury his ashes at sea, but then I changed my mind. He stayed on board in a small bronze urn on a shelf in my studio. The inscription on the urn reads, *"Truffle--a spirit pure of heart and a good companion in troubled times."*

When I finish my memoirs, the dedication will read the same.

EPILOGUE

One night when *The Golden Fleece* was docked at a small exclusive island with gardens of exotic flowers, the four of us were sitting topside drinking champagne. Above silhouettes of palms, the full moon shone and lit the landscape with a soft glow.

Suddenly, at the prow of the ship I noticed two wisps of smoke. At first, I thought it was evening mist, but they swirled taking on the shapes of two ghostly people. Cap and Fey.

Although the evening was soft and warm, I suddenly felt cold and my body tingled. Tonight they looked different than in my dreams. They no longer had blue skin and hollow eyes full of agony, but were smiling and dressed in clean, dry white clothes. They looked almost normal, except that I could see the lights of the shoreline through them. Fey's long dark hair fell in soft ringlets around her shoulders. Cap's grey hair was curly around a handsome face. I realized what an attractive couple they must have been when they were alive.

I grabbed Max's arm. "Get me paper and pen."

"Oh, no," Max said. "Here we go again. Sylvia is communicating with the ghosts."

"No kidding?" Lucia slid closer to me. "Can we talk to them, too?"

"Shh," Max said, "Sylvia will handle this."

I felt the paper and pen in my hands.

I write, *"Do you know that you have been avenged?"*
"Yes."

I write Cap's answer. The others watched over my shoulder.

"Justice is ours and our names are cleared."

"Are you at rest now?"

"Almost," Cap says. *"You shifted the energy of the island for us. We owe everything to your special powers. We wanted to say thank you and good-bye."*

Fey says, *"You and your friends brought good energy to the island. But it was mainly due to you, Sylvia. Unfortunate, the way things happened. We might all have been great friends."*

Cap says, *"Don't be sad, Fey. It will only delay our departure."*

I was almost glad to have this last visit with Cap and Fey. Almost. But with relief, I realized this was our last conversation.

"Just one thing to ask before you go," I write. *"The shard I found on the windowsill of our cottage. And the shell on my napkin. Did you put them there?"*

Fey says, *"It was a way of showing you we were around."*

Cap salutes and says, *"Thank you for helping us make peace with the Universe."*

Fey gives a little smile and waves.

They fade away.

Exhausted, I closed my eyes and put my hands over my face. The tingling in my body stopped. I was free. I hoped. "They're gone."

"Let's toast Cap and Fey," Lucia said, holding up her champagne flute. "May you have fair winds and following seas."

We lifted our glasses to the sky. Lucia went below and brought up a vase of white lilies from the saloon. We each tossed one onto the black water and watched them as they drifted farther and farther away and disappeared into the night.

The moon painted silver streaks on the water as we sat quietly together. Sky was looking at the stars with a telescope. Max was twiddling with his moustache, probably thinking about the next party he would cater. Lucia stood by the mast, the moonlight shining on her blonde hair. Suddenly she bent her head back and gave her wolf howl. It was full of loneliness, frustration, longing, anger. Maybe it was a eulogy to Cap and Fey or sadness that she lost her home on the island--probably, a little of both.

I wanted to eulogize all that, too, and I remembered a cliché that seemed perfectly fitting, so I stood up and sang into the starry night, "Ta, dahh!"

The fat lady sang, but her adventures were far from over.

THE END

ABOUT THE AUTHOR

Alexandra Wallner was born in Germany. Not able to speak English when she immigrated to the United States, she almost flunked first grade. But with the help of comic books--Uncle Scrooge, Donald Duck, Katy Keene, Little Lulu--she learned her new language. Words and pictures together lit the spark for her future career.

After graduating from Pratt Institute's Fine Art Program with an MFA and enjoying a brief stint in magazine design, she started collaborating with her husband John in creating children's books.

Not limited to a love for children's books, Alex and John have a passion for renovating and working in old houses. In Woodstock, N. Y. they renovated an 1850's farmhouse. They restored an 1865 townhouse in Philadelphia and remodeled a 1920's Maine island cottage.

During the long Maine winters, Alex started taking notes for a story about Sylvia and Max Saltwater and their encounters with island folk. The notes evolved into PINOCCHIO ISLAND.

They started thinking about warmer places to live when Alex became weary of slipping on ice. Breaking precedence, they moved to a warm climate into a newly built Florida house. Unfortunately soon after, they experienced three hurricanes in six weeks.

Continuing their gypsy ways, they moved to Merida, Yucatan, Mexico where they restored a mid-nineteenth century casa and added two studios in the back of the garden.

They care for an elderly Jack Russell, a family of cats, a rambunctious iguana, and a sprinkling of geckos.

Alex threw out the moving boxes and swears this is her final home.

www.ingramcontent.com/pod-product-compliance
Lightning Source LLC
Chambersburg PA
CBHW081149170626
46813CB00009B/3130

* 9 7 8 1 6 0 1 7 4 9 1 0 9 *